He walks to the door with authority, closes it and snaps the lock. "None of the other guys're in the house. Just you an' me."

"Okay."

I'm a pledge again, like when I first joined the fraternity…and Carl knows it!

He goes to the window, and he looks out, maybe remembering when he lived here. He closes the drapes abruptly, plunging the room into warm shadows, and he turns back, unbuttoning his shirt and peeling it off. The massive muscles ripple across his broad shoulders and arms, and the slick black hair glistens on his massive chest.

Christ, I'd almost forgotten what a solid-built sonofabitch he is! I take a deep breath, and a flush of sex-heat storms into my groin.

Hypnotized, I watch him take the paddle from the wall and heft it in his bear-like paws. His fingers are short and thick-knuckled, and dark silk lines his fore arms.

"Pledge," he gro

"Yes, sir!" I snap

"Assume th' po

GW00728092

SOME LIKE
IT ROUGH

Clay Caldwell

Badboy

SOME LIKE IT ROUGH

Introduction:
Rough-and-Tumble with Clay Caldwell
Aaron Travis

Clay Caldwell can give it to you rough. Clay Caldwell can give it to you easy. And sometimes, Clay Caldwell can give it to you both ways at once....

A few years ago, Clay, who lives in the desert in Southern California, was up in the Bay Area and dropped by for a visit. He asked me to come out to his car. He opened the trunk. Inside was a cardboard box filled with old porno paperbacks—over sixty in all—every one of them written by Clay. In that box was the collection of a lifetime—literally.

Clay wanted me to have all those books. But how could he part with them? Well, he said, seeing that he was semiretired from the writing business, and I was anything but retired, he figured he should pass those books along to me, in case I had any use for them....

That's how I became the keeper of the Clay Caldwell Collection.

Some stats. Clay's first "adults-only" novel was *Cruising Horny Corners,* published in 1967 under his first pen name, Lance Lester. It was a humorous look at a naked young innocent's journey through the backyards of an imaginary gay suburbia. The sexiness was largely tongue-in-cheek, but *Cruising Horny Corners* was a ground- breaking book. In 1992, John Preston included an excerpt from it in his own groundbreaking anthology, *Flesh and the Word.*

In the next sixteen years, Clay would write sixty-two more books, using twenty-three pen names. The pen names he used most often were Clay Caldwell, Lance Lester, David E. Griffon, Rod Hammer, Thumper Johnson, Jeff Lawton, and Lance LaFong. His last novel was

Workin' Out, published in 1983. After a brief hiatus, he began publishing new short stories in gay mags like *Inches* in the late 1980s, and he has yet to retire his much-abused typewriter.

In recent years, Badboy Books has republished several classic Caldwell titles, including the novels *Tailpipe Trucker, Queers Like Us* and *Ask Ol' Buddy,* three volumes of science fiction, *All-Stud, Service, Stud,* and *QSFx2* (the last a shared anthology with Lars Eighner), and *Stud Shorts,* a collection of Clay's more recent short stories.

But browsing through the Clay Caldwell Collection recently (purely for professional reasons, of course), I realized that some of Clay's most memorable work (and certainly the stories that had the most influence on my own imagination and writing) had not yet been rediscovered. I'm talking about his SM short stories— powerfully concentrated tales of dominance and slavery, kidnapping and incarceration, training and submission, bondage and sexual torment, mentoring and self-discovery. To me, these stories are Clay's most potent legacy. I think his SM writing will stir readers as deeply as that of more recognized authors like John Preston and Larry Townsend. To that end, Badboy presents *Some Like It Rough,* a collection of the best of Clay's SM short fiction.

Clay evolved into a master of SM but he began as a comic writer; even in his harshest fantasies, there's often a note of humor and a touch of romance. Sometimes Clay allowed the humor and romance to dominate, and that happens nowhere with more satisfying results than in his stories about athletes and college jocks. The dick-stiffening smell of the locker room…a smirking topman's cocky swagger…a hunky stud down on his knees, hungry with hero worship…blustering buddy-talk that turns shy and seductive…butt-blistering rites of passage…deliciously predictable role-reversals—these are the elements of Clay's jock tales. You'll find the best of them collected in *Jock Studs,* which features footballers, swimmers, runners, way-cool surfers, ski bums, frat pledges, and tennis brats.

Meanwhile, I'm off to do more reading from the Clay Caldwell Collection. Strictly for professional reasons, you understand…

FINDING OUT

F rank slouched behind the steering wheel of the lumbering truck, relaxed and at ease. He'd made the run to Oakdale dozens of times, and it was strictly easy money.

His dark eyes shifted from the roadway ahead to the rearview mirrors and back automatically, and he dropped one hand to the full-mounded crotch of his Levi's, stroking his hidden genitals.

"Pushing this goddamn rig makes me horny," he muttered aloud, and then he snorted. "Shit, *everything* makes me horny!"

Frank was in his late twenties, with short-clipped black hair and strong masculine features. His worn work shirt outlined his solid, burly physique.

"Maybe I ought to get me a partner...a copilot...a cocksucker." He always talked to himself on long lonely runs like this one. "I don't want anybody behind this wheel except me, but I wouldn't mind having a copilot who'd work on my dick." He shrugged. "Get sucked off...fuck ass...let some prick-licker have it at the next piss stop."

He'd never given a damn how he got his rocks off.

Yeah, maybe that was one reason for being a trucker.

Lots of cock-hungry queers on the road, waiting to gobble trucker meat...and Frank had plenty of meat to offer, damn it!

"Remember that one stud?" he said to the stiffening flesh-column inside his pants.

"Remember how he sucked...wanted to get fucked... wanted to do anything... I wonder what he meant— 'anything'..."

He was rolling up the climb to the summit, and he

downshifted, the diesel motor growling and thundering, the rumbling sensations running up his legs into his groin.

"Goddamn, I'm horny!"

Ahead, he spotted a blond youth at the side of the road, thumb offered.

No, there were two of them. A burly dark-haired man stood in the shade of a tree, letting the youth swelter in the hot sunlight. Both wore Levi's, and the blond's shirt hung open, showing a glimpse of his trim bronzed torso.

"Good-looking stud," Frank commented aloud. He eased up on the gas pedal. "Hell, I can use some company." He braked to a stop and leaned across the wide seat, opening the door on the far side. Hop in, guys."

"Thanks," the man in the shade acknowledged, and he came forward, shoving the blond toward the rig. "Get your lousy butt in there, punk!"

The blond scrambled into the cab and sat, head down, beside Frank without looking at him, and his companion followed, slamming the door.

"I'm headed for Oakdale." Frank released the brakes and started the truck forward again.

"Good enough," said the man at the other side of the cab. "I'm Duke. This pile of shit's Tim."

"I'm Frank." He glanced at the two studs from the corner of his eye. "Tim doesn't talk much, huh?"

"He does what he's told." Duke jabbed the blond in the ribs with his elbow. "Butt me, peckerhead!"

Tim pulled a cigarette from his shirt pocket, lit it and passed it to Duke, then hunched head down again.

Frank frowned, wondering what the hell went with these two hitchers.

Tim was a handsome blond athlete-type, while Duke was swarthy and rugged-built. Plenty of muscle beneath that denim shirt!

Yeah, Duke looked tough as nails, but Tim was no weakling…and Tim did whatever Duke told him to.

"Tim's your copilot, Duke?"

"Huh?"

"'Copilot.' That's what a trucker calls a pal who travels along with him, lighting cigarettes so he can keep his eyes on the road, riding shotgun in case Smokey Bear is out there—"

"Shit!" Duke interrupted, flicking cigarette ashes on the floor of the cab. "Tim's no pal of mine! He's—"

"Use the ashtray," Frank grumbled, suddenly annoyed. "I don't like having my rig dirtied up."

"Hell, Tim'll clean it up for you when we get to

Oakdale," Duke bragged. "He'll clean it up with his *tongue* if I tell him to."

"Use the ashtray!" Frank repeated sharply. He waited until the man had tapped his cigarette into the dashboard ashtray, then relaxed. "I guess you don't understand, Duke. A trucker's rig…it's like a home…and a wife…a living room and a bedroom…a lover.…"

"Wild, man," Duke snorted. "Real wild!"

They'd reached the summit, and Frank concentrated on hammering through gears as they pulled out onto the flat tree-banked highway, then dug for a cigarette.

Tim moved fast, taking the cigarette, lighting it, tucking it between Frank's lips. For an instant, their eyes met.

Yeah, Tim was one good-looking stud…but kind of strange.

"Thanks, Tim." Frank centered on the roadway again. "That was like how a copilot'd light up a trucker's weed."

"What th' hell're you takin' that asshole for?" Duke sneered. "I trained him t' do that. Crap, he'll do anything I say. Right, Tim?"

"Yes, sir," the blond murmured, slumping back. "Anything you say, sir."

"Damn right!" He looked over at Frank. "Ever have a copilot who'd do 'anything'?"

"No. I've always run solo…no copilot…but I've heard about copilots who—"

"This blond fuckface'll do anything I tell him to," Duke declared. "He knows what'll happen if he doesn't."

"What'll happen?"

"See this belt?" He ran his fingers over the wide leather band buckled about his waist. "I'll lay it on him bareass till he crawls like a goddamn dog. Or maybe I'll work on his nuts. He's got big ones, but they're tender as hell."

"It sounds like you're pretty rough on him," Frank said, squinting at the highway ahead.

"He expects it." He reached over and spread Tim's unbuttoned shirt from his strong, tanned chest, and he grasped one large amber nipple, twisting it viciously. "Right, punk?"

"Yes, sir!" Tim hissed, wincing in pain. "I'm your slave, sir!"

Duke settled back, apparently satisfied, and Frank finished his cigarette, his expression thoughtful.

These two hitchers were the strangest he'd met…the handsome blond stud who obeyed every order from the other man…the black-haired guy who bragged about working over his companion….

"What'd Tim mean, Duke?" he asked at last. "About being your 'slave,' I mean."

"You don't know about slaves an' masters, huh?"

"I think I'm finding out."

"Tim needs a stud like me t' kick th' shit out of him." Duke stretched and cocked one booted foot on the dashboard. "I tell him what t' do an'—"

"Get your foot off of there!" Frank barked. "You're scraping dirt on the deck!"

"Hell, Tim'll lick it clean."

"I don't want him licking my rig, not unless I say so! Get your goddamn foot down!"

"No sweat, pal," Duke half-apologized, pulling his boot back, and he shot Frank an uncertain look, then shrugged. "You sound all wound up inside. Like you're horny, maybe."

"Shit!" He realized he'd yelled at the cocky bastard… and he sure as hell was horny! "Okay, maybe you're right."

"How about a blowjob? Tim's not bad when it comes t' suckin' cock."

"Jesus!" Frank almost laughed. He'd never had a stud

offer his buddy, but Duke and Tim weren't buddies. "Hell, if he wants to gobble on my meat—"

"What *he* wants don't mean a fuckin' thing," Duke interrupted. "If I tell him t' suck, he'll suck." He pawed the crotch of his Levi's. "Make up your mind, trucker."

Frank recognized the challenge in the man's voice.... The sonofabitch was right—Frank's prick was already swelling sex-hot in his pants.

Man, it'd be good to jam the blond down on his dick and shoot off a load!

"There's a place, another mile or so...down by the creek...lots of bushes and trees...I'm going to pull off and take a leak."

"Sure, Frank...sure." Duke turned to Tim. "You're goin' t' give him th' best blowjob he's ever had, right?"

"Yes, sir."

Frank hammered the rig down the highway toward the cutout he'd found long ago.

He eased up on the gas pedal and braked in smoothly, landing on-target off the road.

"Piss stop," he announced, swinging from the cab.

"Me, too," Duke said and turned to Tim. "C'mon, creep!"

Frank strode around the truck and into the clearing

18

beyond the border of overgrowth, knowing that Duke and Tim were following.

He unfastened his fly, hauled out his heavy, thick-shafted cock and let it dangle as he took a leak.

The golden spray slashed on the dried grass, and he rested his hands on his hips, swaying from side to side.

Finished, he turned back and—goddamn!

Tim was on his knees in the center of the clearing, his shirt and pants spread open, his genitals exposed, and Duke stood over him...pissing on him!

The stream poured from Duke's lean finger-held prick and washed over Tim, and the handsome blond let it soak his body and clothing without moving!

Frank buttoned his fly and sauntered toward them as Duke finished.

"Clean him up, Duke," he said quietly. "I don't want him stinking up my rig."

"He can wash up in th' creek." Duke shoved his cock back into his Levi's. "He's a goddamn slave, and—"

"You pissed on him, *you* clean him up!" Frank ordered. "Lick him clean the way you wanted him to clean up after you!"

"Go to hell! I'm no piss-drinker!"

"Lick!" he repeated and he slammed one bearlike

paw against the side of the man's head, knocking him backward.

"Fuck you, trucker!" Duke barked, and he cocked his fists, his dark eyes blazing. "I'm goin' t' make you crawl just like I made Tim crawl!"

His fist smashed into Frank's belly. It was like hitting a stone wall.

The two men were well matched, about equal height and weight, and they fell on each other, cursing and pounding and ripping and gouging.

A livid welt rose on Frank's cheekbone, and a truckle of blood came from the corner of Duke's mouth.

They punched each other repeatedly, neither one giving an inch.

Duke grabbed Frank in a clinch and rammed his knee into the trucker's crotch.

"Christ!" Frank hissed in pain, wrenched free, and clobbered Duke square on the jaw. "I'm going to bust your nuts for that!"

Duke's head snapped back from the force of the blow, and Frank moved in fast, hammering his midsection until he slumped to his knees, then sprawled back, unconscious.

Frank filled his lungs triumphantly and then peeled off the tatters of his shirt.

His barreled, hair-thatched chest glistened with sweat droplets, and raw bruises showed on his burly torso.

He turned and found Tim still on his knees, gazing at him without expression.

"Get out of those clothes, Tim. Then strip Duke."

"Sir?"

"He's going to lick you clean, like I told him to."

Tim got to his feet slowly and began undressing. His shoulders and arms were well muscled and tanned, and his wide hard-plated chest was dusted with sun-bleached peach fuzz, large dark nipples at each side.

Automatically, he peeled off his piss-soaked Levi's, and his long, thick prick fell loosely from the patch of pubic hair at his groin.

Yeah, Tim was a damn good-looking stud...and his naked body glistened with streams of Duke's piss.

He started toward Duke, then hesitated.

"Frank...sir...Duke's my master.... You don't understand about slaves like me and—"

"I'm finding out," Frank muttered. "Strip him, dammit!"

"Yes, sir!"

Tim hunched over Duke and worked him out of his clothing.

Finished, he faced Frank again, head-down.

21

"Stretch out on your back," the trucker ordered, then picked up Duke's Levi's and jerked the belt free from the waist loops. He ran the strap between his fingers and moved over to Duke, kicking him in the ribs. "Wake up, 'master.'"

"Huh?" The nude swarthy stud blinked his eyes open, focused, then growled at Frank. "Sonofa—"

"Tim's waiting to be licked clean."

"Shit!" His dark eyes flashed with anger, and the stain of dried blood at the corner of his mouth cracked. His solid chest heaved beneath a glaze of black silk, and his thin, limp cock curled over his dangling testicles. "He's a goddamn slave, an'—"

Frank brought the belt down across Duke's chest with a brutal snap, raising a wide crimson welt from one small nipple to the other.

Duke gasped with surprise and pain, then twisted over on his stomach to protect himself.

Frank followed and whipped Duke again, laying the strap across his back over his shoulder blades.

Duke cursed softly, and his muscles knotted beneath his taut skin.

Frank took his time, belting the cringing man's back until it was lined with burning marks. An unsuspected sense of mastery over his victim filled him.

22

Slowly, mercilessly, he beat hell out of the groaning sonofabitch!

"No more!" Duke whimpered at last. "I give up!"

"Crawl!" Frank ordered, a flush of sexual excitement racing through him. "Crawl over there and lick your stinking piss off Tim!"

Tim was lying back on the grass, arms and legs spread, eyes clamped shut, his bronzed, athletic, piss-gleaming nakedness offered.

Duke crawled to him…lay out on top of him…let his face press against his slave's acrid-wet chest.

"Okay, Frank?" he mumbled. "I'm doing what you said, right?"

"Lick!" He slammed the belt down on the upturned cheeks of Duke's pale ass for the first time, aroused by this new experience. "Start at his shoulders and lick all the way down! Put your tongue to work! Lick!!"

He whipped Duke's butt again, and Duke began licking…lapping at Tim's shoulders…chest…nipples…armpits—doing what Frank'd ordered him to do: licking his slave clean!

He laid the strap on Duke's quivering butt again…and again…whipping the pale buns red-hot… watching Duke lick faster and lower….

"Sir!" Tim gasped, tensed. "I'm getting a hard-on!"

"So what?" Frank looked down at the naked blond and realized that Tim hadn't been talking to him, he'd been talking to that piss-licker Duke! "What's wrong with getting a hard-on, Tim?"

"I'm a slave.... Duke's ordered me not to get a hard-on.... I—I've got do what he says."

"Yeah?" He saw Tim's cock thicken and swell as Duke tongue-lapped the tangle of pubic hair at his crotch... dammit, Tim was hung! And he belted Duke's pinked tail again. "Get down there and suck his balls! *And* his asshole!"

Duke obeyed, shifting down to lick Tim's bulging nuts...raising his legs and tonguing the hair-spiked ridge leading toward his tail...then burying his face in his slave's exposed ass!

Tim whimpered, thrashing on his back and locking his hands into fists as if fighting his sex excitement. His massive, full-swollen prick slapped back against his taut belly.

Shit, Tim was nuts-hot horny...like a goddamn trucker on a long haul!

"Suck his dick!" Frank ordered, sure that Duke'd do whatever he said. "Suck him off, 'master'!"

"No!" Tim begged feebly. "I'm Duke's slave…. He doesn't suck…never has…isn't—".

"Suck!" Frank repeated and laid the belt on Duke's quivering ass one more time. "Suck!"

Duke lowered Tim and took his rigid cock in his mouth, choking, gagging…then sucking.

Frank looked down at the burly stud, his back welted and hunched over to obey. He ripped open his pants and tugged them from his legs.

His cock bobbed free, full-hard.

He spat in his hand and applied the juice to his throbbing iron.

He knelt behind Duke and drove his prick into the cocksucker's asshole.

Duke howled, the sound muffled, and Frank gripped the back of his head, jamming him down on Tim's rod again.

Frank hip-pumped, ramming his prick into Duke's clenching butt repeatedly…getting his rocks off… trucker-style….

"AGGGHHHHH!!" The climactic roar broke from his throat. His come belched into Duke's guts. "AHHH! AHHHHH!! AGGGGRRRHHHhhhh!!!…."

and he was vaguely aware that Tim was also yelling… also getting his rocks off…

both of them....

with Duke sucking cock and getting fucked in the ass... "master"..."slave"...

Frank relaxed slowly. When he opened his eyes, the three of them were still locked together.

"We'd better clean up in the creek, Tim." He withdrew his heavy, softening ram from Duke's battered tail and swung to his feet. "You can wash your clothes at the same time."

He sauntered through the trees to the swift-moving stream and dove into the cool water. When he surfaced and looked back, Tim was approaching, his piss-soaked pants and shirt in his hands.

Good-looking stud...blond...tanned...strong, athletic build...plenty of meat...you'd never guess he's a slave....

Tim scrubbed his clothing and piled it on the bank. Then he plunged into the water, splashing and washing his virile nakedness rapidly. Suddenly he focused on Frank, as if noticing him for the first time.

"Want me to wash you, Frank?" He sloshed across the creek to stand in front of the burly trucker, head down. "Duke lets me scrub him in the shower."

"Hell, I'm not shy."

"Thank you, sir." He cupped his hands, filled them

with water, then poured it over Frank. He stroked the darkening bruises on the man's torso. "Duke put up a pretty good fight."

"He's a rough sonofabitch."

"So're you." He watched his hands move slowly over Frank's thickly haired barrel chest. "He's never done that before...licked me...rimmed my ass...sucked me off."

"How do you usually get your rocks off, Tim?"

"He does whatever he wants with me. If I please him, he lets me jerk off while he works on my balls." He stroked lower over Frank's solid, naked torso. "You're bigger than Duke...bigger all over...understand?"

"Like I've said before, I'm finding out." He pulled away and tramped toward the bank of the creek, palm-wiping himself. "I didn't bring any towels, so I guess we'll have to sun dry."

"Yes, sir."

Frank went back to the clearing.

Duke, the rugged stud he'd fought and beaten and whipped and fucked, lay face-down on the grass, his welt-streaked back and ass exposed.

Tim, Duke's slave, followed, laying out his freshly washed shirt and pants on the turf.

"Butt me," Frank ordered quietly. "Butt both of us, Tim."

"Yes, sir." He went to the pile of personal items he'd emptied from his pockets, dug two cigarettes from the crumpled pack, lit them, then came up to Frank, pressing one of them between his lips. "Yes, sir!"

"I don't like being called 'sir,'" Frank muttered. "I had enough of that...before I started highballing a rig." He inhaled smoke, then put his free hand on Tim's peach-fuzzed chest, stroking the taut curves and hard-tipped nipples. "That's another thing that makes me different from Duke."

He let his hand move downward, over Tim's muscled stomach and into his crotch. He gripped Tim's large slippery balls deliberately.

Tim stiffened. He gritted his teeth as Frank's fingers tightened.

Frank pressured steadily, watching intently until his victim's expression indicated the level of pain, and then he eased off and released the sensitive globes.

Tim exhaled audibly, and his heavy prick thickened slightly.

They finished their cigarettes in silence.

"Duke works on your nuts a lot, Tim?"

"Whenever he feels like it," the blond acknowledged. "He's my master."

"He is?" Frank asked pointedly, and he nodded toward the whipped male sprawled on the grass. "Go piss on him."

Tim hesitated, bewildered, and then he turned and walked slowly to Duke, standing over him and tugging his dangling cock.

The first spurt came reluctantly, and then the full-force stream was pouring down on Duke's hair and shoulders, his welted back and ass.

Duke squirmed and clawed the grass beneath him, but he seemed to accept his humiliation without speaking.

Finished, Tim walked back to Frank, knelt in front of him and lip-worshiped his exposed genitals.

Frank forced himself not to move, and the handsome blond licked his crinkle-sacked testicles...sucked them gently, first one and then the other...then his fast-rising prick, bulging head to choking base...all the way!

"Good enough," the burly trucker growled, shoving Tim back from his newly aroused ram. "I've got a rig to push to Oakdale; that's the only reason I don't want you to make me pop again."

"Uhh—sir—Frank?"

"Hang your shirt and pants on the rearview mirror. They'll be dry by the time we get there." He waited while the naked blond got to his feet, gathered up his clothes and headed for the truck, and then he sauntered over to Duke, nudging him in the side. "It looks like you've lost a slave and I've picked up a copilot."

"Crap!" Duke sneered. "You don't know how to keep that shit-eater in line, asshole!"

"I'm finding out," Frank declared once more, stooping to pick up Duke's belt from the grass. "I'd better take this with me...in case Tim needs to be reminded who he belongs to."

PLEDGE-SLAVE

I'm one of the pledges to the college fraternity, and we're in the middle of the traditional initiation.

There're ten of us, all stripped to our Levi's, and we've all been paddled and humiliated and done everything our "brothers" have demanded.

"Line up!" Carl orders. "Line up, you fuckin' pledges!"

Carl's the pledgemaster and a senior classman, and

we line up at attention across the frat house dining room. Frank's on one side of me, swarthy and tough as nails, and Johnny's on the other side, blond and chunky and my best buddy in the group.

"Ass inspection!" Carl commands, slapping the wooden paddle against the flat of his palm. "Strip!"

We peel off our pants. We've been through this before during the initiation, taking off our jeans and showing the members how much damage they've done to our butts with their paddles.

But this time, Carl's the only senior in the room.

He starts at the left end of the line, beyond Frank, and I know he's looking at the marks on each guy's buns. I know mine must be black and blue. Yeah, I've taken my swats…and a lot more than the rest of the pledges…. I guess I've worked on getting paddled—it's sort of a turn-on.

Carl's in back of Frank now, murmuring something to him. Frank tenses and sucks in an audible breath.

Carl moves behind me, and his big, pawlike hands cup my asscheeks.

"You can really take it, pledge," he whispers in my ear, and his fingers dig into my warm flesh-curves. "I like that."

The coarse-clothed crotch of his Levi's rasps against

the crack in my butt, and for an instant, it's like he's ready for a stand-up fuck!

He lets go and moves on to Johnny.

Christ! I wonder what it'd be like, having that paddle-swinging stud screw my ass!

The heat rushes to my groin, and I concentrate on not throwing a hard-on. Sure, I've been getting my rocks off with guys, but I don't want my fraternity brothers to know.

"Get-acquainted time!" Carl announces. I guess he's finished his ass inspection. "Left face, pledges!" We turn, forming a single column, and I can't help noticing Frank's wide, muscled shoulders and tapering back... and slick pale butt. "I want you all t' be true brothers, which means that you all perform th' sacred act of friendship. See th' can of shortnin' on th' table over there?" I've heard about this initiation ritual, and I think it's sort of funny, having rough-and-tough Frank in front of me. "You're goin' t' march around that table, two steps at a time, an' when you get t' th' grease, you're goin' t' lube th' friendliest finger you've got an' shove it up th' butthole in front of you until th' friendship circle's completed. Any questions?"

"Shit!" one of the guys at the back of the line objects. "I'm not going to stick my—"

Whack! Carl's oak paddle strikes bare ass.

"Want t' drop out, pledge?"

"No…no, sir…I want to be a brother…sir!"

"Start marchin' around th' table, you finger-fuckers!"

We start the march…two steps at a time…halt…a curse…two steps…an embarrassed giggle…two steps… a frightened whimper…two steps forward…

Ahead of me, Frank's at the table…reaching for the lubricant…hesitating, unsure…sticking his whole god-damn hand into the can.

He's showing off, and I know it!

A grunt from the guy ahead of Frank…a fingertip inserted, perhaps…

Two more steps forward…my turn!

I grease the index finger of my right hand. I can't help wishing it was my dick as I nudge it between the tight round cheeks of Frank's butt. Yeah. I sure wouldn't mind fucking the hunky athlete!

I locate the crinkled opening, lube it for a moment, then slip my finger inward to the first knuckle.

"Bastard!" Frank hisses.

"Golly!" I whisper, innocent-like. "I'm only doing what Carl ordered!"

And I give Frank's little asshole another knuckle's worth of finger.

Two steps forward.

I spread my legs slightly and feel Johnny's greased finger probe into my tail warily.

Hell, pal, give it to me! I'm no goddamn virgin, that's for sure!

His fingertip rests against my pulsing asshole, and I shove back, taking it easily.

Man, this is wild! Plugging Frank's butt while my buddy Johnny plugs mine!

Two steps forward, and when Frank stops, I give him my finger all the way to the base. Yeah, and I get all of Johnny's!

I feel Johnny's body warmth almost touching my back. Dammit, he's the best pal I've got! His hot breath explodes across my bare shoulders, and I know he's getting the finger treatment from the guy behind him.

We're moving again, completing the circle.

I screw Frank's clenching hole slowly, knowing he can feel each thrust, each turning and twisting and kneading. He sure as hell doesn't object!

And Johnny's close behind me, his finger resting in my ass…not his cock…shit!

From the corner of my eye, I can see the other pledges in the circle, stripped, hand-to-asshole…a couple of cocks puffed a little, like mine…a couple of studs kinda turned on, like I am, maybe—

"Halt!" Carl commands, and we obey. "Fingers out!" We obey. "'Bout face!" We obey. "Make another friendship circle, you lousy pledges!"

I'm facing Johnny's back. He's blond, and his shoulders are wide and muscle-thick. He's a chunky stud, and he's my buddy. He's got a pale ivory butt, the bubbled arcs pinked from being swatted.

He gets to the can of lard on the table first…sticks a finger into it…reaches forward to the guy in front of him—

We all move two steps ahead.

The grease is on my left side this time, and I stick my left forefinger into it.

That finger's shorter and not so thickly knuckled as the one I shoved into Frank.

I push it into Johnny's tail. The passage is already slick, the opening spread.

I slip my finger into him. He doesn't curse or resist.

Two steps forward.

Frank's behind me now, and I'm not surprised when he finger-rams me. It's his way of getting even.

Hell, I've had bigger pricks than his finger shoved up my butt!

I pressure into Johnny gently, and he squirms, adjusting to the penetration as we move again. Yeah, he sure as hell isn't objecting!

We complete the circle once more, and I stretch the rest of my fingers, stroking the soft-haired ridge between Johnny's thighs. My fingertips brush against his large, loose-swinging balls and—

"Fingers out!" Carl bellows. "Hit the latrine, then shower! You've got exactly five minutes!"

We dash down the hall to the latrine across from the downstairs dormitory. The lights aren't working, and we stumble into the blackness of the small shower room. There're only four sprays and ten of us, and we're packed together, naked, trying to get wet and find the soap and—

A hand brushes against my crotch, and lingers, examining my cock and balls, then pulling away.

Man!

"Hey, guys!" That's Pete's voice, the short, stocky joker in the group. "I'm getting a hard-on!"

"Hell, who isn't?" someone snickers.

"But this is the first one I've thrown since this goddamn initiation started!" He gasps kiddingly, "Oh, Frank! You mustn't play with it like that!"

"Shit!" Frank growls from the other side of the room. "I'm nowhere near you, you asshole!"

"Well, one of you studs is!"

We all laugh, and I'm surrounded by squirming nude male bodies.

A wet dream come to life!

No one can see me in the darkness, so I let my hands wander…a sex-tight pair of testicles drawn up to an already-hard prick…another one of the pledges, turned away from me, his slablike asscheeks marble-smooth and taut…

a sudden blast of shower water drenching me as I'm shifted under one of the sprays…

reaching for…getting a bar of soap shoved into my hand…lathering the grease from my fingers, the fingers I had up Frank and Johnny's butts…

soapy palms rubbing over my chest and downward…

groping the unseen stud while he gropes me…

Jesus! I've got the biggest hard-on I've ever felt in my fist, and I can't tell who it belongs to!

I'm pushed away from the shower and the huge man-iron.…

silence except for the gushing water…all of us just writhing together in the darkness…touching…exploring…testing…

yeah, a real, live wet dream!

all of us cock-and-balls stripped, matching rigid pricks, slithering about in the blackness...

a short, chunky guy pressed up in front of me, solid and barrel-chested...Pete...his arms locking around me... both of us holding each other...it's got to be Pete... hunky, what-the-hell joker...no joking right now—

"One minute!" Carl announces from the doorway to the latrine. "You goddamn pledges've got one minute t' finish gettin' showered an' haul your butts back down th' hall. One swat for every second you're late!"

Peter jerks away from me. We're both trying to get under the showers to rinse off...and so are the other guys....

and we're pouring out into the main room of the latrine and finding towels and drying fast....

There goes my hard-on!

Yeah, I don't want to show how I've been turned on by what happened in the showers...and I don't want to get paddled bareass for being one second late—or do I?

I go along with the rest of the guys, running back to the dining room and lining up at attention facing Carl, Frank on my left side, Johnny on my right.

Carl moves along in front of us, rugged and full-muscled, stripped to the waist and hairy-chested, flipping the paddle from one hand to the other.

Christ, he's burly and tough and looks like—

"You goddamn, ass-pluggin', finger-fuckin', horny cock-grabbin' pledges—" He steps back and shows his teeth in a wide, pleased grin. "You've all made it through th' initiation!"

The sliding doors behind him open, and there're all the frat brothers, some dressed, some half-stripped, all no longer our seniors in the fraternity.

"C'mon in," the President motions, laughing at our shock. "The bar's open…brothers!"

The initiation's over!

Shouting and laughing, we crowd the bar and grab for liquor-filled glasses.

Dammit, that booze tastes good!

"Hey!" Johnny saunters up to me, blond and tanned and grinning. "I guess we're really buddies now, huh? Asshole buddies!"

"I guess so," I chuckle, remembering how he squirmed his butt back on my greased finger. "Kinda crazy, huh?"

"Hell, it wasn't—" He shrugs and turns away. "I'm going to get loaded!"

I watch the easy shift of his pale, lightly pinked ass

as he crosses the room toward a group of our brothers, and I wonder how he'd feel about our being buddies if he knew I dig having sex with guys.

Maybe he suspects. Maybe he doesn't.

I spot Carl standing alone in the shadows. His rugged features are set, and the slick black hair glistens on his massive chest. He's put away that swat-paddle, but he still looks like a pledgemaster should. Christ, he's a tough sonofabitch!

I wander over to him.

"How's it going, Carl?"

"Not bad." He views me coldly with his narrow, slitted eyes, and his thin lips barely move when he speaks. "Your butt's goin' t' be black-and-blue for a week or so."

"Maybe I bruise easier than the other pledges."

"You took more swats than any of them." He has me nailed with his gaze. I remember how he cupped my asscheeks and toyed with them during the last inspection. "It was like you were askin' for a real beatin'."

"Bullshit!" I'm trying to defy him, but my voice doesn't sound as confident as it should. "I made it through the initiation, right?"

"Yeah." He shows the hint of a pleased grin. "You were a damn good pledge."

"Thanks." I look down, avoiding his steady, command-ing gaze, and I feel like he's always going to—

"Your glass is empty," he notes quietly. "Go for a refill, pledge."

"Yes…sir."

He's not the paddle-swinging pledgemaster anymore, and I'm not a pledge anymore…but he called me "pledge." And I answered "yes, sir"…and I'm obeying him.

I go back to the bar and refill my glass.

Pete comes up beside me to mix another drink for himself, and I expect one of his goddamn jokes.

"Thanks for kissing my ass in the showers," he murmurs intimately.

"Crap. I didn't kiss your ass, joker."

"You must've." He turns and rests back, his elbows on the bar, his glass in one hand, the other wandering idly over his taut-muscled torso. I remember looking up to him in the blackness of the shower room. I wonder if he knows it was me. "There were ten of us in the show-ers, and I counted nine kisses on my butt."

"Maybe someone kissed twice."

"Shit, I never thought of that!" Pete runs his fingers downward over his pale flat-curved belly, stopping just short of the tangle of pubic wire and the loose-dangling cock. "It must've been Frank. He's always wanted to kiss my tail. Sometimes at night, I hear him at the other end of the dorm, beating his meat and groaning about how he wants to—"

"Yeah?" I've got a crazy idea. Maybe Pete's joking about Frank, or maybe— "You were on the other side of Frank in the friendship circle, Pete?"

"Yeah." Suddenly he's serious, staring straight ahead. "He's a real rough-and-tough stud, but when I stuck my finger—" He jerks his hand from almost touching his heavy dick, and he drinks fast, becoming the joker again. "I hope you bastards don't line up to kiss my ass every time I take a shower. You'll wear the goddamn thing out!"

He tromps across the room to play the joker with some of the other guys.

I wonder what happened when Pete finger-fucked Frank. I wonder if they stumbled on each other in the blackness of the shower room, the way Pete and I did. I wonder if—

Christ! Maybe Frank's the one who threw that king-sized rod!

Some of the brothers are beginning to head for their rooms, and I relax, drinking and feeling liquor-mellow.

I survey the naked ex-pledges, and I wish I could tell which one gets that giant hard-on when he's hot. Maybe I should suggest we take another gang shower, only with the lights on.

I see Carl still standing in the shadows, massively built and rugged. Frank's talking to him, only it looks as if Carl's doing most of the talking. His thin lips barely move, and Frank stands there, head down, nodding occasionally.

I wonder if Frank has that always-a-pledge feeling I have about Carl.

"Goddamn, buddy!" It is Johnny stumbling up beside me. "I'm gassed!"

"You look it." His large brown eyes are glazed, and a shit-eating grin is spread across his handsome features. "Better hit the sack and sleep it off."

"Good idea…if I can find my room."

"C'mon." I wrap one arm about his shoulders. "I'll put you to bed."

Johnny's room is right across the hall upstairs from the four-bed dorm where I live. He had a roommate until a couple of weeks ago when the dumb bastard flunked out of school.

I guide Johnny toward the stairs and upward, and he leans against me, letting me support him.

"Want to move in with me, buddy?" he mumbles. "We'd make good roommates."

"I'll think about it."

"It'd be real good…you're my best pal…."

I feel the warmth and strength of his naked body against mine, and I wonder what would happen if we roomed together.

Damn it, I'd like to have sex with him! Yeah, and I'd like to do more than just finger-fuck his ass!

We reach the second floor, and I guide him down the hall and into his room.

"Hit the sack, Johnny."

He stumbles to one of the two beds, and I close the door behind us.

"Jesus, I'm loaded!" he mutters, sprawling on his back and covering his eyes with one arm. "Maybe I oughta take a cold shower and sober up."

"You already took one shower tonight, remember?"

"Yeah…that was…all of us in there t'gether…after th' friendship circle…messing around…best pal…" His voice trails off. "Yeahhhh…"

Maybe he's passed out…. And maybe he hasn't.

I cross to his bed, and he's lying there, naked and nuts-pulsing sexy. His blond hair is mussed, and his broad, muscled shoulders melt into the slow-heaving curves of his solid chest, golden silk sprayed toward the dark nipples at each side. He's got that arm flung over his face, and more silk fills his wide exposed armpit. His flat tanned stomach is muscle-marked by the rise and fall of his breathing, and his legs are spread, his heavy cock dangling outward and down over his bulging testicles.

Maybe he's as drunk as he claimed…and maybe he isn't.

Shit, I don't care! If we're going to be roommates, Johnny'd better find out right now that I dig getting it off with guys, not cunt! Yeah, and if he yells "Queer!" I can always claim I was as drunk as he is!

Hell, I'm hot for the sonofabitch, and I know it!

I sit on the side of his bed and put one hand on his chest lightly. He doesn't make a move to push me away. Maybe he really is passed out!

My dick starts to get hard, the sex-hungry heat rising in my groin.

I watch my fingers stroke Johnny's heaving chest…the corn silk—covered arcs…the firm nipples… the rib-etched sides…the masculine physique…the shorts-marked line at his hips…his crinkle-haired groin.…

his cock...

his balls!

Yeah, I've got him by the balls, the way that guy back at the gym grabbed me by the nuts and—hell, I can't squeeze the way Stan squeezed my nuts.

I bend down and tongue-lap Johnny's prick, and I remember how Stan jammed me down to suck him off...and how he ordered me to blow the others—Tommy, the horny studs on the football team, his other pals.

Johnny doesn't move, and I shift onto the bed, kneeling between his spread thighs. His full-crowned prick throbs and begins to stiffen, and I take the swelling head into my mouth, tongue-washing it slowly and thoroughly.

Christ, it tastes good!

The shaft hardens, slick and solid, and I gulp down on it hungrily. Yeah, he's hung for sucking! Not too big, just right!

I suck his iron all the way into my throat, hold it for a moment, then ease off halfway. He's acting like he's still asleep, but he's breathing harder, faster, one arm still covering his eyes.

Shit, he knows what I'm doing!

I release his balls and let my fingers creep back toward

his asshole, just like I did in the friendship circle. The cleft between his buns is still slippery with grease—sure, none of us had time to really wash up in the shower room—and the crinkled lips of his little hole—

My finger slips inside easy as hell!

All the way in!

Like he wants it in his clenching nest again!!

Or, maybe, he wants something bigger…like my cock!!!

I suck his iron again, tip to base…again…again …and again…and he digs his heels into the mattress, raising his ass and pumping his meat into my mouth— and laying his butt wide open—

I suck his iron and stick a second finger up his rear…. I've got him squirming on two fingers now… first burst of precome in my mouth…

Yeah, buddy! Get your rocks off! shoot your cream into my guts! Come! COME!

COMMMME!

Johnny lets go, thrashing back on his shoulders, stifling his cries with gritted teeth. For an instant, I'm afraid I'm going to cream right along with him. Man, what a turn-on!

I swallow fast and pump my fingers into Johnny, matching each potent spurt…again and again.

I run my free hand over his arched, quivering, muscled torso, and he sags back, moaning softly.

I suction the last of the heavy flow, then hold his slow-fading cock in my mouth and tongue-lap it gently, and he shudders with the aftershocks of his climax.

That's something damn special, taking a buddy off and feeling him come down afterward! No matter what Johnny says tomorrow, when he's wide awake and sober, I'm glad I've cooled his nuts tonight, damn it!

He's lying still now, and I let his dick slip free from my mouth and raise my head. He's sprawled back, naked and sweat-glistening in the dimness, one arm still flung over his eyes. I wonder if he's really passed out or if he's peering at me and my sex-hot prick.

My fingers are still buried in his asshole when a new idea hits me. Yeah, I'm going to fuck him! I've got a feeling he won't object—not if he didn't object to what I've already done!

But I've got to grease my ram. He'll never be able to take it bare.

I ease my hand from under him, and he kind of grunts as my fingers slip free. Maybe he knows what I've got in mind.

I swing to my feet and take my time crossing to the

door, giving my hard-on time to soften. Shit, I don't want any of our frat brothers to catch me coming out of Johnny's room with my rod at full-mast!

I open the door. The hallway's empty and silent. I guess everyone else has hit the sack. I head down the corridor to the latrine, needing to take a leak and knowing there'll be some kind of pecker lubricant there.

There're no lights on in the can, but I have no trouble finding the urinal in the dimness. I tug my loosened cock and begin to piss; there's nothing like taking a leak to loosen up before screwing a stud's ass!

The stream spatters into the trough. As it ends, I hear sounds from the shower alcove beyond the half-wall at the end of the room.

Curious, I flip the last droplets from my dick and tiptoe to the opening, and—

Awww-shit-goddamn-Keerist!

Carl's standing there in the shadows, his head thrown back and his eyes clamped shut, bare-chested and rugged as hell, muscles tensed, Levi's down around his knees…and Frank's kneeling in front of him, naked, face to crotch—sucking cock!

My rod snaps up full-hard again.

Carl's like a god looming over Frank. A belt dangles

from one of his hands…and there're faint welt-stripes marked across Frank's back, all the way down to his tight-clenched ass.

Yeah, Carl's made Frank pledge himself—like a slave—

I look up. Carl's eyes are open, glued on me…seeing me naked and prick-hot and he raises the belt and brings it snapping down across Frank's shoulders.

Jesus, what'd it be like if I was in Frank's place?

Numb, I retreat, and I'm balls-aching hot. Damn it, I've got to get my rocks off!

I find a tube of hair grease one of the guy must've left on the shelf over the washbasins. It'll do.

I haul back down the hallway. I don't give a shit if one of the guys catches me. I'm going to screw Johnny's butt!

I slip into his room and lock the door behind me. He's turned on one side on the bed, his back to me, and the creamy-pale cheeks of his ass seem to glow in the dimness.

I cover my throbbing iron with lubricant. If Johnny's a virgin, he sure as hell won't be one in a few minutes!

I ease onto the bed behind him and run my palms lightly over his shoulders and back. The corded muscles shift beneath the smooth flesh, and I wonder if he knows I'm there—and what I plan on doing. I let my hands slide downward to his tail…cup the firm, rounded cheeks…spread them slightly…slip my fingers into the crevice and locate the puckered target.

Johnny moves, turning farther away and cocking his upper leg. Maybe he doesn't know he's exposed his little asshole even more…or maybe he does!

I grip the turgid shaft of my dick and nudge the slick head into the relaxed passage…center on the hidden opening…pressure—

Christ, it's like a knife cutting into warm butter!

Johnny chokes a breath, and I hold still, collar-deep between those clenching lips. I run my fingers over his solid shoulders again, and—man, he's shoving his butt back, taking more and more of my iron!

I wrap my arms about him, and he plants his tail in my crotch, my cock buried balls-deep in his guts.

Goddamn! He's got to be wide awake, and he knows damn well who's fucking him!

I stroke his broad chest and pebble-tipped nipples, and I hip-pump once, deliberately.

"Still want me to be your roommate, Johnny?"

"More than ever, buddy," he whispers. "More than ever!"

Yeah, he's asking for it! I'm going to cock-ram him all

night long, slow and sure until he begs for more...and every other night for as long as we room together... yeah, make the good-looking blond stud beg for it!

I clench him back in my arms and close my eyes, plugging his butt...and I remember seeing Carl in the latrine showers, massive and pants down, towering over Frank and making the swarthy weight lifter suck him off, laying that belt across his shoulders when he catches me watching—

It's my graduation day from college, as well as the annual Homecoming for the alumni, and I'm in my room at the frat house. Most of the guys have already left, and the place is silent, deserted.

I've stripped off my rented robe and hauled on an old pair of Levi's. I wonder where to start the job of packing my gear. I don't have to move out for a couple of days yet, but I've collected one helluva lot of crap in the past four years.

I scratch the hair on my bare chest, trying to decide what to pack and what to throw away, and there's a knock on the door.

"C'mon in," I call, and blink with surprise as the door opens. "Carl!"

Christ, I haven't seen the burly stud who was pledge-master of my initiation since he graduated at the end of that semester, and he looks even more rugged than he did then. His black hair is clipped short, and his narrow-slitted eyes fasten on me as his thin lips flicker a grin.

"Hi, brother." He gives me the fraternity handshake. His grip is steel-hard. "Moving out, huh?"

"Yeah, I finally got my diploma." Just seeing Carl again makes me feel like a goddamn pledge! "What brings you back?"

"Homecoming." He looks around the room. "I lived here when I was a senior, remember?"

"Sure."

"You were rooming down the hall with Johnny when I graduated.

"He transferred to State last year."

"Frank?"

"He's around somewhere." I can't take my eyes off Carl...the sport shirt clinging to his muscled physique, glistening chest hair showing at the open throat... swollen biceps...crotch-bulging wash pants slung low on his hips. "Maybe he's down at the beer bust on the quad."

"He couldn't hold his booze worth shit." He prowls

around the room, inspecting it. "You were damn lucky, having this place to yourself like I did."

I've never thought about Carl's having lived here. It's the best room in the house, except for the one reserved for the frat president, and I got it when I was elected pledgemaster last semester. There was a good view of Sorority Row from the front window, and a private latrine, and—

Carl's checking it out like it's still his room, like he's still my pledgemaster, like nothing's changed.

"The pledgemaster always gets this room," I mumble, trying to explain. "You know."

"Yeah." He spots the oak paddle hung of the wall, the "sacred club" of the fraternity initiations...the one he used on me. "Were you any good as th' master?"

"Okay, I guess." My muscles tense, and my heart's pounding with sudden excitement. "You were better."

"Man, you were a damn good pledge." He turns back to face me, studying me intently. "Better than all th' others...includin' Frank."

"Thanks." I remember seeing Frank after the initiation was over, muscular and naked, on his knees in the shadows of the latrine shower room, his heaving shoulders and back welt-marked, his head bobbing against

55

Carl's exposed crotch…and the belt dangling from Carl's hand. "Want me to see if I can find Frank?"

"No." He walks to the door with authority, closes it and snaps the lock. "None of the other guys're in the house. Just you an' me."

"Okay."

I'm a pledge again, like when I first joined the fraternity…and Carl knows it!

He goes to the window, and he looks out, maybe remembering when he lived here. He closes the drapes abruptly, plunging the room into warm shadows, and he turns back, unbuttoning his shirt and peeling it off. The massive muscles ripple across his broad shoulders and arms, and the slick black hair glistens on his massive chest.

Christ, I'd almost forgotten what a solid-built sonofabitch he is! I take a deep breath, and a flush of sex-heat storms into my groin.

Hypnotized, I watch him take the paddle from the wall and heft it in his bear-like paws. His fingers are short and thick-knuckled, and dark silk lines his forearms.

"Pledge," he growls.

"Yes, sir!" I snap automatically.

"Assume th' position!"

"Yes, sir!"

I bend over, hands on knees, but willing. Yeah, I'm a pledge again!

Carl's pledge!

From the corner of my eye, I see him move into position to swat me. I haven't tasted the paddle since initiation, and I wonder if I can still take the beating I know he's going to give me.

I'm his pledge, damn it!

He barely taps my upturned ass with the paddle, showing me where he's going to place the first swat, and I feel the sting through the worn denim covering my cheeks.

I clamp my eyes shut and grit my teeth. I know he's flexing and winding up—

Whaccckkk!

The paddle hits my tail…Jesus!…smashing pain… the blond kid getting spanked by the coach when I was at the gym…flashing memories—

Whhaaaccckkkk!

…the male-scented smell of the locker room, and Stan twisting my balls until I knelt to suck him off—

Whack! Whack!

…getting fucked for the first time…the fraternity initiation—

57

Thwackkk!

...finger-fucking Frank and Johnny in the "friend-ship circle"...and, afterward—

Tthhhwwwaaaccckkk!

"Sir!" The word whistles from my throat. "Sir!"

"Ass inspection! Strip!"

I straighten and peel off my Levi's. I'm showing him the marks he's left on my ass, like before...but this time, my cock's standing out, iron-hard! Yeah, this time it's just me and Carl!

He's behind me...palms cupping my buns, fingers tracing the crack between them...gripping tightly....

"Remember when you saw me an' Frank in th' showers after th' initiation?" he growls. "Maybe I should give you th' same treatment I gave him."

I picture Carl standing over Frank in the shadows, the belt dangling from one hand. "I can take anything he can, sir."

"Get over on th' bed," he orders. "On your hands an' knees."

"Yes, sir!"

I climb onto the bed, kneeling on all fours with my butt toward him. His rugged features are set and cold as he draws the wide leather belt from his trousers. He doubles it in one hand, and I close my eyes again; bracing myself for the first blow.

Yeah, I'm going to get my first taste of leather!

The lash whistles through the air and rips across my bare asscheeks.

Christ! Shit! Goddamn!

A ribbon of fire streaks into my flesh. I see pain flashes on the inside of my eyelids. I fight back a scream, and the pain mounts, then numbs slowly.

The sex heat intensified in my loins, and my rigid cock quivers.

Another brutal stroke…another…pain—and pleasure!

Yeah, I'm wallowing in the combination of agony and sensual excitement…naked and crouching before the whip-wielding pledgemaster…accepting each blow… showing him that I can take it…more!… MORE!

I want to feel the lash across my shoulders and down my back.… I want to crawl before him.… I want to serve him, to please him, to—

The whipping's stopped! Jesus, I hope I didn't yell or cry out or do anything that made Carl quit! I want him to be proud of how his pledge can take all the pain he feels is necessary!

I catch my breath and open my eyes. Carl's standing

in front of me, his bulging crotch at eye level. His fingers unfasten the fly of his pants and spread the flaps. He isn't wearing shorts, and a lush growth of black silk trails downward from his cratered navel over his pale, flat belly to merge with the flare of crisp pubic wire at the base.

He shoves his trousers down, and his prick and balls snap free. I grin to myself because he's hung the way I've always thought he'd be—like a stud bull in rut! The flesh-column is long and thick...twisted veins bulging along the shaft...almost no indentation at the broad collar...massive crown, mallet-shaped and glistening...a bead of wetness bubbling from the deep-marked well... large testicles swinging in their crinkled sack.

Whipping me's sure turned him on! Damn right, I'm glad!

He grasps the ram and pushes it toward my face.

Sonofabitch, I'm going to suck that iron!

I press my lips against the tip...kissing it...inhaling male scent...letting my tongue wash the precome from Carl's prong, tasting and swallowing it...taking his swollen cockhead into my mouth...slathering it with spit...gulping down on it hungrily.

I remember that gang shower during the initiation

and the huge hard-on I felt in the darkness. Maybe Carl really did sneak in there with us pledges!

His hands rest on the back of my head, urging me forward, and I don't care how choking-big his dick is—I want it! All of it!

My lips smash against the lush tangle of wiry hair at his groin, and I've shown him that I can take every goddamn inch of his giant! I can't breathe, but I don't give a shit... I'm doing what he wants... I'm serving him!

He pulls back, letting me up for air, and I grip his solid hips for support. He holds my head in place and rams his iron down my throat again, as if challenging me to take it.

I'll show you, Carl! Anything you want...sir!

I suck willingly, and my hands roam down his legs and upward over his burly torso.

Anything, sir!

He jerks away, freeing his pulsing tool. Then he grabs my hair, wrenching my head back. He holds the base of his spit-wet rod, spanking it back and forth across my upturned face, and I welcome each stinging slap.

"Anything!" I whisper aloud.

"Yeah!" It's as if he's been reading my thoughts. He

pulls his full-hard prick back against his belly. "Lick th' sweat off my balls! Make love t' them, pledge!"

I lunge forward, burying my face in his crotch and nuzzling his exposed testicles. My tongue darts out to lap them...separate them in their thin-skinned sack... suction one and then the other...I can't quit!

I reach up to stroke his silk-haired chest...full-arched chest...wide, sharp-tipped nipples...sac-tight nuts stuffed into my mouth—

I'm hunched on the bed, naked and ass-whipped, and I'm prick-stiff, obeying the pledgemaster...my master!

Yeah, I'm ready to do whatever the rugged bastard wants!

He jams my head down from his balls, and I lick the sensitive linings of his thighs...the deep-marked valley at each side of his groin...the wiry hair surrounding his powerful genitals...shit, I'm slobbering over him like a dog in heat!

Hell, I don't care! I don't care about anything except being—

"I'm goin' t' fuck you," he says, pulling back slowly. "Right, pledge?"

"Yes, sir!"

"Grease?"

"In the bathroom…sir!"

I heard him grunt and tromp to the can…fumble around, finding the tube of lubricant…come back… position himself behind me. I picture him standing there, naked and brawny, his massive ointment- gleaming cock aimed at the crack in my blistered ass.

He grasps my buns and spreads them, and I tense involuntarily as his huge prickhead centers squarely on my sensitive opening.

Shit, he'll split me wide open with that telephone pole!

He pressures…eases…pressures again…thrusts hard!

I open my mouth in a silent scream as the bulging crown drives collar-deep into me, and he rubs his palms over my straining asscheeks. The stab of pain fades, and my muscle ring relaxes, accepting the powerful invader.

"Settle back," he orders quietly. "Take it, pledge!"

"Yes, sir."

I grit my teeth and shove back, and the rigid column inches deeper into me. He rests his hands on my hips and stands motionless, and I can feel the taut veins rake my super-sensitive lips as more of the turgid shaft slides inward.

I'm sweating with the effort, but I want to prove to him that I can do what he orders. Shit, it's like getting a length of steel pipe jammed up my butt!... The biggest goddamn chunk of stud meat I've ever taken...and Carl's making me do it all by myself...more...more!... Crisp crotch hair against my buns!!

Yeah, I've done it! I've worked all the way on my pledgemaster's massive dick! I've obeyed his orders!!

His fingers grip my hips securely, and he gives a final thrust, burying his iron in my guts...pain...pleasure!

He eases back to the flange, almost taking his ram from my hungry asshole...I don't want him to pull it out! He slides it balls-deep into me again.... Thank you, sir!

"You want me t' fuck you," he says, as if he's reading my mind. "Right, pledge?"

"Yes, sir."

"Say it!"

"Fuck me, sir!" The words come pouring out, uncontrolled. "Anything you say, sir!" I'm on my hands and knees, stripped and butt-whipped, and Carl's prick throbs in my asshole. "Fuck me! I can take it! Give me your horny dick! Get your rocks off! Please, sir!"

"Yeahhh!" He brings one foot up, planting it on the bed beside me, draws back, deep-rams, and the width of his groin hammers against my tail. "Damn right!"

Head down, I open my eyes, and I can see my own

cock flopping between my spread thighs, no longer full hard, a droplet of clear liquid dangling from the tip. I watch it stiffen with each potent thrust into my guts.

Carl moves onto the bed, planting his knees outside mine. He grips my shoulders for added leverage as he pumps in short, vicious strokes. Yeah, I'm getting fucked like never before!

He jams me down until my chest is on the bed, my arms spread, my ass arched up to his crotch. He mounts me dog-style, angling his huge prick into me as if probing every inch of my guts. He's gulping for breath and grunting with each penetration, and drops of his sweat splash down on my back.

Christ, he's tearing me apart…and I don't care!

"Yes, sir!" I mumble. "Anything you say, sir! I can take it! I'm your—"

I can't say the word I'm thinking—slave! No, I'm not ready to say it…not yet!

Carl's muscled arms lock about me, and he hauls me back to sit on his fence post as he settles on his haunches. His sweaty chest hair presses against my shoulder blades, and his fingers claw at my exposed torso. I flail the air helplessly with my hands, and I throw my head back, mouth open in another silent howl. I'm pinned down on his brutal invader, and he corkscrews his hips slowly, reaming my throbbing asshole.

"Goddamn good!" he hisses in my ear. "Good pledge!"

Yeah, I'm his fraternity brother…his pledge…his ass-plugged slave!

His fingers wrench and twist my bare flesh as they work downward…into my crotch…bypassing my aching-stiff cock…clenching my balls!

He's got me by the nuts!

Flaring pain!… Take it, man!… Yes, sir!… Ass prick-plugged!… Rugged pledgemaster!… Good pledge serving his master!… Pleasure-pain! He releases my testicles and slams me down flat on the bed, and he falls on me, screwing for all he's worth. I'm pinned beneath his surging nakedness. I dig my fingers into the mattress beneath me, welcoming his fury.

Yeah, I want it! I want—Jesus, I'm going to shoot my wad!

My steel-hard dick plows into the bedsheet, and I stuff my mouth with the cloth to stifle my cries. I don't want to cream until Carl does, but—

Aggghhhh!

I crash into the searing ecstasy of climax…come-shooting…explosion after explosion in rhythm with the male ram pumping into my guts...ultimate pleasure... slobbering pledge submitting to his master!

"PLEDGE!"

Carl wrenches his massive iron from my pulsing asshole and pulls up over me. The first heavy spurt of come splashes into the small of my back and— ARRGGHH! He slams his convulsing ram back into my gaping hole!

He's pouring his sperm into my guts!

I've served him! I've been a good pledge! I've taken my pledgemaster's sex-hot dick! I've made him pop his load!

Yes, sir. Anything you say, sir!

I clench my butt muscles, milking the last of the male flow from his massive ram, and he blankets me with his powerful body.

I float in dazed satisfaction, exhausted and totally pleased...secure...mastered...wanting to stay in the new world I've discovered. Yeah, Carl's paddled and whipped and fucked me...pain and pleasure...master!

I'm trapped between his burly nakedness and the come-wet sheet beneath me. Both of us are sweating like worn-out athletes in the locker room. I remember the gym locker room where Stan made me suck cock for the first time.

Carl's prick is still firm in my tail. He hasn't gone soft yet. Maybe he wants to go right on and get his rocks off again. I've heard about studs who stay hard and fuck and fuck and—

His lips graze over my shoulder, and he raises himself, breaking the bond of come and sweat between us.

"I've got t' clean up," he mutters. "I've got t' catch th' night plane back home."

"Carl—" I grit my teeth as he withdraws his still-swollen ram—I want it, sir!—and I feel empty when it's gone. "Shit!"

He chuckles and slaps me on the butt, easy and almost playful, and he hauls up from the bed and heads for the latrine.

I lie still, listening to the shower start, and I wonder if I've ever felt so completely satisfied before. Maybe it was crazy, letting Carl whip me, obeying him, submitting to whatever he wanted…. I'll have to think about that later.

I hear the spray stop, and I turn my head to see Carl come sauntering from the bathroom, dripping wet, a towel in one hand, his heavy cock curved outward and down from his hair-filled crotch. Christ, what a stud!

"Worn out, Carl?"

"Hell, no!" He rubs the towel over his loosened genitals, his narrow eyes viewing me, and I know he can see the smear of come he left on my back and the glowing cheeks of my upturned ass. "I would've kept on goin', if I'd had more time. I like t' get my gun a couple of times before I quit." He raises the towel to his barreled chest, drying lazily. "I should've messed around with you instead of Frank when I was livin' here."

"Why didn't you?"

"I figured you were makin' out with Johnny." He continues drying off. "He dug screwin' your tail, huh?"

"No. He liked blowjobs and getting fucked—that's all."

"Shit!" He grins. "I should've humped both of you!"

I swing up from the bed, leaving the large wet stain marking my climax on the sheets, and I cross to the bureau against the far wall.

"Cigarette, Carl?"

"Yeah." His reflection in the mirror over the dresser shows he's looking at my backside as I light a pair of cigarettes. "Ever take a paddle or belt bareass before?"

"No." I turn and hand him one of the butts. "Here."

"Thanks." He takes a drag and lets the cigarette dangle from the corner of his mouth as he continues toweling himself, powerful muscles rippling and shifting beneath his taut bronzed skin. "Better not let th' guys see your tail for a day or two. I left some marks."

"Okay."

I can't take my eyes off him while he finishes drying. I'm not calling him "sir" anymore, but I've still got that weird feeling of being his pledge…his slave.

He tosses aside the towel and hauls on his pants. He leaves the fly spread open, his huge prick and balls hanging out as he reaches for his belt.

"Is Frank stayin' here t'night?" he asks.

"I think so."

"He acts tough as shit, but if you lay some leather on him, he'll suck or spread his buns for you."

"I'll remember that."

Carl's threading the belt through the loops of his trousers. I try to recall the fiery pleasure-pain slashing across my bared ass. Yeah, I want more!

"Frank didn't take half as many strokes as you did th' first time," Carl mutters, tugging on his shirt, "You always were a better pledge than he was."

"I—wanted to take it…at the initiation…and this afternoon."

We finish our cigarettes and douse them, facing each other, and I remember the initiation…goading Carl into giving me more paddle swats than any of the others… my first experience in pleasure-pain…the ass inspection when my pledgemaster pressed the bulging crotch of his Levi's against my blistered butt and whispered "good pledge"…and afterward, when I put Johnny to bed and sucked him off…and went to take a piss and get some grease to lube my dick before I fucked him—and saw Frank whipped in the shadows of the shower room, sucking Carl's cock…

and the pledgemaster's right here in front of me, half-dressed, his genitals hanging out of his fly.

"Assume th' position," he growls knowingly. "Assume your new position, pledge!"

"Yes, sir!"

I know what he means about the "new" position, and I kneel before him. His thick-shafted prick seems to beckon me, and I plunge forward, pressing my lips to it…kissing it…worshiping it.

Yeah, Carl's more than my pledgemaster now!

"Good pledge!" he murmurs, then pulls back. "I've got t' haul ass."

I stay where I am. I don't want him to leave. I want to do it again…go even further…go as far as he wants me to go!

He buttons his shirt, stuffs the tails into his pants, tucks his spit-slick cock and nuts inside, fastens his fly.

"Damn it, Carl—"

"Don't tell Frank I clued you in on what he digs." He turns and saunters toward the door. "I'll keep in touch… pledge."

I'm still on my knees, head down. I hear the door lock snap…Carl's going…the door closes behind him.

Maybe he'll change his mind and come back.

He doesn't.

Hell, we got our rocks off, that's all.

I stand up, and there's my reflection in the mirror over the bureau. I look the same as before, the same face and build and all, but I sure as hell don't feel the same!

I twist around and look back over one shoulder, and—yeah, my asscheeks are red and burning from the paddling Carl gave them, and livid streaks mark where he belted me.

I reach back and rub my buns. Maybe I couldn't take another whipping. Maybe I could've. Maybe—

I watch the reflection of my fingers stroking each welt darkening across my buns. Carl said I took it better than Frank did. Frank's always put on the rough-and-tough act around the frat house—

I wonder what it'd be like, laying a lash on his butt, watching him crawl, fucking his muscle-clenched ass.

My dick bobs, starting to get full hard again, and I head for the shower. I'd better clean up before I take on Frank.

Yeah, I'm going to give him what Carl gave me! Man, I'm going to…

WORKSHOP

It's Saturday and I don't have to go to work, but I wake up at the regular time.

Clear sunlight is pouring through the open windows, and I can hear Chet's slow, sleep-filled breathing beside me.

I slide carefully out of bed. I've learned to get up without disturbing Chet.

I've learned a great deal since he first brought me here.

75

I walk silently into the bathroom and close the door, and I go to the toilet and tug my prick before taking a leak. My cock is morning-warm and heavy, and as I piss, I reach lower to fool with my slippery, loose-sacked balls, enjoying the sex hunger filling them.

Finished, I go to the washbasin and splash my face with cold water. As I dry off, I check my reflection in the shaving mirror. I see that glistening metal chain around my neck, and I can't help smiling.

Chet padlocked the chain on me when he began training me, and he's the only one who can take it off.

I go back to the bedroom, and he's still sleeping peacefully, the single sheet covering him pushed down on his hips.

I should make a pot of coffee so it'll be fresh and hot when he wakes up, but I don't.

I sit on the side of the bed and look at him.

Damn it, he's an ugly sonofabitch!

His face isn't just tanned, it's weather-beaten like old leather, and there's a thick scar hacked through his right eyebrow.

Even when he's asleep, his eyes are narrow slits between his heavy brows and high, jutting cheekbones, and his nose is wide and flat at the bridge from being broken, maybe more than once.

He's got more scars on his cheeks and jaws, and his thin lips are spread just enough to show his chipped front teeth.

Yeah, he's just plain ugly!

As though his face didn't already look as if an Army tank'd run over it, he likes to keep his black hair clipped short in a military cut. Most guys want a haircut that helps cover up the flaws, but not Chet. I know, because he's taught me how to trim it just right.

The first time I tried, it came out all wrong, and he disciplined me by shaving every bit of hair off my body. My hair's grown back, and I've learned how to cut his the way he likes it.

Yeah, I've learned so goddamn much from the ugly bastard!

I sit on the edge of the bed watching Chet. His bare shoulders are wide and lined with ropy muscles. His chest is broad and slicked with black silk, and his nipples are amber circles at each side, flat and hard.

One of his powerful tanned arms lies outside the sheet half-covering him, and I remember the torturing strength of his thick-knuckled fingers.

I wait patiently for him to wake up.

At last, he squirms lazily, and his dark eyes flick open. He yawns and then his gaze focuses on me.

"What're you starin' at?"

"You," I reply and take a deep breath. "You're ugly."

"Tell me somethin' I don't already know." He settles back again, his arms folded behind his head, and the sleek hairs gleam in his wide armpits. "Got th' coffee ready?"

"No." I put one hand on his solid chest, and I smooth the silky strands against the firm muscle plates. "It's Saturday."

"So?"

"Neither of us has to go to work." I let my fingertips outline his tits. "You're the ugliest stud I've ever met."

"Yeah?" His eyes tighten into a cold squint. I feel as if he's reading my mind. "If I bust that handsome face of yours, you'll be as ugly as I am."

"I'll never be that ugly, no matter what." I keep my voice quiet and challenging. The hint of a grin crinkles the corners of his mouth. I know he understands what I'm thinking, and I pull my hand back, trying to hide the hunger mounting inside me. "Want me to plug in the coffeepot?"

Chet grunts and rolls away, swinging to his feet. He ignores me, stretching again with catlike ease.

His physique tapers from those wide shoulders and chest to his slim waist, and his heavy cock dangles outward and down from the forest of pubic wire at the base of his taut pale belly.

He's hung like a goddamn stud bull, and he knows it!

He reaches down to scratch his bulging nuts, and his full-crowned dick flops toward me tauntingly.

"C'mon," he orders and turns toward the sliding glass doors leading to the patio.

I follow him, and we go out into the warm, bright sunshine.

There are no neighbors near Chet's place, but he had me build the brick wall that now surrounds the lawn and house.

I know what he expects, and I kneel on the lush grass in front of him.

He fingers his dick and takes careful aim, and a golden stream of piss sprays out, washing over my bared chest.

From experience, I know he pisses like a racehorse when he first wakes up, and I bow my head so the hot liquid can play across my shoulders and stream down my back and into the cleft in my ass.

The acrid stench wafts into my nostrils, and I rear back, exposing myself completely.

The stream sluices down over me, and when it centers on my crotch, my dick soars up full hard.

I remember the first time I got a hard-on from having Chet piss on me.

When he's finished, I hunch forward and take his bulging cockhead into my mouth, lapping up the last droplets.

I wash the slick crown thoroughly, but when I try to gulp down on the still-soft shaft, he pulls away.

He knows I'm hot to suck him off, but he isn't ready to give me his come.

"Stand up," he orders quietly. The bastard never yells at me because he knows I'll do what he says.

I get to my feet, and he turns the garden hose on me.

The water is ice cold, but I try not to flinch.

He blasts the spray on me, and I fight to keep from covering my crotch as he aims deliberately at my exposed genitals.

My prick shrivels, and my nuts tighten at the stabbing pain.

He drenches me front and rear, even squirting the stream into the crack in my ass to scour out his piss. I know he won't quit until I'm clean enough to suit him.

I've heard about guys who keep their slaves in filth, but Chet's just the opposite. He's neat as hell himself, and he expects me to be the same.

At last, he's satisfied, and he leaves me shivering with cold.

I know better than to object.

He comes back and rakes me with a coarse towel.

"Thank you, sir," I murmur when he's finished drying me.

"Still think I'm ugly?" he asks, studying me narrowly.

"Yeah!" I whisper defiantly, goading him. "You're ugly!"

He spins me around and shoves me forward across the lawn.

At the back corner of the patio is the concrete block building Chet calls his "workshop." The sex excitement renews inside me as we walk toward it.

There are no windows in the building, and the walls are soundproofed. I know, because this is where Chet kept me until he'd trained me.

He opens the heavy metal door, and I step into the humid darkness.

Warm air laps over my nakedness, but the floor is cold and rough beneath my bare feet.

Chet slams and locks the door behind us, then flicks on the single overhead light.

The room is large, and pulley-hung ropes and chains dangle from hooks in the ceiling. All the torture machines I remember are still here. The far wall is still lined with the shelves of neatly placed equipment.

Right from the first, Chet called all those whips and belts and gadgets his "equipment."

I see all of it in an instant, and I feel as if I've come home.

Yeah, this is where Chet brought me that first night... where he worked me over...where he kept me until I submitted willingly to everything he demanded.

I know what he expects, and I move under the hanging chains.

He steps in front of me, naked and cock-soft, and he attaches the bindings to my wrists, then hauls on them to pull me up, arms over head and stretched taut, helpless.

Damn it, Chet is one ugly bastard...and a real sadist... and he's finally brought me home!

He leaves me hanging by my wrists as he crosses to the collection of whips, examining them thoughtfully, and a quaking tension grips me as he chooses a length of thick black leather.

I remember when I'd hung here while he made that

lash, drilling rows of holes in it so it'd whistle through the air and land squarely, oiling it so it'd curl and lap at the curves and hollows of my unprotected flesh, then fashioning one end to fit around his wrist and across his palm for maximum control. I remember how he flogged me into total submission.

Chet moves behind me, and I know he's positioning himself before delivering the first blow.

I tense every muscle, trying to prepare myself for what I know is to come.

And nothing happens.

Yeah, the sonofabitch knows he's torturing me by waiting, by making me stand there naked and chained, by making me sweat, by making me concentrate on the memory of how he's beaten me before.

A glaze of perspiration breaks out across my shoulders, and a drizzle of wetness trickles down over my rib-etched sides from my armpits.

I try to hate him for being a goddamn sadist.

Just before I'm ready to whimper and beg him to get it over with, he starts.

The lash sings as it streaks through the air, and I feel so goddamn good when it whacks across my back from my right shoulder to below my left armpit.

There's an instant of numbness, and then the wrenching pain as the welt is given time to rise and turn blood red.

Okay, I know what my back looks like after that first stroke because Chet's made me watch while he's whipped some pickup he's brought back from the bar where he found me.

From experience, I know he'll let the fiery pain sink in before laying the lash on me again.

Yeah, the bastard never rushes anything! After all, he took weeks to break me down to being his goddamn slave!

I recover from that first stroke and tense again and grit my teeth, and when he's damn good and ready, Chet straps me, this second stroke carefully placed just below the first.

He continues the flogging, slowly, patiently, methodically.

He lines my back and ass with slashes of fire. I struggle to keep from crying out.

I am dripping with sweat, and I can feel my full-hard cock bobble in the air with the force of each new blow.

He returns to my shoulders, this time whipping from

left to right. When the new welt crosses an earlier one, an agonized groan breaks from my throat.

He does not react, and the lash continues searing my raw flesh at the same brutal cadence.

My groans become curses, then hoarse screams.

Chet doesn't give a shit!

I clench my eyes shut, and a warm numbness seems to close over me.

I can hear the whip whistle through the air and strike with a wrenching snap, and I can feel the streaking pain, but I seem to be separated from the torture. It's as though I'm standing in the distance watching some poor bastard naked and hung up by his wrists and showing a hard-on while his Master whips him mercilessly…and I am that poor bastard!

I want to crawl to Chet, to kneel before him, to confess my servitude, to endure any humiliation that will please him, to welcome his tortures…to belong to him completely.

Damn it, I want to—

The beating has stopped.

That sonofabitch's done it again! He's eased off just before I would've passed out…or babbled that he owns me.…

Goddamn sadist!

I'm hanging in Chet's workshop, my backside beaten raw and tender, my head down and my chin on my chest, stripped bare…with a hard-on!

I know he's giving me time to clear the numbness from my brain. When he's sure I'm ready, he releases me from the chains.

I crumple to the floor, gulping for air. My beaten back and ass burn with pain.

I open my eyes and see his bare feet in front of me.

I let my gaze rise up his powerful legs to his crotch, and his massive prick juts toward me, solid and potent. The huge, blunt-rounded crown blends into the broad shaft with almost no indentation at the flange, and the long thick column is lined with taut throbbing veins.

Yeah, he's hung like a stud bull, and I feel proud that whipping me has aroused him.

I rock forward and press my lips to the tip of his ram, nibbling lightly and tongue-stabbing the deep clearly marked well.

Sometimes Chet holds me in place and jams his iron into my throat brutally, but now he stands motionless, letting me worship his masculinity.

I take the cockhead into my mouth, licking it gently, and swallow the lush, taunting taste of his sex-hot flesh.

I inhale the all-male scent of his crotch and suction downward on his potent shaft.

I remember how he's forced me to watch other men go down on him and how they choked and gagged. My own rod pulses with pride because he's trained me to suck him off the way he likes.

His turgid column plunges deep into my throat, and I nuzzle the crisp tangle of pubic hair at the base to show him that I've accepted every inch of his giant club.

An aching hunger to drink his spurting come fills me, and I suck eagerly, aggressively.

He grips my hair and jerks my head back, and I stare up at him. He looms over me, his eyes narrowed and cold, his harsh features set, his muscled physique glazed with a light sweat.

Yeah, the bastard knows what I want, but he isn't ready to give it to me yet!

He grasps his spit-wet cock and slaps it across my upturned face. It stings, and I try futilely to get it back into my mouth.

He slaps again and again until I whimper in frustration.

With a grunt, he hauls me across the room to a low table.

He lays me down on my back and attaches my wrists

and ankles to metal clamps. I am spread-eagled, unable to move.

My rigid prick snaps back against my belly, a drop of clear liquid dangling from the tip toward my navel. He views me coldly, as if I were a slab of meat laid out for his inspection.

I can't keep from staring back at him, worshiping his masculine nakedness, his rugged features, his spit-gleaming cock.

He goes to his equipment shelves again and returns with the gag he made especially for me.

Chet uses a gag only when he expects me to howl and beg for mercy.

He doesn't like to hear me beg; that's the kind of bastard he is.

The gag is one of those soft rubber pieces athletes use to protect their teeth, only Chet added a metal bar that digs into the corners of my mouth and holds down my tongue.

He fits the gag into my mouth. Now the only sound I can make is a strangled choking from my throat.

More precome bubbles from my dick.

He gets another item from his collection. I tense and strain at the bindings holding me when I see it.

The metal ball-stretcher!

Yeah, Chet made the goddamn thing for me when he decided that his leather ones weren't painful enough. He measured and remeasured just how far he could force my nuts down in their sack, and then he let me watch while he made the hinged clamp.

Christ, I can still remember how I howled when he locked it in place the first time. Like most guys, my testicles pull up tight when they're worked on, but he dragged them down until the stretcher fit and held them in place, bulging like a couple of goose eggs. And once I got used to the pressure pain, he added more weight to the metal sheath…and then the strap to spread my balls as far apart as possible.

He comes back to the table where I'm tied down and grabs my nuts, stretching them and applying that torture device without noticing that I'm trying to scream against the gag in my mouth.

He snaps the strap in place. He knows he's strained my nuts to their limits.

He drops them, and lightning bolts of pain stab through me again as they bounce between my legs.

Chet doesn't give a shit about how much I hurt…the sadistic bastard!

Aching, I watch him go back to the shelf once more and pick up—the switch!

I remember the day we went swimming bareass down at the creek, the day he cut the long, thin branch from the willows growing by the water. He peeled off the light green bark, and then he made me bend over while he lashed my butt with the supple stick. Each blow raised a welt of crimson flesh, and for days afterward, I was reminded of that beating whenever I sat down.

I want to beg him not to use that goddamn switch, and now I know why he's gagged me.

He's going to use it on my front side, not my ass!

I cringe as he positions himself beside the platform table, but I can't take my eyes off his rugged nakedness and his soaring prick.

He raises the switch and brings it down with a sure, well-placed stroke. It sings through the air and snaps across my chest. A trail of fire races from one nipple to the other.

I thrash helplessly at the bindings holding my wrists and ankles, and he hits me again...and again...and again....

The blistering blows crawl slowly downward over

my chest and muscle-tightened stomach, and the pain-pleasure numbness engulfs me once more.

I close my eyes, and I'm floating away, standing back and watching the sadistic master discipline his naked, cock-hard slave.

But I am the body stretched spread-eagled, and I am writhing and trying to scream against the gag in my mouth as Chet lays stroke after stroke of the switch on my quivering flesh.

He pauses, giving me time to wallow in the fiery agony as if knowing I'm on the verge of exploding in sexual climax.

I no longer hate Chet, but I don't love him, either.

I am his slave—that's all.

I force my eyes open, and he's staring down at me, viewing my battered body, his rigid prick glistening with heat. I am pleasing him, and that pleases me.

He reaches down and runs his fingers over the narrow, ridged welts he's raised on my chest and stomach, emphasizing the marks he's given me.

"Still think I'm ugly?" he growls, speaking for the first time since he started this torture. "How about it, asshole?"

I want to tell him he's so goddamn ugly that he's

beautiful, but I know he gagged me because he didn't want me to beg or cry out or speak.

Hell, he doesn't give a shit about what I think or how I feel.

Yeah, he knows he's made me his slave.

He gives me the hint of a smile, and he moves down the platform to my hips, letting the switch drag over my exposed genitals.

Then he slams it down on my upper thigh. My muscles contract into the granddaddy of all charley horses.

Christ, it hurts!

When I was at the gym, one of the guys used to sneak up on me and ram his fist into my biceps or thigh muscles to give me a charley horse. He got a charge out of seeing me hurt and hearing me curse his brutality...and he made me suck his cock in return for not hitting me that way...and I lost interest when he quit punching me and took it for granted that I'd go down on him whenever he wanted.

Chet continues to hammer my thighs, first one and then the other. The pain is as bad as any I've ever known.

He ends the torture by tapping my stretched and separated balls lightly with the switch, and I almost pass out.

No, Chet won't let me lose consciousness. He doesn't want me to miss a second of the torture he's inflicting on me.

He runs his palms over my whipped nakedness and toys with my sensitive nipples. I know what he's going to do next.

He gets the tit clamps he made especially for me, the ones with large metal springs that gouge the pincers into my flesh, and when he applies them, I shriek into the gag in my mouth.

He watches me struggle, his massive prick throbbing. We both know he's taken me to the limit of my endurance.

The pain overwhelms me, and my only thought is to serve Chet in any way he wants.

He's taken me into total submission. Once again, I'm warmed with the pleasure of being his slave.

And the sonofabitch knows it!

He moves to the foot of the table, unfastening my ankles and attaching them to chains hanging from the ceiling.

He steps back and hauls on the chains, wrenching my legs upward until I'm doubled back on my shoulders. I admire his harsh, set features and the play of his powerful muscles beneath his bronzed, sweat-slicked skin.

Maybe I *do* love the bastard.

Shit, how can a slave love the stud who's used him the way Chet's used me?

I'm hanging upside down, my weight pressing down on my chest and making it hard to breathe, much less scream or beg for mercy. My butt is exposed to his cold gaze.

Yeah, he's going to fuck my belt-stroked ass!

I remember the first time he rammed his pile driver into my tail. He'd whipped me and tortured me, he'd made me suck his cock, he'd pissed on me, he'd expanded my limits step by step, but it wasn't until I gave up completely that he doubled me over and fucked me.

Christ, it hurt! I felt like a goddamn virgin, and he plowed that iron into my guts as if he wanted to rip clear through me.

Yeah, when Chet's horny, he fucks ass like few men and no boys at all!

I see him bring a tube of lubricant and climb into position on the table. My asshole twitches hungrily.

Damn it, I want him to screw me, to shoot his load into me, to get his rocks off!

He rubs his palms over my punished buns and

spreads them, and he presses his grease-covered fingers against my unprotected hole. His face is still expressionless, but I know his cock's as hot as my butt.

He lubricates the pulsing opening, spreading the puckered lips slowly and working the slick ointment inward. He always greases my tail, never his prick.

His dark eyes are fixed on me, watching for my reaction as his fingers probe and knead the tender flesh ring. If it weren't for that goddamn gag, I'd be begging for his hand, his arm...all of him!

He straightens on his knees, looming over me, and his sinewy muscles quiver as he brings the tip of his massive ram up to the center of my throbbing asshole.

Fuck me, Chet!

Fuck me, sir!

He presses slightly, knowing he's torturing me in a way his whips and chains and toys never could.

Stinking, lousy, sadistic, ugly bastard!

He relents and nudges his blazing cockhead into my quivering hole, and I try to drag him all the way into me.

No dice. He's going to do it his way...like always.

He inches that fuck stick into my tail so slowly that I can feel the ridged veins along the shaft.

He takes his sweet time, but he goes all the way to his tightening balls.

Give it to me, sir!

He hunches over me, sweat-glazed and rugged and when he's damn good and ready, he begins pumping.

His hips slam against my tortured testicles, and his cock slithers into my guts.

He rocks forward between my upturned legs and grabs my shoulders to increase his leverage, and the sweat from his body splashes down on me.

My nuts are hammered with each penetration and the pain makes my asshole clench around his iron-stiff ram.

That's what the sonofabitch wants, damn it!

He increases the tempo slowly, and his excited breathing echoes mine.

He jerks the clamps from my tits, and I writhe in the agonizing afterpain.

He rakes his work-rough hands over my welted flesh. His huge rigid cock is slamming into me with mounting fury.

Give it to me, you bastard! Fuck the hell out of me, you ass-busting stud!

Master!

He's using me without mercy, and the mixture of hate and love swirls in my brain.

Yeah, I'm your whipped and beaten slave, you fucking prick!

He throws his head back and roars a hoarse bellow of conquest, and his butt-ripping iron convulses in my guts.

Christ, he's beautiful when he blasts his load!

I'm trying to howl, bound and gagged and lost in the ecstasy of serving him. He grips my steel-hard dick, jamming his fist down from the swollen head to the hair-nested base and my aching balls.

Agggggghhhhh!

I'M COMMING!

My sperm spatters on my belly and chest and spurts all the way up to my face. I know Chet is still pouring his climax into my guts.

I slump back, exhausted, floating in the ultimate dazed numbness.

I hear Chet's voice from far off, but I can't tell what he's saying to me.

I don't care.

Hell, he doesn't know the special feelings only a total slave can enjoy when he's served his Master!

I feel him relax, and he scoops up my come and spreads it over my belly and chest and face.

I want to lick his fingers clean, but he's gagged me so that I can't.

I want to lick his fingers and body and cock.

I want to taste his sweat and come.

I want to serve him totally!

I wonder if he recognizes my attempt to smile gratefully...

With a grunt, he drags his still-firm iron from my clenching hole. Now I feel weak and empty.

Chet moves off the table and releases the chair holding my legs, letting me down to lie on my back, arms spread.

He gazes down at me for a long moment, and then he turns and saunters from the room.

I know he's going back to the house to take a shower, and I ache to go with him.

He's trained me to shower with him. He likes to stand under the cool spray while I soap him from head to toe, front and back. I've learned to scrub him spotlessly clean.

I'm lying with my arms stretched and my wrists chained down, naked, my mouth gagged. I try to hate

Chet because he hasn't let me wash the sweat from his body, the come from his cock, the shit from his asshole.

Hell, I'm no good at hating the sonofabitch!

My body still aches from the beating he's given me. My back and ass are streaked with whip lashes, and my chest and belly and thighs are lined with crimson welts from the switch. The gag fills my mouth, and the metal sheath stretches my balls and holds them painfully tight.

I wonder what other torments Chet has in store for me, and my dick quivers with renewed strength.

He returns with a steaming cup of coffee and a cigarette, and my iron snaps to full hardness at the sight of his rugged, freshly washed nakedness.

He puts down the coffee and cigarettes and unhooks the stretcher from my nuts, then grips them in his fist.

It hurts, but I'm willing to submit to anything he wants to do to me.

I'm his slave, and he knows it.

He releases my balls and runs his fingertips over my pulsing hard-on.

His long thick cock flops tauntingly between his thighs as he moves to the head of the table. I want to touch it, to suck it, to make it blaze with heat, to satisfy its master.

Without a word, he takes the gag from my mouth,

props my head up and feeds me some of his coffee, then gives me a drag on his cigarette.

"Thank you, sir," I murmur.

He doesn't answer.

He releases my wrists, and I rub them to restore the circulation.

He leans back against the shelves holding his torture equipment. I realize that each of the ones he's used was made especially for me.

Yeah, the lousy sonofabitch made all of them just for *me!*

Christ, only a slave like me knows how important that is!

I roll from the table and crawl across the floor to kneel in front of him.

His legs are fleeced with black silk over muscle, and I press my lips to them and lick hungrily.

I don't give a damn that I'm acting like a dog in heat.

I want to please him!

I lap upward toward his loose-falling cock and bulging testicles.

Shit, I'm horny for the fucking bastard!

I inhale the potent masculine scent of his crotch.

I nuzzle his large, slippery balls, wash them with my tongue, suction them gently.

He stands motionless over me, but his prick is swelling with excitement.

I caress the broad satin-smooth head and massive shaft.

"Still think I'm ugly?" he growls.

"Yes, sir!" I wrap my arms about his hips and press the side of my face against his flat-curved belly. "You're getting uglier and uglier, damn it!"

"Asshole!" I feel him chuckle, and he scratches my scalp with his fingernails. "We've got our Saturday chores t' do, but afterwards, I'm goin' to bring you back in here for some more trainin'."

"Anything you say, sir."

"I've made somethin' new for you." He reaches back to the shelf behind him. When I look up, he's holding a length of iron, a crescent-shaped piece of metal welded to the tip. "It's a brandin' iron. Think you can take it?"

I picture the half-moon heated white-hot and searing into my flesh, marking me with his initial.

I'll be branded the way cattle are branded by their owners.

I'll belong to Chet forever.

"Yes, sir," I whisper. "Yes, Master!"

†††

I sure as hell don't understand Chet!

It's Friday night and all of a sudden he said to get dressed in this shirt and these pants because we're going out.

The shirt is like the one I was wearing when he first brought me here from that bar, and so are the pants.

He's standing there, watching me get dressed, doing what he's ordered.

These aren't the same clothes I was wearing that first night.

I remember how Chet tied me up and ripped off that shirt and those pants...locked the chain around my neck...whipped and beat me...tortured me until—

I'm his slave.

I already have my balls stretched and bound tightly to my cock with the sheath he made for me, and I feel the pressured heaviness keenly as I pull on my pants.

This is the first time he's let me choose the bondage and put it on myself, and I know I pleased him by picking the one I did.

Don't ask me how I know he's pleased. He sure doesn't look it.

He just stands there expressionless, watching me dress.

He's wearing the old work shirt and Levi's he was wearing the first time I met him.

I pull on the shirt, button it and stuff the tails inside my trousers.

I glance at my reflection in the mirror and see the chain glistening about my neck.

Chet padlocked the chain on me the night he brought me here, and I can hide it by buttoning my shirt higher.

I don't.

"Let's go," he says, rubbing my ass meaningfully.

I remember the first time he said "let's go" to me…in that bar where I'd gone looking for the end of the rainbow…yeah, I could've said "no, thanks" or "fuck off, chum".… But I went with him.

I go with him now, and his hand stays on my butt… on the right cheek.

He's always liked to feel my tail, but that right bun— hell, he's made it his, and we both know it!

We walk outside. Chet's battered car is sitting in the driveway.

He gets in on the driver's side and I slide in from the other side.

I sit close enough to him to feel the warmth of his body without actually touching.

Chet starts the motor. We're moving.

I don't know where we're going.

I don't ask.

It doesn't matter.

I look down at my clothes and wonder why he wanted me to wear them.

He drops one hand from the steering wheel and cups my crotch with sureness.

He likes to grope me while he's driving.

His fingers dig inward and press down on my tightly bound testicles.

The sonofabitch knows he's hurting me!

I don't look up, but I can't help smiling.

"You're giving me a hard-on," I mutter.

"Everything gives you a hard-on, cocksucker." He eases up but keeps his hand where it is. "Butt me."

I half turn toward him and reach for the pack of cigarettes in his shirt pocket, and I let my fingers stroke the taut cloth covering his hard-plated chest.

I can feel the hair-thatched flesh and the firm nipples.

Shit, it's better when he lets me mess around with both of us bareass!

I take out a cigarette from his pocket, light it, and put it between his lips.

Chet's got thin, hard lips, a scar on the upper one.

Hell, he's got scars all over his face, and even if he didn't, he still wouldn't win any beauty prizes!

Yeah, he's ugly!

I watch him drag on the cigarette, the glow making ruddy streaks on his battered features.

Okay, so I've gotten used to the way he looks.

I've gotten used to everything about the sadistic bastard.

I settle back. His hand stays on my bulging crotch.

I drop my head again.

I'm his slave.

"Chet?" I call him by his first name because he's taught me what he likes and doesn't like. "Feeling ugly?"

It's a sort of code word between us, my calling him "ugly."

"Maybe." He turns the car from the street and brakes to a stop. "Remember this place, pal?"

I raise my head and recognize the parking lot behind the bar where I met Chet.

I haven't been back since that first time.

We're both dressed the way we were that night, and I wonder why he's brought me back.

Christ, maybe he's going to leave me here!

He swings from the car, and I follow him into the building.

Shit, the sonofabitch wouldn't turn me over to another Master! Or would he?

We enter the large smoke- and sound-filled room, and Chet leads the way to the long bar against one wall.

I don't listen as he jokes with the bartender and orders drinks for both of us, and I can't stop thinking about what it'd be like to serve a different Master.

I feel like shit!

Chet's hand pats my ass—the right cheek.

I want to shout and laugh and cry with relief!

I know the sadistic bastard isn't going to give me to anyone else, not after what he's finally done to me!

"Drink up, chum," he growls, raising his glass. "I'm going to check around a little."

"Sure thing."

Anyone listening might think that Chet and I are just a couple of buddies having a drink together...but I'm wearing the chain he padlocked around my neck... and the harness he made for my cock and balls...and the clothes he's bought me to replace the ones he shredded the first night we met here....

He drifts off into the crowd.

I taste my drink and lean forward, my elbows on the bar.

I gaze about the room.

A number of the men are wearing leather jackets and trousers, some decorated with metal studs, some with chains.

Chet never bothers dressing up in leather.

A husky young stud stands in a pool of light, bare-chested, thumbs hooked defiantly in the belt loops of his Levi's. A man walks up to him and sticks one hand in his face. The youth licks the man's fingers.

"Piss, you fuckin' dog!" a voice hisses behind me.

I turn and see a burly leather-clad man glaring at a tall, handsome blond. The blond's shirt is spread open, and a small gold hoop dangles from one large crimson nipple. He sighs, and a dark, wet stain traces down the inside of one pants leg.

I finish my drink, and the bartender brings another.

I know Chet sent it, and I search for him.

He's standing partway down the bar, right where he was standing the first time I saw him. I can't help grinning at him.

He gives me the hint of a smile, and I know he's thinking about that first time, too.

I came to this bar looking for a rugged, good-looking Mr. Wonderful…and I ended up with Chet.

He's plenty rugged, but he sure as hell isn't good-looking! He's goddamn ugly!

I concentrate on my drink.

My prick's beginning to swell, tightening the pressure on my sheath-tied testicles…the bindings Chet made for me…the bondage I chose to wear tonight….

I focus on Chet again.

He's talking to a short, chunky stud. The stranger has burr-clipped black hair and heavy eyebrows, and his features are strong but almost boyish. His thick neck spreads into wide, weight-lifter shoulders, and a white T-shirt clings to his barrel chest.

Chet says something to him, and he hesitates, then nods in agreement.

Chet brings him over to meet me.

"This is Gary," he says to me.

"Hi, Gary," I murmur.

"Hi."

He looks me over, and his dark eyes fix on the chain about my neck.

I know he wants to feel the weight of a slave collar around his own neck, and I grin at Chet.

"C'mon," Chet growls, and he leads us toward the rear of the bar.

I know where we're going, and a surge of warmth rises in my loins.

The three of us walk down a short corridor and into a darkened room.

The air is humid and scented with sweat-leather-sex. As my eyes adjust, I see moving figures…a naked youth hangs suspended by his wrists, his face twisted in pain as weights are tied to his balls…the blond I saw at the bar is on his knees, swallowing repeatedly as his Master pisses into his mouth…eyes closed, another man displays his totally shaven head and body.…

I remember when Chet brought me to this room to let me know what kind of treatment he had in store for me, and my prick snaps to full hardness inside my pants.

I look at Gary, and his broad chest heaves with his sharp breathing as he takes in the scene.

From experience, I know the combination of tension and excitement he feels.

Chet takes us to one side of the room and mutters something to Gary.

Gary steps in front of me, short and chunky and avoiding my gaze.

He stares at the chain around my neck, then he reaches up to touch it, almost caressing it.

I stand motionless, arms at my sides.

He unbuttons my shirt all the way down and spreads it open.

He watches his fingers stroke over my exposed chest and taut nipples.

I know he's wondering if he can take the torments I've been through to earn my slave chain.

His hands move downward.

He opens my trousers and pushes them down on my thighs. My throbbing hard-on snaps free.

He stares down at it...touches it...finds the straps separating my nuts and binding them to the base of my cock.

I'm pleased that I tied the sheath Chet made for me as tightly as I could, and I sense that Gary's thinking about having his own genitals in the same kind of bondage.

I feel his fingers tremble as he examines the bindings, and I hear his breath hiss between his clenched teeth.

He releases my testicles and moves behind me.

He raises my shirt and runs his hands over my back as if searching for welt marks.

110

Chet's never scarred me…he's left me with bruises and black-and-blue marks…but no scars…except for one.…

Gary's fingers move downward to my ass…roam over it…find the crescent-shaped scar.

I tense, remembering the night Chet gave it to me.

He'd tied me facedown on the torture table in his workshop so securely that I couldn't move…he'd let me watch him heat the branding iron he'd made…*C*—for Chet.

He'd waited until it was white-hot, and then he'd asked, "Still want it, pal?" He'd already shown me the iron, but he gave me that last chance to back out.…

"Hell, yes, I want it, you sonofabitch!" He burned his initial into my right buttock "where I can see it, whether I'm fuckin' you faceup or facedown!"

I feel Gary examine the scar with trembling fingertips.

He sinks to his knees and outlines it with his lips and tongue.

I see the pleased look on Chet's face.

"Get dressed," he orders me quietly, and Gary gets to his feet as I pull up my pants and force my hard-on inside. "Let's go."

They start toward the hallway, and I follow, still fastening my fly.

Gary has a trim bubble-butt and his buns bounce up and down as if he were marching in a parade, while Chet has an easy, macho gait.

We cross the main room of the bar to the door, and I see Chet's hand cup over Gary's right asscheek.

I wonder if Gary expects to get branded tonight.

You've got to earn Chet's brand, Gary—I ought to know!

Outside, we get into the car, Chet behind the steering wheel, Gary in the middle, me on the outside.

Chet takes off, and I know he's headed for home.

Gary drops his head, staring down at himself.

I remember that night when Chet took me home from this same bar...the second thoughts I had when we were in the car, just the two of us...the uncertainty about what I was getting myself into....

Chet lets his right hand fall from the wheel to cover the bulging crotch of Gary's jeans.

That's what Chet did to me that first night...put his hand down between my legs...pressured my hidden genitals almost gently—as if both warning and reassuring me....

Gary squirms, maybe hurting.

He doesn't raise his head...just as I didn't.

Chet is still driving with his eyes watching the road

ahead. He reaches over to take my hand and bring it down into Gary's crotch.

I press down...full-hard prick bulging...Gary's hung! Upfront balls...push down on them....

He tenses but doesn't shy away.

I ease the pressure. I know I've hurt him—just a taste of what Chet's done to me—and he's accepted it the way I've accepted everything from Chet.

I keep my hand right where it is.

Yeah, I know just how Gary feels!

And I know what Chet's going to do!

My cock throbs, still hard.

We pull into the driveway and get out of the car.

Chet claps Gary on the shoulder and steers him toward his concrete block "workshop" in the back patio.

I saunter into the house and head straight for the bedroom.

I peel off my shirt. As I skin down my pants, my dick bounces free, stiff as hell.

I know Chet's beginning Gary's training in the workshop, just as he began mine.

I fold my clothes carefully and put them away.

I unfasten the straps stretching and separating my sex-hot nuts.

I remember the first cock-balls bondage Chet used on me, and I'm damned pleased that he's taught me how to take heavier and heavier torment.

Shit, the sonofabitch knew right from the first that I'd end up being his goddamn slave!

I wrap up the device Chet made for me.... I whimpered like a beaten dog the first time he put it on me...and he let me choose it and put it on all by myself tonight...and I showed him by binding it as tight as I could...and he gave me that half-grin that says he knows I'm trying to please him....

Chet's a real all-out fucking sadist!

That cocky stud Gary's out there in Chet's workshop right now, and I bet he's finding out what a bastard Chet is, getting hung up and blindfolded and stripped and worked over the way I got worked over my first night here.

I wander into the living room.

I mix two drinks: one for Chet, the other for myself.

I wait for Chet.

He comes in, stripped to the waist, droplets of sweat beaded on his soft chest hair.

"Been working hard?" I ask, handing him his drink.

"Not as hard as I worked on you, asshole." He settles in his armchair, and I light a cigarette and pass it to him. "Gary's not as good a cocksucker as you are."

"I wasn't very good the first time I went down on you." I sit on the floor at his feet, leaning against his leg...like a good slave. "Going to train him to take that stud meat of yours the way you trained me?"

"Yeah."

"Good." I feel his hand on my shoulder, then his fingers on the chain about my neck. "Gary wants a chain like I've got, Chet."

"He's got it."

I remember when Chet padlocked his chain on me.

I take a long swallow from my glass.

I let my free hand touch his ankle...creep up beneath his pants...stroke his hairy calf....

I like touching the rugged bastard, damn it!

"You're ugly, Chet."

"You knew that when you came here with me. So'd Gary."

"Going to brand him?"

He doesn't answer.

We finish our drinks in silence.

"Back t' work," he mutters, getting to his feet.

I look up at him, and I know what he wants. It's crazy how I've learned to read his thoughts.

I pull up on my knees and run my palms over his powerful thighs.

I unbutton his fly and drag his Levi's down to his ankles. His massive prick tumbles free, the broad head blending sleekly into the long thick shaft.

I rock forward and run my lips over his cock and loose-swinging balls.

His ram stiffens quickly.

Yeah, he's horny! Goddamn horse-hung stud!

"Ease off," he growls, covering a chuckle, and steps back. "We'd better see how Gary's doin'."

I stand up. For a moment, we're facing each other, both naked, both showing our hard-ons, both kind of grinning.

Shit, the fucking bastard's so ugly he's beautiful!

He heads for the door to the patio, and I hustle to catch up with him.

He's going to let me work on Gary with him!

Outside, I fall in step with him, and we start toward the windowless building at the back of the patio.

"How long do you think it'll take to train Gary, Chet?"

"Not as long as it took with you." His hand moves to my

right asscheek and rests there. "You put up a good fight."

"I was fighting myself," I confess. "It wasn't easy to give in to you totally."

He grunts and opens the heavy metal door to his workshop. I go inside.

The small lightbulb glows overhead, and Chet's torture devices are partially hidden in shadows. Gary is stationed in the center of the room, blindfolded and stripped, the shreds of his clothing scattered on the floor. His arms are stretched, and his wrists are fastened to ropes hanging from the ceiling. A slave chain is padlocked about his short, thick neck.

I remember when I was hung up like Gary is now, and I know what Chet expects me to do.

I step up to the husky naked stud and toy with his chain. He stiffens, wondering what's in store for him.

I run my fingers over his muscular shoulders and down to his broad high-arched chest, and I know from experience the emotions filling him. The black hair is silky and flat-lying, and I stroke it lightly, tauntingly.

His nipples are firm and dark. I grip and twist each hardened tip.

He hisses and thrashes at the bindings holding him.

I want him to experience everything Chet's done to

me! I want him to moan and groan with pain…to howl…to beg for mercy…to know each and every torture until he learns the freedom of total slavery!

I watch my hands wander downward over his short stocky physique to his crotch.

His cock thrusts iron-stiff from the lush nest of crisp wire at his groin, mallet-crowned and almost as long and thick as Chet's…almost, not quite…hell, every stud can't be hung like that goddamn Chet!

I examine Gary's iron with my fingers and discover the narrow straps spreading and clutching his testicles.

It's probably the same one Chet used on me the first time.

Shit, Chet's trained me to take a lot heavier ball bondage since then!

I bounce Gary's nuts on my fingertips, and he whimpers softly.

I kneel in front of him and see the droplet of clear liquid dangling from the tip of his inflamed prick, and I lick it away.

I take his blazing cockhead in my mouth, and he shivers with surprise.

I gulp all the way down on his throbbing iron, pressing my lips into the tangle of pubic hair at the base.

I show him how well Chet has trained me!

I feel Chet move behind Gary, and I know he's spreading our victim's asscheeks and greasing his exposed hole with his fingers.

I begin suctioning Gary's turgid ram as Chet finger-fucks him.

He writhes helplessly, trapped between us.

I know he's about to pop, and I grip his balls tightly.

He bellows a hoarse cry, and his come spurts into my mouth.

Christ, he lets go like a goddamn fire hose!

I get every drop without swallowing any of it.

When he runs dry, I hop to my feet and embrace him, pressing my lips to his and forcing his sperm into his mouth.

He swallows and sucks my tongue clean.

I hold his stocky, muscular body to mine, my rigid prick jammed against his still-firm, spit-wet tool.

Yeah, I know just how he feels!

I release him, and Chet motions for me to trade places with him.

I move behind Gary and examine his powerful back and trim ass.

I grasp his buns and spread them, and I nudge the head of my cock against his well-lubricated hole.

I remember how Chet always greases my butt—never his prick—and I ram my rod in collar-deep.

"Shit!" Gary curses. "You're wrecking me!"

"Bullshit!" I growl, surprised at my own aggressiveness. "I'm just warming up your tail for that telephone pole of Chet's!"

I lock my arms about his chunky frame and inch inward slowly.

I haven't screwed a stud in the butt since before I met Chet, and I'm balls-aching hot to plow Gary!

I plug in all the way to my nuts and hold him squirming on my pulsing iron.

I see Chet in front of Gary, cock-hard and grinning at me, and I return his grin.

I wonder if this is how Chet feels when he's fucking me.

Damn it, I hope so!

I start thrusting, driving my hard-on in and out of the clenching muscle ring.

Chet moves in closer and goes to work on Gary's nipples and testicles.

Gary is trapped between my plunging ram and Chet's tormenting fingers.

I pound steadily against the sleek, muscle-pinched cheeks of his ass.

Chet reaches around to embrace me, sandwiching Gary between us, and I know his knee is grinding into Gary's unprotected crotch.

I increase the tempo of my thrusts.

Gary throws his head back against my shoulder and groans with tortured ecstasy, and I feel him quiver as his second climax rips through him and pours out against Chet's nakedness.

"You're going to clean Chet up!" I bark, hammering into him furiously. "When he cuts you down, you're going to lick him clean!"

"Yes, sir," he whispers, his tail pressed into my groin. "Yes, sir!"

Jesus, he called me "Sir!" I'm Chet's goddamn slave, and Gary's called me "sir!"

My come breaks loose and smashes into him.

I howl with pleasure and claw at the short, husky young man getting my load.

Man, I'm giving him everything I've got!

Yeahhhh!

Dazed and exhausted, I cling to him and struggle for breath.

I feel Chet beside me, his hand on my right ass-cheek reminding me that I'm wearing his brand.

Hell, I don't need to be reminded, no matter what!

I ease free from Gary and face Chet. His belly and crotch glisten with Gary's spattered cream.

I bend down and lick his massive rigid cock clean.

"That's Gary's job," he grumbles, tugging me up by the chain about my neck. "Go get washed up."

I stumble across the workshop and leave.

Outside, I fill my lungs with cool night air, and I start toward the house, suddenly chuckling.

That goddamn Chet! He's given me a taste of being a Master, but he never had any doubts that he'd trained me to be his slave forever!

I wonder what else the sonofabitch has planned for me…and for Gary!

I head for the bathroom off the room I share with Chet.

I wonder where Gary will stay. Maybe in the spare bedroom. Maybe with us.

Hell, it'll be a long, long time before Chet takes off Gary's blindfold, much less lets him out of the workshop.

I remember how Chet kept me blindfolded at first… how I didn't know night from day…how I lost track of time…how he worked me over…how he fed me and washed me and took care of me...how I learned every nook and cranny of his body without being able to see him...how he trained me!...

and how he continued to keep me in that windowless room after he finally removed the blindfold...how I was chained and tied to his various torture machines... how he let me watch him make the new "equipment" he'd chosen just for me, the whips and stretchers and clamps...how he brought me to the moment when I was willing to be his slave...

and how he'd finally let me live in the house with him...how I realized that he was always my Master, no matter how much we joked around like buddies...

and how I said yes when he was ready to brand me.

Okay, so I hope Gary'll learn all that I have.

I hop into the shower and blast myself with the tepid spray.

I grab the soap and start lathering myself carefully, head to toe.

Chet wants his slave to be neat and clean.

Some Masters don't. Some Masters want their slaves to live in filth and all that shit...and some slaves want that.

There're so many different kinds of Masters and slaves!

I wash front and back thoroughly, rinse and wash again. Chet wants me spotless.

I used to clean up like this because I had to. Now, I *want* to.

Chet opens the shower curtain and steps naked into the stall with me.

I stand back and watch him drench himself...burr-clipped black hair...rough, scarred features...wide shoulders and strong, tapering physique...long, thick cock flopping between his powerful thighs....

He positions himself with his back to the spray, legs spread, relaxed and sure. I step forward automatically to wash him.

I rub the soap over his shoulders and hair-glazed chest, and my goddamn prick starts to stiffen.

He's right—everything about him gives me a hard-on!

"Did Gary lick you clean, Chet?"

"He tried. He's not very good at it."

"He'll learn, like I did." I watch my soapy palms slide over his taut, plated chest and wide, firm nipples. "He's built like a weight lifter."

"It's his hobby. We'll get him some weights so he can keep in shape."

That settles it—Gary's going to stay!

I'm not surprised that Chet's found out about Gary's hobby. Before he's done, he'll know everything about the hunky stud...everything....

He raises his arms, and I lather his silk-filled armpits.

I remember the repeated question-and-answer sessions Chet's put me through when he's had me tied down...the events I thought I'd forgotten... childhood... first jerk-off experience...blowjob...school...growing up...sucking and getting sucked... fucking and getting fucked...pain... slave desires... everything!

"Gary wants to be your slave," I murmur as I scrub downward over Chet's sleek bronzed torso.

"What makes you think so?"

"It takes one to know one, remember? Going to put him through everything you put me through?"

"Yeah."

I remember the beatings...the tortures...the humiliations...the long, slow, painful road to the total freedom of being Chet's complete slave.

I kneel before him to wash his crotch, and his cock is just hanging there, soft and long and thick.

My dick is iron-hard, and he knows it.

I hate that! I hate the way he can stay soft and make me wait!

Maybe that's another thing that makes him a Master and me a slave.

I soap his huge prick and sensitive balls gently.

"The first night I was here," I blurt out. "You worked me over...got me started...tied me down when I was worn out...and pissed on me—"

"You can mop up th' workshop t'morrow an' get Gary cleaned up th' way I like."

"That isn't what I'm getting at!" I explode, knowing damn well that I'll do whatever Chet says, including washing his piss off Gary. Shit, I've learned to do worse than that! "I mean—did he call you names?"

"Yeah, just like you did."

"Did—Did he figure out you're ugly?"

"Goddammit, nobody's ever called me 'ugly' except you, asshole!"

Everything falls into place!

Chet's made me witness everything he did to me that first night we met...going back to that bar dressed as we were the first time...picking up Gary the way Chet picked me up...going through all of it the way it happened the first time, only this time I was Chet's slave watching and working with him.... Chet's known all along that would—

126

"You're ugly, Chet!" I jump to my feet, laughing. "You're so fucking ugly that—"

"Wash my back," he growls and turns around. I get to work. "I never saw you screw a stud in th' ass before t'night. You plowed him damn hard."

"It—It was like I was you." I'm scrubbing his back and tail, and it isn't easy to put my thoughts into words. "I—I was you, and Gary was me. Understand?"

"He's goin' t' fight harder than I thought. Like you did."

"How come?"

"I told him he's goin' t' be your slave. I guess that's about as far as a guy can go, bein' a slave t' a slave. Right?"

Christ, he's giving me Gary!

"Right, Chet!"

"Think you can train him, shitface?" He spins around, and his cock juts rampant from his crotch.

"Think you can train him t' take my pecker down his throat or up his ass as good as you do?"

"Hell, yes!"

Shit, I love Chet…but I'll be damned if I'll tell him so!

Yeah, no matter what, I'm his slave, and I know what he wants right now.

I turn around and bend over, bracing myself against the tiled wall of the shower stall.

I feel him move in behind me.

He's soaped his hands, and he rubs them over my butt, outlining the brand he gave me…his initial—the same as mine—the one I'm going to give Gary when he earns it!

He spreads my asscheeks and lathers the passage between them.

He always lubes my hole, never his massive ram.

He centers the tip of his swollen cockhead against my puckered opening.

"You an' me'll train Gary," he promises. "He'll learn t' do what you say…but you'll always be mine, right?"

"Yeah…yes, sir." He shoves his aching-hot ram into me…not just head deep…all the way to the hilt!…uniting us, his fucking cock jammed all the way into my goddamn asshole! "Yes…MASTER!"

MUTT

B rad eased his foot on the gas pedal and turned the delivery van onto a narrow, tree-lined road. A glance at his watch told him it was almost noon, and he relaxed, dropping one hand to paw the heavy-curved crotch of his trousers.

Brad was in his late twenties, and his black hair was clipped short in a military cut. His tanned features were harsh and brutally masculine, his dark eyes set in narrowed slits, his thin lips fixed and unsmiling, and his taut shirt outlined his thick-muscled shoulders and powerful chest.

The road came to an end in a small turnaround, a single house half-hidden behind a heavy bank of brush. Brad braked the truck to a stop.

"Mr. Phil Jackson," he read the label on the small package on the tray beside the steering wheel. "What th' hell's he bought this time?" He picked up the box and raised his thick eyebrows with surprise. "Whatever it is, it's heavy."

With a shrug, he swung to the ground and started up the walkway toward the house, the heels of his work shoes clacking against the pavement. He moved with a sure—almost cocky—gait, stomping up the two steps to the porch of the house and ringing the bell sharply.

There was movement inside, and then the door opened.

"Hi, Brad."

"I've got another package for you."

Phil was about Brad's age and height, blond and tanned, a bath towel hooked about his hips.

"Come on in."

"Thanks."

Brad tromped into the sparsely furnished living room. Raw wood beams formed a false ceiling below the peaked roof. There was a kitchen alcove at the end of the room, a hallway door standing open at one side.

"I just got out of the shower," Phil apologized as he closed the front door, then tucked the towel tighter about his waist. "I haven't had time to dress and—"

"No sweat," Brad interrupted, and he put the package on the coffee table in front of the leather-upholstered couch. "This is my last stop before lunch."

"Want to have lunch here? I've got a lot of stuff in the—"

"I'm goin' down to th' café. There's a cunt there I'm workin' on screwin'." He glanced at Phil, cold-eyed and rugged. "Maybe she's got a friend for you. Know what I mean?"

"Yeah." He looked down at himself—his full-arched chest and taut stomach and the towel bunched around his hips—and he pulled in a slow breath. "You—You sound horny."

"Damn right." He tugged his bulging crotch openly. "I've gotta take a leak before I haul ass."

"Down the hall and through the bedroom."

"Thanks."

Phil watched the man saunter through the doorway, and then ran one hand over his chest. He was good-looking and solidly muscled. He brushed the soft, sun-bleached hair spreading toward his wide, dark nipples. His palm moved downward over his tightened stomach, and he fumbled the heavy genitals hidden beneath his towel. At last, he followed Brad down the hall.

The bedroom was neat and furnished masculinely, an open door at one side leading to the bathroom. Phil heard the rush of water as the toilet was flushed and he started toward the clothes closet opposite.

"You've got a pretty good pad here," Brad muttered.

"It's not bad." Phil turned to find Brad standing in the doorway, his pants spread open and one hand shoved inside as he shoved down his shirttails. Their eyes met for a moment, and then Phil looked down at the gaping trousers and the man's slow-moving fingers. "I—I was just going to get dressed."

"Yeah?" Brad pressed his hand deep into his crotch. "What're you starin' at?"

"Nothing."

"I've had queers stare at me th' way you're starin'," Brad mocked. "You queer, Phil?"

Phil watched Brad draw his hand up, raising his shirt slightly and displaying the fringe of lush pubic hair at the base of his flat, pale belly. He swallowed fast.

"Yeah, I—I go for guys," he admitted hesitantly. "I thought, maybe—if you're horny—maybe you'd let me—"

"You want to suck my goddamn pecker?" Brad interrupted with a snort. He sauntered toward Phil. "Hell, gettin' a blowjob ain't like screwin' a cunt, but I don't give a shit."

Phil looked at the rugged truck driver standing in front of him and shivered as he brought both hands up to stroke his shirt-covered chest.

"Look, Brad—"

"Don't fuck around," he growled. "If you're so hot to suck, get down there an' suck!"

Phil dropped to his knees obediently, paused, then ran his hands up the man's thighs and fingered the wide leather belt laid open at the waist of his pants.

"Dammit, Brad, I can't help wanting—"

"I ain't interested in hearin' your sad stories, fairy! Get t' work on my dick!"

"All right."

He gripped Brad's trousers and jerked them down below his knees. The man's genitals tumbled free, his long, thick cock curling outward and down from his hair-filled groin, his loose-sacked testicles swinging heavily beneath it. He slammed forward, rubbing his face against the warm, sweaty organs hungrily, and the musky scent of maleness flooded into his nostrils as he ran his lips and tongue over the dangling shaft and slick prickhead.

"Sheee-it!" Brad snickered. "You sure as hell are queer, chum!"

Phil felt the column quiver with the first shocks of hardness, and he nuzzled it, then gripped Brad's bare hips and ducked lower to lick his tightening balls. He heard the man grunt, and work-rough hands pawed over his shoulders, dragging him closer.

"Yeah!" Brad muttered. "Work on my goddamn nuts... shit, I don't give a damn...so fuckin' hard up... yeahhh!"

Phil tongued the slippery organs eagerly and drew them into his mouth. The man's swelling cock slapped against his face as he sucked gently. He let his hands slide upward from Brad's hips and found his shirt had been spread open. He stroked the bared torso, trembling with growing excitement.

Suddenly he released Brad's testicles and sank back on his heels. The man loomed over him, dark eyes narrowed into cold slits, powerful chest gleaming under a thick mat of flat-lying hair, black silk trailing down over his muscled stomach and spreading across his taut, pale belly to merge with the lush, tangled hair at his groin. His rigid prick thrust potently from his crotch, the long, thick shaft marked with pulsing veins. A bubble of moisture formed at the tip of the broad-rimmed crown.

"Lie down on the bed," Phil whispered. "Let me touch you all over...lick you and—"

"What th' hell for? You want t' queer me, you lousy fairy?"

"No, I just want to—"

"I don't give a fuck what *you* want!" Brad spat, stepping forward to jab his turgid cock at the kneeling man's face. "Get back on my pecker! Suck me off, goddammit!"

Phil lunged forward again, gripping the man's legs for support and taking the glistening cockhead into his mouth. He gulped down the taste of maleness thirstily, and then he was sucking the fullness of the column until his lips pressed against the prickly wire at the base. He held there, his face buried in Brad's crotch, and then he felt the hands clench the back of his head again and heard the cold, rasping voice.

"That's more like it, cocksucker!" Brad thrust hard,

drawing his cock partway back and slamming it into Phil's mouth again. "That's what you want, ain't it? A goddamn dick to blow on, that's what all you fairies want!" He snickered as Phil choked and fought to control the plunging column. "Suck, y' fuckin' sonofabitch!"

Again and again, Brad drove his pulsating cock into Phil's throat, holding him helpless between his clenching legs and jamming his head back and forth rhythmically. He felt the sex heat rise in his loins, and he tensed, every muscle straining as he surged toward his climax.

"You're gonna get it, y' goddamn fruit! I'm gonna pop off a load like…" He broke off, arching his back as he rammed brutally. "Aggghhh, y' stinkin' bastard! Queer! Yeah—ARGH!"

He clutched Phil down on his convulsing prick, and his hot come came sluicing out.

"SHIT! AWW, GODDAMN! YEAHHH!! He pumped again, slowly, deliberately. "TAKE IT! SWALLOW THAT HORNY JUICE, Y' CREEP! GULP IT DOWN! SUCK… SUCK!" He took a fast breath. "COCKSUCKER!"

His climax slowed and ended. Then he stood motionless for several minutes, the strength ebbing back into his body. At last he eased his wilting prick from Phil's mouth and slapped it lightly against his face.

"You like swingin' on that chunk of meat, chum? Hot to take it again sometime?"

"Okay."

"Goddamn fruit!" He snickered as he stepped back and saw that the towel had slipped from the kneeling man's hips. "Shit, gulpin' my dick gave you a fuckin' hard-on!"

"I couldn't help it." Phil looked down at the massive crimson-crowned cock thrusting from his crotch. "After you leave, I'll jerk off."

"Who said anythin' about leavin'?" Brad peeled off his shirt and flexed his powerful arms. "I've got plenty of time left on my lunch hour."

Phil stared as the brawny, cock-flopping truck driver kicked off his pants.

"Wh-What are you going to do, Brad?"

"What th' hell d'*you* care, queer?" He sat on the side of the bed and hunched forward, unlacing his work shoes and pulling them off. "I ain't wore out yet, if that's worryin' you." He glanced at the still-kneeling blond and broke into a slight grin, then stripped the leather laces from his boots. "Crawl over here. I'm gonna tie you up till I'm ready to give you another load of come."

"Wait a—"

"Want me to work you over, ya stinkin' homo?" His narrowed eyes blazed. "Want me to bust that good-lookin' face? Kick those horny balls? Stomp on that goddamn hard-on?" He saw Phil shiver and his voice hardened. "Get over here an' stick your hands out!"

Sucking in a sharp breath, Phil shuffled over to the man on all fours and offered his hands held together, his head down.

"Please, Brad, don't—"

"Shut up, cocksucker!" He wrapped the leather thong about Phil's locked wrists, grinning again as he saw the blond wince when it dug into his flesh. "That's more like it, chum. Now, you just relax while I see what I can find to eat. Then maybe I'll feed you my cock for lunch."

Snickering at his joke, Brad sauntered naked from the room and down the hall to the main room of the house. Without pausing, he went into the alcoved kitchen, opened the refrigerator and found a plate of fried chicken and salad. Grabbing the plate and a can of beer, he started back to the bedroom.

Phil was still on his haunches, head down, his tied hands half-covering his rigid cock and bulging testicles. He was deeply tanned except for the pale stripe at his hips, and his thick neck melted into wide, full-muscled shoulders and a broad, hairy chest. His husky torso tapered sharply to his slim waist, and his thighs and legs were muscled powerfully.

Brad put his plate of food on the top of the dresser at one side of the room, popped open the beer can, and took a long drink before looking down at the crouching man.

"You ain't like th' other queers that've sucked me off," he said casually. "How come you ain't got crystal chandeliers hangin' around this dump?"

"I don't go for chandeliers."

"You're a fruit, ain't you?"

"Yeah, I guess so."

"Then you're supposed to fruit up th' joint where you live." Brad grabbed a leg of fried chicken and bit into it, chewing and talking at the same time. "How come you don't have a fancy apartment in th' middle of town like th' rest of th' fairies?"

"I like living out here, where it's quiet."

"Shit, I'd think you'd want to be humpin' up an' down Main Street, lookin' for more cocks ta suck." He viewed Phil while he scratched his balls with his free hand. "You're built damn good for a queer. Most of them're built more like cunt than like guys."

"I work out…played football in college…you know."

"How th' hell would I know?" He swallowed another mouthful of his lunch. "Maybe a good-lookin' stud with a body like you've got turns on th' other queers, huh?"

"Dammit, that's not why—"

"Shit!"

Brad finished his lunch and threw his head back to drain the beer can. Some of the foam drizzled down his chin and spattered onto his barreled chest, and he rubbed it into the lush black hair lazily.

"Want another beer?" Phil asked, his gaze intent on the ruggedly built man. "There's plenty more."

"I ain't about ta get drunk while I'm workin'." Brad let his fingers trickle down to his loose-hanging prick, flipping it toward the kneeling blond. "How 'bout you? Want to drink more pecker juice?"

Phil's shoulders sagged. Then he nodded slowly.

"Okay."

"Hey, how come you're so horny for my dick, chum?"

"It isn't that," Phil admitted. "You're plenty big and tough and—"

"Hell, all you goddamn fruits turn on like cunt when you get a stud's pants down." He snorted and sauntered toward the clothes closet. "I bet you've got a whole rack of dresses ta wear when you an' your fag pals get t'gether, huh?" He opened the door and stared at the line of plain, neatly hangered shirts. "Goddamn! How come you ain't got lace on th' cuffs of your shirts?"

"I don't wear that kind of clothes."

"Why not? You're queer, right?" He started to turn back, and he blinked as he viewed the inside of the closet door. "Christ! What's all this crap?"

"Nothing," Phil murmured, his head dropping again. "Just—Just some things I—I've sort've—collected."

"This looks like a dog leash." Brad pulled a leather collar and chain from a hook. "You ain't got a dog, so what do you want with this?"

"A guy I know…a couple of them…they like having me make them wear it…like a dog.…"

"Jee-zus!" Brad exploded. "You fuckin' fairies're a bunch of creeps! Yeah, real creeps!" He nodded to the other things hung on the back of the door. "How about these paddles an' straps an' shit?"

"If the guy doesn't obey me—" Phil's voice was whisper-tight in his throat, and he clenched his eyes shut. "Hell, you wouldn't understand."

"You whip 'em into shape, huh? An' then you suck 'em off like you did me, huh?"

"No. They have to suck me…or get fucked…whatever I say."

"Christ, you're queer as hell! You couldn't wait t' blow me, but you've gotta get your kicks by makin' some other fruit crawl like a goddamn dog!" He spun around to the hunched blond, the leash in his hands. "Maybe I oughta treat you like you've treated them, huh?"

"Dammit, Brad—"

"Cocksucker!" Brad jerked Phil's head up and snapped the collar around his neck. "How do you like that, fruit? How do you like bein' on th' dog's end of th' leash?"

Phil struggled for a moment, then doubled over again.

"Lemme go, Brad."

"Hell, doggy, I ain't taught you any tricks yet." He snickered. "Think you could learn t' sit up an' beg? Or fetch a stick? Hey, mutt, roll over!"

Phil started to object, and Brad jerked the leash sharply. The blond choked, then groaned and sprawled flat on the floor, twisting onto his back. His bronzed body gleamed in the soft light, his bound hands cupped over his crotch.

"Stretch your goddamn arms out behind your head," Brad ordered, hunkering down beside the man. "I wanta take a good look at my little puppy dog."

"Okay," Phil murmured, obeying. "You win."

"Damn right!" Brad smiled, thinly. He rubbed one hand over Phil's face playfully, chuckling as he felt the man's tongue lick his palm and fingers hungrily. "Yeah, good doggy!" Suddenly he swung over to kneel across Phil's chest and rock forward, his heavy cock and balls dropping onto the blond's upturned face. "Here's what you really want to lick, ain't it?"

Phil's tongue washed eagerly over the burly trucker's loosened testicles and slow-hardening cock. He felt the flesh column stiffen, but when he squirmed to take the swelling cockhead into his mouth, Brad pulled away.

"Let me take you off again," Phil groaned. "Please!"

"You like suckin' on my bone, doggy?"

"Yes!" the blond whispered. "For chrissakes, Brad—"

"You'll get my dick when I'm good an' ready, cock-sucker!" He shifted to hunker beside Phil again and mussed the golden hair on the broad chest. "I ain't finished checkin' you over, puppy."

"Please!"

Phil shivered as Brad's work-hardened fingers scraped over one of his broad amber nipples, and he started to raise his arms to reach for the man. Brad gripped the tensed nipple and twisted brutally.

"Lie still, mutt!" He saw Phil wince and fall back. Then he pinched the other nipple deliberately, ignoring the man's pain-filled gasp. "That's so you'll remember to do what I say."

"Yes...yes...sir."

Brand's hand moved tauntingly over Phil's muscle-tight torso, touching and patting and inspecting. Finally he seemed to notice the blond's full-masted cock. The shaft was thick and strong, lying back against his flat belly, and the massive crown was dribbling colorless liquid into his navel.

"Tell me somethin'," the trucker said, his voice suddenly relaxed and inquisitive. "You like to fuck th' other queers in th' butt, right? Well, don't a ram th' size of yours rip a guy's asshole wide open?"

"I keep a tube of grease over there in the top drawer of the dresser," Phil murmured. "If a stud wants to get screwed—"

"Goddamn! You tie him up an' use them whips on him, an' then you plug that horny prod into his tail! Yeah, you're queer as hell!" He drew his fingers upward to graze over Phil's hard-pointed nipples once more. "I've heard about you bastards stickin' pincer-things on a guy's tits ta make him yell. You got any of them?"

"Yes…sir."

"Maybe I oughta clamp them onto your tits. Or maybe I oughta hook them onto your goddamn balls!" He swung to his feet, naked and rock hard, one hand tugging at the leash locked to the dog collar around Phil's neck. "Too bad I ain't got time ta try some of that crap on you. C'mon—up on th' bed, chum."

"Wha—What are you going to do, Brad?"

"Fuck your ass."

"No! I don't want—"

His words were cut off as Brad wrenched the collar choking tight, and then he was clawing at it, half-dragged to the wide, neatly made bed.

"C'mon, doggy," the man coaxed mockingly. "Climb up here like I said to!"

Phil sprawled facedown on the bed, gulping for breath as the collar loosened.

"You could've choked me to death!" he gasped. "You dumb truck driver, what if you'd killed me?"

"Shit, who'd ask questions about a goddamn faggot?" Brad dropped the leash and stepped back, viewing Phil's outstretched body thoughtfully. "You're th' one who was so hot to suck a trucker's prick, right?"

"Hell, Brad—"

"Shut up, mutt." He shook his head, concerned. "It seems like you ain't been trained right. You're lyin' there wearin' that dog collar, but you still ain't learned as much as a puppy." He shrugged and sauntered to the dresser. "You've had your butt screwed, right?"

"A couple of times," Phil admitted. "I—I don't go for it."

"Tough." He opened a drawer and pulled out a tube of lubricant and a folded towel. "I'll train you t' go for it, puppy dog."

He dropped the towel and grease tube on the bed, and Phil raised his head to watch him cross to the open closet.

"What are you looking for?"

"A trainin' strap." Calmly, Brad selected a long, narrow belt from the collection hung on the door and turned back. "Th' next time you're told to spread your buns, you're gonna do what you're told, right?"

Phil watched the naked man position himself beside the bed, the belt held securely in one powerful hand, his partially softened cock swinging loose between his taut thighs. Then he tore futilely at the thongs still tying his wrists.

"Cut me loose, Brad!"

"Lie still, ya goddamn fruit!"

The belt whistled through the air and slashed across

Phil's unprotected back. The blond gasped as a ribbon of fire seared downward from one shoulder to the opposite side.

"Christ!" he hissed, squirming helplessly to escape. "Knock it off, you—"

"Lie still!" Brad growled again, and he whipped a second belt slash across the man's back, paralleling the first. "You're gonna get yourself trained, doggy."

Phil groaned, then let his head drop and shut tight his eyes. He was sprawled across the bed, naked and defenseless, his arms and legs dangling over the sides, and he tensed as he heard the lash whistle through the air again.

"Brad—owww!"

"Shit!" Brad muttered, dropping the narrow strip of leather. "That fairy belt ain't big enough for *real* trainin'!"

Determined, the burly truckdriver went to his piled-up clothing and drew the belt from his trousers. The strip of black leather was almost two inches wide, a double line of small holes running its length. He ran it through his fingers slowly as he strode back to the bed.

He paused and fumbled his full-swollen prick as he studied the heavy-breathing blond, and suddenly he bent down to stroke Phil's shoulders and lash-striped back lightly.

"I'm gonna train you right, pup," he murmured almost gently. "You've gotta learn to obey when I tell you somethin'. Understand?"

"Yeah," Phil whispered. "Yeah…yes, sir."

"You're learnin' already," Brad announced with satisfaction. He straightened, his gaze intent on the motionless man. "I'm gonna see to it that you don't forget!"

He raised the belt deliberately, biceps bulging, his muscle-ridged frame tensed. Then he brought it down across Phil's solid shoulders with a brutal crack. A wide strip of whiteness cut the tanned skin for an instant, then darkened. Brad paused, then wet his lips and laid on another blow carefully.

Phil gritted his jaws and ground his nakedness into the mattress beneath him.

Brad brought the lash down again.

And again.

And again.

Phil writhed, a wash of sweat pasting his chest and belly to the coolness beneath him. The belt snapped across the upturned cheeks of his ass repeatedly, turning the pale flesh a bright pink.

"Brad!" Phil's pleading voice was tight in his throat. "Sir!"

With a grunt, Brad dropped the belt and reached for the tube of lubricant on the bed.

"Yeah, you're learnin', doggy." He studied the helpless blond as he greased his rigid cock. "Climb up on your knees. I'm gonna plug that hot little ass of yours."

Phil hesitated, then worked himself into position on all fours. The shadow of a smile turned the corners of Brad's mouth. Without speaking, the rugged trucker finished coating his massive iron with lubricant, then moved in behind the crouching man, rubbing his palms over the burning asscheeks. His grin widened, and he smeared more grease on his fingers and pressed them deep between Phil's buns, slicking the hairy passage and the tight-clenched opening.

"I'm gonna fuck th' hell outta you," he threatened. "I'm gonna spread your goddamn asshole wide open, fairy!"

"Brad—"

"Lousy queer!" He pulled his hand free and gripped his turgid prick, nudging the gleaming head into the shadowed crack between the sleek flesh-arcs of the man's tail. "Yeah, now you're gonna get it!"

Phil gasped as the steel-hard knob centered against his

quivering asshole and thrust steadily. Brad tensed and pumped his hips forward slightly, then again with more force. Suddenly the potent iron drove inward collar-deep.

"AGGGGHHH!"

"Goddamn!" Brad swore softly and grinned down at his partially buried prick. "You like th' feel of my pecker in your butt, chum?"

"Christ! You're wrecking me!"

"Bullshit!" He rubbed his palms over Phil's back, then gripped his hips securely. "Slide back on it, doggy."

"I can't!"

"Th' hell you can't!" His fingers dug into the man's skin, holding him in place. "Want me ta ram all th' way in?"

Phil groaned and let his head drop between his heaving shoulders, and he forced himself back on the unyielding giant. Brad watched the thick-veined shaft inch deeper and deeper into the clasping crevice, and he chuckled proudly.

"That's th' way, pal…yeah, keep takin' it…shit, there ain't nothin' like pluggin' int' a tight little asshole!… Man, you're gettin' there…c'mon…all th' way.…"

"No more," Phil whimpered haltingly. "Honest, Brad, I can't—"

"Want me t' use my belt on you again?"

"No...please...don't—"

"Get your goddamn butt all th' way back here before I kick th' piss outta you!"

Phil's breath whistled between his clenched teeth as he writhed back on the swollen ram. And then his arched asscheeks were nested against the crisp hair at the trucker's groin.

"Jesus!"

"See, puppy? I told you that you could take it." Still holding Phil in place, he pumped slowly, deliberately. "Yeah, I'm gonna train you real good."

"You're tearing me apart!"

"You'll get used to it." He continued his steady, potent thrusts, tracing his fingers over the blond's pink-streaked buttocks. "Once I get you broke in, you won't have no trouble takin' any cock that comes along.

"Finish it!" Phil groaned. "Hurry up and finish it!"

"Shit, I'm not about t' rush a good fuck like this one." His throbbing cock still buried in Phil's tail, he pushed him forward on the bed and eased up to kneel between his spread legs. "You like it better this way, doggy?"

"Awww, Brad—"

Phil's words were cut off by a hoarse gasp as the

burly trucker began pumping ruthlessly. Again and again, the huge, throbbing prick drove into his guts, heavy testicles slapping at the backs of his thighs. Then Brad's thick arms locked about him.

"C'mere, pup! I'm gonna teach you to sit up and beg!" Brad sank back on his haunches, dragging the writhing man in his embrace with him. "I'm gonna teach you to sit up on my prick an' beg ta get fucked!"

"Aggghhh!"

"Beg, you peckerhead!" Ramming his solid cock inward in short, violent strokes, he clawed his fingers over Phil's arched chest and firm nipples. "Want me to stick those pinchers on your tits? Whip you all over with my belt? Tie weights on your goddamn balls?" He gripped the blond's genitals with both hands, twisting his rigid dick and clenching his testicles threateningly. "Beg, ya sonofabitch!"

"Please!" Phil whispered, wrenching back against the brutally violent man. "Please...fuck me!"

"Louder!"

"FUCK ME! PLEASE! ANYTHING YOU SAY, SIR!"

"Damn right!" He slammed Phil facedown on the bed again and fell on him, plowing into his upturned tail with increasing fury. "I'm gonna fuck...work you over... train you right, puppy...."

"ANYTHING YOU SAY!" Phil bellowed again. Suddenly he cried hoarsely, "CHRIST! I—I'M GOING T'— AHHHHHGGGGGHHHHH! I CAN'T HOLD IT! I—"

"GODDAMN FAIRY!"

"I'M COMIIIINNNGGGG!"

"SHITHEAD! COCKSUCKER!" Brad rammed into the thrashing man and clung to him. "HOT LITTLE ASS-HOLE! SQUEEZE DOWN! TAKE THAT PRICK!... YEAH!... TAKE IT!"

"AHHHHHH!"

"YEAHHHHHHH!"

Howling in ecstasy, the two men were locked together, squirming and thrashing and pouring out their mutual climax. Brad pinned Phil beneath him and spewed the fiery explosions into his clenching asshole, grinding his nakedness against the blond's back and butt as if trying to melt their bodies together. Phil struggled against the thongs still binding his wrists together, aching to reach back and clasp the man dominating him.

The instant of eternity ended, and they were two men sprawled across the bed, one with his cock still buried in the other's ass...the rugged trucker named Brad...the blond queer named Phil.

"Shit," Brad murmured, raising his head from Phil's shoulder. "I'm sweatin' like a goddamn horse!"

"Want me to lick it off?"

"You like that? Lickin' th' sweat off a guy after he's fucked your butt?" He reached up to tug at the dog collar fastened around Phil's neck. "Once I get you trained, maybe I'll bring along another stud for you to lick while I'm screwin' you."

"If—If you want me to."

"Damn right, pup. You do what I say or you're gonna get worked over till you learn your lesson."

"Y-Yes, sir."

"Good doggy." He patted the blond's head, then reached for the towel on the bed. "I gotta clean up an' get back ta work."

He pulled up on his knees and jammed the towel into Phil's ass as he withdrew his heavy, limp cock. With a grunt, he swung to his feet and sauntered into the bathroom.

Phil heard the shower start, and he twisted onto his back, rubbing his bound hands over his chest and belly, then cupping his sticky, relaxed genitals. He closed his eyes, and a contented smile turned his lips.

Fresh scrubbed, Brad came back into the room, still toweling his brawny nakedness.

154

"Asleep, chum?"

"No." Phil opened his eyes and studied the power-fully muscled man. "Too bad you can't stick around."

"What the hell for?" He caught the blond's hungry gaze and flipped his heavy prick mockingly. "You want some more of that, cocksucker?"

"If you want to."

"Maybe I oughta get a bunch of th' guys at work t' stop by an' keep you busy." He tossed the towel aside and started to climb into his pants. "There's one stud—Jack—shit, he's got th' biggest dick I ever saw. Maybe I'll bring him around ta fuck your goddamn face while I whip you into line." He picked up his belt and began working it through the loops in his trousers. "That'd be a boot in the balls, showin' Jack what a good cocksucker my little doggy is."

Phil watched Brad tug on his shoes and socks, and then he offered his still-tied wrists.

"Want your shoe laces?"

"Keep 'em. I've got another pair in th' truck."

"Aren't you going to untie me?" Phil asked nervously. "What if something happens? What if somebody comes by?"

"One of your fruit pals? Shit, that'd be somethin', one

of your goddamn queers findin' you tied up an' wearin' your doggy collar!" He pulled on his shirt, leaving it unbuttoned and hanging loose. Then he grabbed the leash attached to the collar around Phil's neck. "C'mon, chum, we're goin' for a walk."

Phil scrambled from the bed.

"Brad—"

"On your hands an' knees, dammit!" He slapped the end of the leash across the blond's back sharply. "You're gonna walk dog-fashion!"

"Yes, sir!"

Phil dropped on all fours and scrambled along behind Brad as the burly trucker led him down the hallway to the living room. Spotting the package he'd delivered earlier on the coffee table, Brad nodded to it.

"What's in that box? It's damn heavy for bein' so small."

"I...I sent away for some...some chains."

"Chains? What th' hell for?"

"Some guys, they like to be chained up."

"Jesus! Shit, maybe I oughta do that to you!" He glanced up at the cross-beamed ceiling and snickered. "Yeah, I could hang you up over one of them beams an' give you some real trainin'. Stick them weights on your balls, twist your nuts an' tits, belt you all over, front an' rear...man, I bet you'd be a real good puppy after that kind of trainin'?"

Phil sucked in a fast breath, and then he rubbed the side of his face against Brad's pant leg.

"I'll be a good puppy, sir."

"Fuckin' queer!" He tugged the leash and started toward the front door. "C'mon. Maybe I oughta chain you up outside so you don't shit all over th' house, pup."

Phil choked back a whimper as he was dragged outside and down the steps to the walkway.

"Christ, Brad—I'm bareass-naked!"

"Damned if you ain't!" Chuckling, Brad dropped the leash and stretched, flexing his biceps and filling his massive chest. Then he reached down to scratch the back of Phil's neck. "Hey, doggy, I just figured out why you live out here in th' middle of nowhere. There ain't nobody around t' see or hear when you're fruitin' around with them whips an' chains, right?"

"I—I guess so."

"Once I get you trained, maybe I'll take you up there in th' trees an' teach you ta fetch, an' shit like that. It'd be kinda good, me an' my doggy goin' bareass in th' woods t'gether."

Phil nudged up against Brad's leg again.

"Ever had a dog before?"

"Yeah, when I was a goddamn kid," Brad answered quietly, still stroking the nape of the crouching man's neck. "I guess I didn't train him right 'cause he ran away."

"I won't run away."

"Damn right, you won't! Not when I get done trainin' you!" He spun to face the kneeling blond. His features were cold and hard, his shirt falling open from his powerful hairy chest and taut stomach. "Show me what you've learned t'day, pup!" He ripped open his fly and pulled out his heavy cock and balls. "Sit up an' beg!"

Phil hesitated, then rose on his knees, his bound hands raised.

"Please…let me have it…anything you say."

"I've gotta get rid of that beer I had for lunch."

"Yes, sir." Head down, he sank back on his haunches to offer his sleek bronzed torso and full genitals. "Anything, sir!"

Brad gripped the base of his prick, stroked the thick shaft and made the broad crimson head bulge, then aimed and grinned as a stream of golden liquid shot out and splashed across Phil's wide chest.

"Anything, cocksucker?"

"Yes, sir!" His prick started to swell as the spray moved

down to his exposed crotch. "Hell, Brad, you know damn well—"

"Shut up, fairy!" Brad held his cock firmly and finished pissing on the motionless blond, then flicked the last droplets from his rod before stuffing it back into his pants. "Yeah, you're a real queer, doggy. Queer as hell!"

"Brad—"

"I've gotta get back to work." Fastening his fly, he started down the walkway to his parked truck. "Maybe I'll be horny enough to come back an' fuck your butt again t'night. Maybe I'll bring along some doggy food an' a bowl to eat it out of."

"Untie me, you sonofabitch!"

"Fuck off!"

Phil twisted over on his back and pawed his piss-drenched torso and swollen cock with his tied hands. The noontime sun shone on his strong bronzed body. He groaned as he heard the truck's engine start and the machine pull away.

"Bastard!... Awww-shit!" He lay back, relaxed, smiling to himself. "Damn you, Brad! That was the best scene you've pulled on me yet!" Lazily, he tugged at the thongs binding his wrists, and they fell away easily. "Yeah, I'm your doggy, and you know it. You'll be back tonight to chain me up and whip me into line...damn right, that's what I need!"

He rolled on his belly and crawled back toward the house, his welted back and ass glistening in the sunlight.

"Yeah, lover, that's what I've always told you I need!"

THE SPOILER

The underground concrete-walled corridor was lit by dull, bare bulbs hanging from the ceiling. Chet felt the body pressure of the guards on each side of him, urging him along. He had dark hair and strong features, and his sweat-streaked work shirt bound to his husky build, his wrists handcuffed behind his back. His dungarees were dirt stained, and his bare feet slapped softly against the cold flooring.

"You never should've tried going over the wall," one of the guards advised coldly. "That wasn't very smart, Chet."

"I damn near made it," the youth muttered.

" 'Damn near' isn't good enough. You'll find out."

"I can take it."

"If you can, you'll be the first."

They stopped in front of a solid fire door, and one of the men threw it open. Chet caught a glimpse of the small, windowless room and the uniformed guard captain standing spread-legged and brawny in the center of it. Suddenly a fist rammed into the small of his back and sent him sprawling forward. He tripped and would have hit the floor if the captain hadn't straightened him with a fast punch to the pit of his stomach. The guards restrained him, and when he caught his breath, the captain was grinning at him.

"Welcome home, punk."

"Miss me, Mr. Wilson?"

"Sure." Wilson was tall—over six feet—and thick, mature muscles ridged beneath his tailored khaki shirt and trousers. Narrow blue-gray eyes dominated his weathered face, and his thin lips pursed in a steady, mocking smile. "I miss every one of you assholes who tries to escape. Have a good time?"

"Yeah." Chet felt numb, knowing what he was in for—knowing what he'd already been through, running away, spending a few crummy days hiding out...and getting caught and brought back. "I had a real ball, Mr. Wilson."

The youth felt the men holding him dig their fingers into his biceps, and he wished to hell Wilson'd get it over with. He watched the captain pick up a pair of leather gloves from the table behind him and skin them on; the gloves would protect the man's knuckles and leave them unmarked, in case anyone asked questions about an inmate who'd been beaten...no, nobody'd ask questions.

"Like I told you," one of the guards said quietly, "you never should've gone over the wall."

"You know Finch, don't you?" Wilson nodded from Chet to the man who'd spoken, then to the other guard. "And Mitchell?"

"Yes"—Chet wished the sonofabitch'd hit him and get it over with—"sir."

Wilson stepped up close in front of him, but instead of hitting him, he ran his gloved fingers over his face slowly, grinning all the time, across his forehead and his dark eyebrows, along his high cheekbones, then down farther to his mouth, his jaw, his chin.

Then the captain hit him for the first time, only it wasn't in the face—hell, no, nothing as expected as that! He jerked one knee up, and Chet gasped as the blow struck his testicles and the pain flamed upward. The men kept him from breaking free, and it was almost a relief when Wilson's fist slashed across his face.

"Yeah, punk—welcome home!"

Wilson hit him again—twice, maybe three times, maybe more—but Chet hardly felt the blows. Then the men released him and he sagged to his knees, fighting the urge to be sick. The warm, salty taste of blood filled his mouth, and his breath rasped in his throat. He clenched his eyes to try to stop the blur of spinning colors. The waves of pain receded slowly.

"Take the cuffs off him," Wilson ordered. "He isn't going anywhere."

They wrenched his arms back and unsnapped the handcuffs, and he dropped forward on all fours. At last, he forced his eyes open. He could see the men's shoes, brightly polished and partially covered by the cuffs of their khaki pants.

"On your feet, kid." It was Finch, his voice quiet and sure. "This is just the beginning."

Chet dragged himself to his feet, trying to replace the

dull ache inside him with red-hot hate—he'd heard a guy could take almost anything if he hated hard enough— and the three men were facing him, Captain Wilson and the two guards, Finch and Mitchell.

Wilson lit a cigarette and inhaled slowly, then blew the smoke toward Chet. The youth wished to hell he could take a drag.

"Strip, punk," the captain ordered calmly. "You've got blood on your shirt."

Chet looked down at the dark stains on his shirt, then wiped the back of one hand across his lips and saw the bright red streaked across it.

"Strip," Wilson repeated.

The youth swallowed and did not raise his head, watching his fingers pick at the buttons on his shirt. He unfastened them, one after the other, and then he tugged the tails free from his trousers and shrugged the shirt from his shoulders. His torso was lightly tanned with strong, athletically muscled shoulders and arms, and his broad chest was sprayed with soft strands of black hair. His nipples were wide and hard at the tips. He took a deep breath, trying to keep his taut stomach from trembling.

"Drop your goddamn pants," Mitchell growled. He

was solidly built and swarthy, and it was the first time he'd spoken to the inmate since he'd been returned by the cops. "When we say strip, we mean all th' way."

Chet hesitated, then eased open his dungarees and let them slip to his ankles. His legs were thick and sturdy and, like all the inmates, he wore no shorts. His genitals dropped free and heavy. His cock dangled broad-shafted and loose, the deep amber head falling well below his large, firm testicles. He kicked his trousers from his ankles and stood naked and defiant—hell, he was used to going bareass in front of the guys in the dorm!

"Not bad," Wilson commented, viewing him narrowly. "You've got plenty going for you, punk. Plenty of prick, I mean. I bet you hustled a lot of queers while you were out in town, huh?"

"Hell, no!"

"Cunt, huh? Get that rod plugged into some babe?"

"Sure," Chet lied. "As soon as I hit town, there was this broad—shit, she was nuts about the way I laid her out, and—"

"That's what all of them say," Wilson interrupted dryly. "All of the punks who go over the wall." He was smiling, amused and, perhaps, a little bored with teenaged bragging. "Yeah, every one of you comes back with the same stories—but you all come back. That's what counts to me." His expression hardened. "You all come back—nobody escapes from here—and nobody goes over the wall twice." He peeled off the leather gloves and turned away while he unbuttoned his shirt. "If you're smart, you won't try running away again. You're stuck here until it's time for you to graduate—remember that."

Chet shifted to the two guards. Finch met his gaze evenly, blond and tanned, his features set, while Mitchell was breathing hard, his broad chest heaving beneath his taut shirt, his eyes fixed and glazed on the youth's nakedness.

Chet had been in for three years and had one more to go...and all the guys said he was tough as hell...and he saw the men...and he was bareass and...and... scared!

"Mr. Wilson—"

"Remember what you said?" Finch broke in, still cold and steady. "You can take it, right?"

Wilson turned back. He was stripped to the waist, his heavy frame etched with swollen muscles, a crisp blanket of dark hair plastered to his powerful chest. Without a word, he pulled the belt from his low-slung trousers, then nodded to Finch and Mitchell.

"Bend him over."

The two guards moved up to Chet and grabbed him by the arms, jerking him over ass-up and holding him firmly. He felt the captain position himself and cock one arm, and he tensed as he heard the belt whistle through the air.

The leather snapped across the youth's pale round ass with a brutal crack, wrenching him forward despite the hands holding him. An instant later, a searing fire ate into his bare flesh. He gritted his teeth as the pain mounted to its zenith, then numbed slowly. A glaze of sweat broke out across his back.

The room was silent except for Chet's hoarse breathing. After what seemed like an eternity, the lash whistled through the air and struck again…and again…and again.

Wilson continued the beating deliberately, allowing time for the full fury of each blow to smash and surge into Chet's brain. He placed the stripes carefully, leaving a neat pattern of ruddy streaks lined across the youth's clenched asscheeks.

Chet's gasps became choked cries, then curses, and finally anguished groans. He fought futilely against the guards holding him. Suddenly they jerked him upright. A fist rammed into the pit of his stomach. His breath shot from his lungs. Then he was being pounded from all sides, his legs turning to jelly. He sank to his knees, then sprawled flat, clawing at the concrete flooring.

"You're gonna get used t' crawlin'," Mitchell mocked. "Yeah, before we're done, you'll wish you'd never thought of goin' over th' wall!"

The guard's voice came through a muffled fog in Chet's brain. After a moment, he became aware of the bruising pain from the combination of beatings. He was naked and sweat-plastered to the rough concrete. He flinched as a bucket of icy water sloshed down over him.

"Wake up, punk," Wilson ordered. "I've got other things to do, so we'll let you off easy today. But I want you to get a good look at what's waiting for you tomorrow."

"Gonna introduce him t' th' spoiler?"

"Yeah. Stick the bracelets on him again."

The two guards wrenched Chet's arms behind him, locking his wrists together with handcuffs, and dragged him to his feet. He forced himself to focus on them—first Finch, blond and handsome and expressionless, then Mitchell, rugged and grinning, then Wilson, massive and sweating and methodical. He tried to hate them, but he didn't have enough strength left to make it work.

"Okay...sir."

"C'mon, I'll give you a tour."

Chet was only vaguely aware of what they were doing as the guards hauled him around the room while Wilson calmly pointed out the wall-bedded chains he'd be hung on while he was beaten, the weights they'd use to stretch muscles and bones until he begged for mercy, the devices he wasn't able to understand at the moment. He knew he'd learn what they were for before Wilson and his pals were done, but at the moment, he didn't care.

Then they had him standing in front of a solid table, an ordinary wood vise attached to one side, the jaws spread wide.

"You're going to get tied down on this table," Wilson continued, still calm and businesslike, "sometimes on your belly and sometimes faceup. And sometimes the spoiler will be here, waiting for you."

The men moved Chet up against the table. Suddenly he snapped awake to what was happening—yeah, he was bareass-naked, bruised and beaten with his testicles being placed between the pincers of the vise. He started to wrench free, but the guards stopped him.

Finch's voice was gentle and relaxed in his ear. "It's too late, kid. You try to pull away, and you'll lose those jewels."

"Goddamn right!" Mitchell muttered from the other side. "Give it t' him, cap'n—give him th' spoiler!"

Chet watched Wilson's thick fingers turn the small handle on the vise and felt the first twinge of pain as the metal clamps dug into his sensitive balls. He hunched forward, a drop of perspiration forming between his shoulder blades and starting to dribble down his spine. The lock clicked sharply as the handle was turned again.

"No…please…Captain…."

Wilson tightened the vise, increasing the pressure systematically. Chet's body was washed with sweat now. A steady trickle ran into his asscleft and down his thighs. The handcuffs ate into his wrists as he struggled involuntarily, trapped between the mounting pain and his fear of what would happen if he tried to twist free of the clamps locked about his nuts.

"Sorry you went over the wall, Chet?"

The youth recognized Finch's voice—cool, almost mocking. He couldn't restrain an agonized groan.

"That's enough for now," Wilson announced unemotionally. "Next time, we'll give you a little more of the spoiler, and even more after that. By the time we're done, you won't want to take a chance on getting caught going over the wall again." He nodded to Finch. "C'mon, Mitchell'll finish up and get this kid settled."

Chet heard the two men leave, and he stared down at his crotch, his testicles still tightly held in the vise, his heavy-headed cock falling limp to one side.

"Th' cap'n let you off easy this time," Mitchell snickered from behind him. "I've seen him work you punks over steady an' slow till it hurts too much t' yell. Sooner or later, you're gonna end up like that."

Chet swallowed hard. "I can take it."

"Bullshit! You'll end up crawlin', just like all th' others. Yeah, a few more sessions with th' spoiler, an' you'll crawl!"

The youth felt the guard step up in back of him, and then the man's grease-slick cock was jammed between the cheeks of his exposed ass. Somehow, he wasn't surprised—he was naked and helpless, his legs spread, his wrists chained together, his balls locked in that goddamn vise—but he gasped as the dagger-tipped rod speared into his narrow opening.

"Christ! Take it easy!"

"Punk!" He jabbed his thin, rigid iron all the way into Chet. He pressed against the youth's back, stripped and brawny and sex-hot. "I'm gonna give you a man-sized fuck! That's what you need—a hot prick shoved up your butt!"

Chet strained to hold still, the slightest movement sending a renewed stab of pain through his tortured nuts. He cursed as the pistonlike penetrations tore into him.

"Damn it, Mitchell...awww, you lousy—"

"You like that, punk?" The guard's voice was hoarse and thick with excitement. He reached around to twist the youth's firm nipples. "I'm gonna fuck you...tight little ass...good-lookin' goddamn stud...make you crawl...yeah, make you—take it! TAKE IT! AWWWHHHH!" His final thrust seemed to merge with the agony filling Chet, and the husky teenager howled in misery. "PUNK! GOD-DAMN RUGGED HORNY PUNK!"

Chet's world was filled with clawing pain. He was only vaguely aware of the brawny guard's climax, the iron-hard cock convulsing in his tail and the come spewing into his guts. Then, as abruptly as he'd begun, Mitchell pulled free, released the vise, and unlocked the handcuffs. Chet sagged into blackness, his hands clutched to his genitals.

When he struggled back to full consciousness, a steady spray of cool water was pounding on his back, and he was hunched on the floor of a shower room. Somehow, he knew that Mitchell was there, washing off and laughing at him for being doubled over on his knees, and he forced himself to his feet. Yeah, that sonofabitch was there, naked and rugged, grinning as if he knew how goddamned much it hurt just to stand up.

"Take a good look, Chet." Mitchell planted his legs wide apart and rubbed his soapy palms over his hard chest and downward to his crotch, fumbling his genitals suggestively. His prick was soft but thick, the arrow-tipped crown barely showing from the loose fold of foreskin, and he tugged it proudly. "You want some more of that? You want to suck on it?"

Chet tried to bring up enough hatred to black out the throbbing pain. "Aren't you scared I'll bite it off?"

"You won't get th' chance," he answered with a pleased chuckle. "That's why I stuck it up your butt... an' that's why I'm gonna keep on fuckin' you whenever I'm worked up." He rinsed fast and sauntered toward the doorway of the small, dank-smelling room. "Clean up, punk. I'll have th' medic waitin' t' check you out before you get locked in for th' night."

Chet showered thoroughly. When he'd finished and dried off, Mitchell was dressed and waiting in the next room with the doctor. The white-coated man examined the youth professionally, noting bruises and contusions and the clearly marked belt slashes across his ass, then applying a burning ointment and letting some of it drip into his brutalized ass when he cursed at the fiery pain.

"He's okay for duty," the doctor muttered with satisfaction. "Yeah, he'll be back in shape by tomorrow."

Mitchell took Chet down the dim-lit hall to a small cell, a cot against one of the windowless walls, a washbasin and open toilet opposite.

"This'll be your home till you've learned your lesson, punk. An' we'll be back t' make sure you learn, believe me!"

He kicked Chet into the room. The youth waited until he heard the iron door clank shut behind him before lurching across to puke into the open toilet; he hurt bad enough to vomit his guts out, but not until that ass-fuckin' guard was gone, damn it!

A single dim lightbulb glowed overhead, and he fell on the bunk, naked and aching and exhausted, clutching his genitals as he slipped into a nightmare of sleep.

Wilson, Finch, and Mitchell came back, just as Mitchell had promised—"We'll be back t' make sure you learn"—and they hauled Chet down to that room again and hung him up by the wrists and whipped him, not just his ass but his shoulders and back and

175

thighs. He braced himself at first, then sagged, then howled and hung limp, too weak to do more than mumble in agony.

That was the worst beating—maybe the doctor really meant it when he examined him and said, "Ease off on this one"—but they kept taking him to the spoiler. Sure, they did all sorts of other things—tied him spread-eagle on that table faceup so he could see them torture him, or facedown so unseen guards could ram his unprotected butt—but the experience that terrorized him in the middle of the night was the fear of another treatment with the spoiler.

Each session began with one of the guards handcuffing Chet's hands behind his back. Then he was taken down the corridor to the room where the vise might be waiting, its jaws spread to grip his testicles and bring the screaming, blinding pain. It got so that when he saw it there, the sweat began dripping and with it, the trembling of fear.

He lost track of time—how many beatings? how many cocks up his ass? how many meetings with the spoiler?—and then Wilson came into his cell alone, locked him in the handcuffs, put a blindfold over his eyes and forced him to lie on his cot. Then there was another man with them—someone Wilson treated with respect and said "sir" to. After the warden was gone, Chet heard the rustle of clothing, then felt the weight of the stranger easing onto the bunk and the brush of thick, pudgy fingers over his face and chest.

"Lovely," the man whispered, and his breath was heavy with stale tobacco and alcohol. "Lovely... young... strong...beautiful stud...male animal...lovely!"

Chet squirmed on his back, his hands chained beneath him, and the taunting caress moved downward over his naked body. He lay still and half-smiled as he felt the fingers slip into his groin and heard the man's pleased sigh.

"Such fine balls...big prick...real horny, huh? Yeah, hard-up and horny...lovely!"

Chet didn't realize that he hadn't objected to having this unknown man examine his sensitive balls or that he'd gotten his first hard-on since being brought back to the school and the torture.

Then the stranger was flat on top of him, heavy and flabby and nuzzling over his bare flesh. For an instant, Chet felt the damp cock jabbed against his own turgid ram. He wanted to laugh because it was so small and kid-hot. And then the man was sinking lower, licking his nuts and tonguing his soaring prick.

"Hey, mister—"

"Lemme, sonny," the man whispered softly. Chet would remember that—the way this stranger he couldn't see called him "sonny"—"lemme do this…just this once…the way it would've been…you and me, sonny.…"

Yeah, Chet'd remember that pain-filled voice, but then the lips were covering the tip of his cock and pressing downward…and he was so fuckin' hot!…yeah, he hadn't gotten his rocks off for so goddamn long, hadn't screwed one of the guys in the showers or made him suck dick…shit, he was all cock- and balls-aching horny… who gives a damn, huh?

"Okay, pal—sure, take me off!"

Chet raised his hips, shoving his sex-swollen ram into the unknown man's throat, and he popped, hearing him choke and gag, feeling him gulp and suck for more.

"Yeahhhh!"

The youth was swept up in the momentary explosion of climax, pleasure and fury and king-of-the-mountain, free of the basement cell and the guards who'd beaten him and fucked him.

But he had to come down again, down to the reality of the fat and flabby sonofabitch who'd gone down on him and was still stroking his bare torso with his soft, hungry fingers. Then the man fell on him, half-suffocating him with his weight, and a squirt of slimy liquid spewed onto his belly.

"Sonny!... Sonny...lovely...yeah, lovely!"

Chet lay still until the man pulled off of him. It kinda bothered him, the way he'd been handcuffed and blindfolded so he couldn't see the guy who'd—

"Thank you," the stranger said quietly, and his clothes rustled as he pulled them on. "Thank you... son."

"Anytime, pal."

As soon as he'd said it, Chet knew it was wrong—but he didn't know why. Hell, the fat old bastard'd taken him off and—"sonny!"—crap, maybe he'd been in too long to know anything more than how good it felt to get his rocks off. Or maybe—shit!

The man left, and Mitchell came in to peel off the blindfold and snicker at the come stains on his belly... and then he was taken down the hall to the room where the spoiler was waiting, and his testicles were jammed between the yawning clamps...

and the metal arms clicked shut, pressing, then digging, then gouging....

and he screamed.

Mitchell let the vise handle slip, and the clamps dug

deeper than ever before—too deep—and Chet howled... and whimpered...and crawled....

Yeah, Mitchell'd said he'd crawl. Right from the first, Wilson had whipped him and Finch had goaded him about being tough enough to take it...but Mitchell made him crawl.

And he fell into a nightmare about that fat, thin-pricked man who'd shot his wad...and called him "sonny."

When he came to, he knew it was all over.

Chet was in his cell again. He couldn't remember how long it'd been since that night when some stranger had sucked him off and Mitchell had let the vise handle slip. Yeah, he'd been beaten and fucked and sucked off for all the years he'd been in; but when he heard the guard's footsteps approaching in the corridor outside, he knew he couldn't take another session with the spoiler.

He sat on the side of the bed, naked and head down. From the corner of his eye, he saw the cell door open and the guard come in. It was Finch, the handsome blond athlete. He held out the handcuffs, ready to chain him and take him to the spoiler.

"Let's go, Chet."

"I can't take any more," the youth murmured, motion-less. "I give up."

There was a long pause. Then Finch dropped the handcuffs and closed the door.

"You've still got a year to go. It'll be damn rough if the warden lets the wolves know you broke down here."

"I—I don't care."

"Make it easy on yourself, kid. Line yourself up with one of us guards, and nobody'll bother you. Mitchell— he wouldn't mind getting into your ass regularly."

"Not Mitchell," Chet vowed. "Not that sonofa—"

"Like I said, make it easy on yourself."

The youth heard the door latch snap, and he drew a slow breath. "You?"

"I get as hard up as any other guard around here."

Chet let his gaze shift across the concrete floor to the man's military-polished shoes, then up his wide-planted legs. Finch had ripped open his fly and spread the flaps, and his prick curled outward and down from a thick nest of tangled pubic hair, the broad, limp shaft capped by a full-rounded amber head. Chet stared for a moment, then understood and slipped to his knees. Without knowing why, he wanted to smile.

"Okay, Finch, I get the picture."

The man stepped forward directly in front of him, and he raised one hand to cup the flaccid cock in his palm and bring it up to his lips. He washed his tongue over the firm crown. Then he took it into his mouth, pressing downward almost hungrily, the lush scent of maleness swirling into his nostrils. He felt the first surge of strength pour into the heavy flesh-column. It was swelling and stretching into his throat. He sucked its full length and held at the base, his forehead pressed to the guard's taut belly. There was something damn good about the way Finch pushed his pants down and gripped his head, holding him securely in place.

"That's right, you've got the picture." He thrust his now-rigid prick with sureness, then pulled back to free it. "Try my nuts—make love to them, kid."

Chet gazed at the slick wet cock and saw Finch pull it aside to expose his large, loose-hanging testicles. He rocked forward again to nuzzle and lick and suck, first one sensitive ball, then the other, then both at once.

And he wrapped his arms about the guard's hips and pressed against him, secure and kinda hot and happy as hell!

"No rush," Finch murmured, stroking Chet's hair. "Climb up on your bunk—you can finish me off there."

Chet ran his hands upward, beneath the man's loose-hanging shirt and over his strong torso. Then he let the sensitive organs slip from his mouth.

"Yeah—sure." He gulped for breath. "Damn it, Finch—"

"On the bunk, kid."

Chet grunted and swung up onto the cot, lying back and watching as the guard stripped off his clothes. Finch was solidly built and tanned, his wide shoulders melting into the broad chest smeared with slick blond hair, his stomach muscled, his belly flat and pale below his sudden tan line, his cock jutting from his crotch.

Chet let himself grin openly.

"You're a real bastard, Finch. I should've guessed that a long time ago, huh?"

"Fuck off," the guard muttered and slid naked onto the bed, fitting himself to the youth and jamming one arm beneath his shoulders to draw him closer. He stroked Chet's hair again with his free hand, then chuckled softly. "All that crap you gave Wilson about what you did while you were in town—that was a crock of shit, right?"

"Hell, no! I picked up this broad and screwed her and—"

"You walked around and looked at things, and you

went to the movies—every movie in town—all by your-self." He eased his rockhard prick against Chet's. "That's what you did, isn't it?"

"How—How do you know?" He laid the side of his face against the man's hair-splattered chest.

"When I was a kid, I did some time in a lousy reform school. I went over the wall once."

"Bastard! I should've known all along that you—"

"I went to the movies and holed up in a crummy hotel, and after a couple of days, I came back and turned myself in." He ran his fingertips over Chet's solid shoulders, his voice quiet and thoughtful. "Yeah, I went back to that fucking reformatory because—shit, it was so goddamn lonely on the outside, and the guys at school, they were—they were all the family I'd ever known."

Chet watched his fingers trickle over the guard's warm bronzed skin. "Did you get worked over when you went back? Is that why you didn't use the spoiler on me or fuck my butt like Mitchell did?"

"Maybe." He wet his lips, then grinned. "I'll get Wilson to move you over to my cottage."

"Okay."

"It'll be good to have a stud around again. I haven't

had a regular sack-buddy for a long time." He chuckled softly. "I sure hope you like to get fucked, kid."

"Horny sonofabitch," Chet muttered and squirmed over on top of the man. "Hell, I don't give a damn."

He pressed his lips to Finch's chest, nuzzling and tonguing outward to the sharp-tipped nipples and back, then downward. He could hear the guard's excited breathing and feel the straining hardness of his cock as he worked lower, and finally he settled between the man's legs, his lips caressing the glistening flesh-column from base to crown.

"Climb on that iron," Finch ordered in a husky whisper. "Bring me off this time!"

Chet opened his mouth to the powerful cockhead and took it without hesitation. Then he was sucking the turgid shaft eagerly, willingly. Once again, the warm, musky scent of maleness filled his lungs, and then the man's legs tightened about him, trapping him in place. His own sex hunger seared hot and demanding into his loins and he clamped himself to the writhing guard.

"Suck! Yeah, suck that meat, kid!" Finch wrenched his hips upward, driving his iron-hard ram into the youth's throat. "Take it! TAKE—AGGGHHH! GODDAMN-JESUS-SHIT-FUCK—AHHHH! The thick hot come shot free,

pouring into Chet's mouth in repeated bursts. "YEAH—
AWWW GODDAMN—TAKE IT, Y' COCKSUCKIN'
SONOFA—cocksuckin'…damn it…awww, man!…yeah…
yeahhh!"

Chet swallowed the last of the heavy come and lay
still, the powerful cock quivering and then fading
slowly in his mouth. At last, he felt Finch's hand on his
head, smoothing his short-clipped hair lazily. He drew
an audible breath, then mussed Chet's hair, chuckling.
"Hey, kid, you popped, didn't you?"

Chet pulled up slowly, letting the heavy prick slip
from between his lips and then resting flat, the side of
his face against Finch's belly.

"Yeah," he murmured self-consciously. "When you
went off—hell, I couldn't hold back."

Finch snorted, one hand still clapped against Chet's
head. "You still got a year to go. You'd screw up again
for sure. Only I'm going to keep you in line."

Chet pulled up slowly, studying the man's flaccid
prick, his tanned, muscular physique, then his relaxed
features.

"You're a bastard, Finch—a real bastard."

Chet swung to his feet, his back to Finch.

"What you said before—about feeling that the guys

were the only family you had when you were in reform—"

"I don't give a shit about you, kid." Finch's voice was quiet and sure, and the cot squeaked as he got up. "Don't get the wrong idea." He moved up behind Chet and embraced him. "You're going to do what I say, and I'm going to make you suck me off or plug your ass whenever I want to—that's all."

"Bastard," Chet murmured, knowing the goddamn guard was lying. "You could've made any of the guys here spread their buns for your prick and—"

Chet relaxed back against the man, feeling the strength of the arms about him, the male nakedness pressed against his back, the heavy cock hanging limp along his ass crevice.

"Okay," he agreed, grinning. "I guess I can do anything you did when you were an inmate like me."

"Punk!"

"Bastard!"

"Goddamn—kid!"

"Yeah…pal."

"Yeah…yeah…yeah, pal."

No Escape

Tony moved cautiously from the brush and trees and viewed the narrow mountain road before venturing into the open.

He was medium tall with close-trimmed hair and mature features. A washed-out work shirt and soiled trousers outlined his well-muscled physique.

The road was empty as far as he could see, and he shrugged and turned back, popping open the buttons on his fly. He groped inside, found his heavy-hanging cock and pulled it out, tugged the thick shaft, then began to piss.

He felt a crazy sort of freedom as he let his mallet-crowned dick dangle from his pants and took a leak in the bushes. He reached inside again to pull out his potent testicles, toying with them proudly.

"Man!" he whispered to himself. "Yeah…man!"

Finished, he milked the last golden droplets from his prick. And then he heard a car motor in the distance.

He shoved his meat back inside his pants and buttoned up as a battered pickup truck came into sight. He studied it for a moment, then hustled to the roadside and offered his thumb.

The truck slowed and stopped.

"Climb in, lad," a deep, masculine voice drawled from the cab. "I'm only goin' a few miles further, but you're welcome t' ride along."

"Thanks." Tony swung up onto the seat beside the man behind the steering wheel. "Rides are hard to catch out here."

"I reckon so." He slipped the clutch into gear and eased the truck forward. He was in his early thirties, sandy-haired, sun-bronzed, sharp-featured, and he wore a bleached khaki shirt and Levi's. "Where're you headed?"

"East." Tony shied away from the stranger's gaze. "Going as far as the freeway?"

"Nearly." He dug a cigarette from his shirt pocket and lit it, his squinted eyes shifting back to the roadway ahead. "I'm Bart. You got a name?"

"Tony."

"Howdy." Bart inhaled smoke, then passed the butt to the youth without looking at him. "You're travelin' light if you're headed east, lad."

"I—I was robbed," Tony lied. He sucked fast on the cigarette. "The last guys who picked me up...they brought me out here and robbed me...my gear...my wallet... everything."

"Lordy! We'd best report that t' th' Sheriff!"

"No!" Tony exclaimed. "I—I don't know their names or anything. And I—I didn't have much with me."

"Sheriff Russell's a friend of mine," Bart explained. "I do believe he'd be glad t' help out a fine-lookin' lad like you."

"Forget it!" Tony sucked on the cigarette again. "He'd probably book me for vagrancy."

"Could be. Rusty ain't much for lettin' fellers wander around here with nothin' but holes in their pockets."

Tony relaxed, grinning. He enjoyed Bart's cool, easy drawl, and he gave the brawny man a quick glance.

"You live around here, Bart?"

"Yup. I've got myself a little spread back off this road." He dug out another cigarette and lit it. "It's a bit of a detour from th' freeway, if you want t' take a look at it."

"How much of a detour?"

"Considerable. I ain't much for havin' folks crowd in on me."

Tony didn't bother to answer. He felt strangely secure with the drawling man...and he sure as hell needed some security!

Without comment, Bart slowed the truck and made a turn onto a side road.

Tony finished his cigarette, doused it, and felt even more secure as Bart wheeled again onto dirt-rutted tracks.

The landscape was heavily treed and increasingly isolated. Suddenly they crested a rise and rolled into a clearing, a small house and barn alone in the wilderness.

"You sure don't like to be crowded," Tony murmured. "I bet no one ever comes wandering in on you."

"Only fellers I invite." He braked the pickup to a stop and slid to the ground. "Come along an' I'll show you around."

Tony followed, studying Bart thoughtfully. They were

a long way from the highway and the outside world, and the drawling stud walked with an easy cowboy gait, showing off what he'd done and planned to do with the property.

The more Tony saw, the more he was sure that Bart's place was the hideout he needed...and Bart was too much of a shitkicker to ever suspect!

"Man!" Tony exclaimed as they finally headed toward the ramshackle house. "You sure have got a great place here! I wouldn't mind living out in the woods like this!"

"'Tain't much yet," Bart muttered, stomping up the wood-plank steps to the front porch of the building. "There's a lot of work t' do, but you're welcome t' stay for a time, if you wish."

"Hey! That'd be neat!" He offered his most boyish smile as they entered the sparsely furnished living room, a fireplace at one side, the open door to a bedr-oom at the rear. "Look, Bart, I don't want to put you out...you know."

"Yup" He matched Tony's smile, open and honest. "It's gettin' late, an' hitchhikin' east'll be somewhat hard, even on th' freeway. Also, I reckon you could use a shower an' all." He nodded toward the bedroom. "You can strip down an' clean up in th' latrine in there."

"Okay." He'd agreed almost too easily but—hell, he didn't want to give himself away. "Sure."

He sauntered into the bedroom, and he heard Bart clomp about in the other room as he undressed and piled his clothes on the wide, neatly made bed.

Naked, Tony stretched and took a long, deep breath, and then he reached down to stroke his loose-hanging genitals. His sun-bronzed physique was a handsome blend of maturing youthfulness and virile manhood, and thickening muscles rippled over his wide shoulders and powerful arms. His broad chest was brushed with dark hair which trailed downward over his taut stomach and flat, suddenly pale, belly to merge with the lush growth at his crotch. His long torso tapered sharply to his narrow waist and hips, and the fullness of his dangling cock and balls was accentuated by his solid, stocky thighs and legs.

He went into the small latrine and started the shower, chuckling as he climbed beneath the warm spray.

Dammit, he'd finally lucked out! He'd hitched a ride with a drawling shitkicker named Bart who dug living in the middle of nowhere…off the beaten path…where Tony could stay hidden for a few days—maybe longer—until the heat was off and he could haul ass out of the state!

He grabbed the bar of soap from the wall holder and

began lathering himself vigorously, pawing his naked-ness, enjoying his muscled masculinity, relishing his now-and-future freedom.

Yeah, Tony had finally lucked out!

He washed thoroughly and rinsed, then hopped from the stall to find a towel and dry off.

There was a razor and tube of shaving cream on the washbasin opposite, and he checked his reflection in the shaving mirror, frowning at the stubble graying his cheeks and jaws.

Instinctively, he started shaving, trying to make his face baby-ass smooth...and saw Bart's reflection in the mirror, stripped to the waist in the doorway behind him and grinning.

"Lordy, lad," the shitkicker drawled. "I'm pleased you found my razor. I'd like t' see you lookin' all cleaned up an' fine."

Bart's thick neck melted into broad shoulders, and the high curves of his chest were blanketed with curly sun-bleached hair. His Levi's dipped low on his hips—no sign of shorts showing—and the crotch bulged with masculine strength.

As he finished shaving, Tony wondered what the man did for sex in this goddamn wilderness.

After washing and drying his face, Tony followed Bart back into the bedroom, only to stop in the entrance, frowning.

"Where're my clothes?" he asked, nodding toward the empty bed.

"I tossed them out," Bart replied with his usual easy-going smile. "They're th' kind of duds th' fellers at th' Sheriff's Honor Camp wear, right?"

"I—I wouldn't know."

"Durn it, I've picked up more'n one of you runaways." He shook his head with annoyance. "I don't know why you tried it, Tony, but they're bound t' catch you. 'Specially wearin' that camp uniform."

"Shit!" Tony's vision of freedom crumbled, and it took a moment for him to suck in a breath and collect his thoughts. "Going to call the Sheriff, Bart?"

"There ain't no phone here."

"So?"

"I reckon we'll just have t' wait till Rusty comes callin'. Then—well, he's always taken th' others back t' camp an'—" He shrugged. "There's somethin' he calls 'extra duty, extra time.' I dunno what that is."

"I do. That's no sweat." Tony wet his lips. "What happens between now and the time the Sheriff gets here?"

"Most times, you runaways do what I say…an' take care of my needs." Bart viewed the naked youth slowly, thoughtfully. "You ain't like those other lads, Tony. I do believe you'd keep on runnin' if I give you th' chance. Yup, stripped bare an' with th' Sheriff chasin' you, I reckon you're th' kind that keeps on runnin' away." He turned to the battered dresser against the wall, opened a drawer, and brought out a pair of handcuffs. "I'd best chain you up till Rusty gets here."

Tony saw the glint of the steel manacles, and he reacted impulsively as the man turned back toward him.

"Shitkicker!" His fist smashed toward Bart's face. "I'm not going back to that goddamn—"

Bart's counterpunch was already on its way.

Bart had dropped the handcuffs and was blocking Tony's blow with one arm. His fist smashed into the naked youth.

Tony staggered back, stunned. His head banged against the wall behind him.

He slumped to the floor.

"I don't like bein' called a shitkicker, boy," Bart grumbled, and he hunched over Tony, picking up the handcuffs. "On th' other hand, I kinda figured you'd stand up t' me." He snapped the clamps on the youth's wrists, then rose and went back to the bureau. "I reckon I'd best chain you well, lad. You ain't quite like th' other runaways I've brought here."

He returned with a length of steel chain and hunkered beside Tony as he fastened one end of it about the youth's neck.

Tony forced his eyes open and shook his head groggily. Then he discovered the handcuffs and chain. He stared at them for a long moment.

"What goes, Bart?"

"How come you're in th' Sheriff's camp, lad?"

"None of your fucking business!" Tony barked, and then he took a deep breath, head down, avoiding the man's steady gaze. "What do you care?"

"I dunno," Bart admitted honestly, his gentle drawl reflecting his uncertainty. "I reckon you must've done somethin' awful wrong. If I'd done somethin' like that when I was a young'un like you, my pappy would've blistered my ass out in th' barn."

"My old man belted me around plenty. That's why—why I left home."

"I did th' same thing," Bart murmured. "But not for th' same reason. I never ended up in a camp like you did—that's for sure." He swung to his feet, tugging on

198

the chain locked around Tony's neck. "Come along, lad."

"Wha—" His air was cut off by the tightened chain, and he stumbled to his feet, clawing at the collar with his manacled hands. "Sonofabitch! You're choking me!"

"Come along," Bart repeated quietly. "We'd best get t' know each other, if you're goin' t' be here till Rusty come t' pick you up."

"Meaning?"

"I'm takin' you out t' th' barn, th' way my pappy would've taken me."

Naked and chained, Tony had no escape, and he followed Bart from the house and across the clearing and into the weathered barn.

The interior was shadowed and smelled of hay and manure. Ropes hung from the overhead beams.

Without a word, Bart attached one of the ropes to the handcuffs on Tony's wrists and hauled him up, muscles stretched.

"Knock it off!" Tony barked, sure of himself. "You lay a hand on me, and the Sheriff'll know it!"

"Like I told you, Rusty's a pal of mine," Bart answered in his gentle drawl. He stepped in front of Tony, smiling honestly. "He knows I've been somewhat rough with his runaways."

"It's against the law to—"

"Lots of things're against th' law. My pappy never thought about that when he took me out t' th' barn." He put both hands on the youth's muscular chest and stroked the bared arcs slowly. He broke off and watched his fingers toy with Tony's crimsoned nipples, then roam lower.

Deliberately, he reached down and gripped Tony's heavy-hanging cock and slippery balls, grasping them securely.

"What the—" Tony tensed, then sneered. "You like playing with a guy's dick, Bart?"

"Yup," he answered without shyness. "Mostly, I play with my own 'cause it's somewhat lonely out here, but it'll be mighty pleasin' t' have you suck on it, lad."

"Go to hell, shitkicker!"

"That ain't a proper way t' talk," Bart cautioned. " 'Specially when I've got ahold of your nuts."

He shrugged and released the youth's testicles. "I'd best whomp some sense int' you." He sauntered across the barn to pick up a length of heavy leather and wrapped one end of it about his wrist securely as he returned. "Want t' tell me why you got sent t' th' camp?"

"It's none of your goddamn business!"

With a grunt, Bart took a stance behind Tony. For a

long moment, he studied his strong bronzed back and pale tight-rounded ass. Then he raised the whip and brought it searing down across the youth's flesh.

Tony gasped at the brutal force of the blow and gritted his teeth, determined not to cry out.

Bart beat him with slow sureness, raising welt after welt on his taut skin. Tony thrashed at the bindings holding him. He fought the mounting pain, and at last an aching groan came from his throat.

Then he was cursing and howling as the lash strokes ripped into him.

Finally he hung limp and helpless, agonized moans coming uncontrollably with each new blow.

Bart stopped the beating and tossed the whip aside. His face and torso glistened with beads of sweat, but his expression showed no strain or emotion.

He released the ropes holding Tony upright, and the youth sagged to the raw wood flooring of the barn.

Bart wet his thin lips, then hauled the teenager to a pile of hay with surprising ease, laying him out facedown with his arms and legs stretched.

"It seems as if a feller needs t' get whomped sometimes, lad. If your pappy'd been like mine, maybe you wouldn't've ended up in th' Sheriff's camp." He sat on the straw beside Tony and ran one work-roughened palm over the young'un's lash-streaked back and ass. "How come you got sent t' Rusty's place, Tony?"

"What do you care?" he snarled.

"Lordy!" Bart sighed. "Ain't you learned nothin' from that whippin'? 'Tain't right for a fine-lookin' lad like you t' be locked up, an' it ain't right for you t' try runnin' away…an' it ain't right for you t' act so—so—well, you're chained up an' stuck with me till Rusty comes for you… an' I'm stuck with you, likewise."

"I stole a car," Tony murmured, all mixed up inside by the shitkicker's drawl and near caresses. "And a lot of other crap."

"You done wrong, lad."

"Yeah…maybe…I dunno."

"You're learnin'," Bart declared decisively. He twisted away to unhook the thong on his work boots. "As long as you're stayin' here, you'd best do as I say. Otherwise, I'll just have t' whomp you some more."

Barefoot, he stood up and began unfastening his Levi's. Tony eyed him warily.

"What're you doing, Bart?"

"Strippin' down." He peeled off his pants, and his prick bobbed forward from his crotch, partially swollen and threatening. "I plan on ridin' that fine little tail of yours."

"Nobody fucks me!"

"'Tain't likely that you're a virgin, not after bein' in th' camp." He brought out a tube of lubricant and began applying it to the bulging crown and thickened shaft of his ram. "I'm mighty fired up, so you'd best relax an' spread your cheeks, lad."

"Knock it off, you sonofabitch!"

"Do what I say, durn it!" He knelt between Tony's legs and slapped his lash-streaked ass hard. "One way or another, I'm goin' t' bust int' you!"

Tony whimpered as Bart's strong hands forced his buns apart, exposing his clenched asshole. And then the grease-slick cockhead was nudging against it.

"No...please don't...Bart...don't!"

Ignoring the squirming youth's pleas, Bart pressured the tip of his iron against the pulsing opening, forcing it to spread. Tony choked back an anguished cry as the potent invader slithered inward collar-deep.

"Lordy!" Bart whispered, pleased and grinning. "That surely is a tight fit!"

"You're wrecking me!"

"No, I ain't. But you'd best stop fightin'; 'cause I've got a ways t' go 'fore all of my pecker's plowed int' you."

"Bastard! Sonofabitch! Fucking shitkicker!"

"Yup."

Tony's bound hands clawed at the coarse straw beneath him, and Bart's turgid prick eased forward... drew back... slid deeper...deeper...again and again...

slowly and almost gently...

all the way to the hairy groin!

Bart was fucking Tony, and the tough-as-nails runaway from the Sheriff's camp was yelling and cursing...and the drawling cowboy's powerful cock filled his guts...

and Tony was helpless to stop it...and didn't want to!

Dazed, whipped and chained, he was yielding totally to the goddamn shitkicker!

"Bart...Bart...Bart!"

"Mighty fine, lad...mighty fine!"

Bart gripped the youth and hauled him up and back to sit on his plunging flesh column, and Tony closed his eyes and submitted completely. He felt the man's powerful arms wrap about him, the callused fingers examining his virile nakedness, and his cock soared iron-hard from his crotch.

Locked together, they sprawled on the hay again, and Bart pumped with growing fury, his hoarse, excited breathing echoing in Tony's ears.

The youth groaned, overwhelmed by the cowboy's masculinity. His climax was churning for release inside him. He threw his head back and howled with pleasure as his come boiled over and spurted into the straw beneath him.

Christ, it felt as if Bart's plunging ram were hammering every drop out of his sex-hot balls!

Then Bart was burying his convulsing iron nuts-deep into Tony and bellowing in ecstasy.

They writhed together, lost in the ultimate masculine sensation. The instant eternity seemed endless.

At last, they sank into the lazy retreat from the summit they'd reached. Tony lay still beneath Bart's naked weight, numb and exhausted.

"Lordy!" Bart sighed finally. "That was mighty pleasin'!" He rose up on his elbows. "I reckon we'd best wash up, lad."

"Not yet," Tony murmured, still floating in the warm afterglow.

"All right." Bart lowered himself flat on the youth's back again. "I ain't never shot my juices int' a finer little tail than yours, Tony."

"It felt like—I dunno…being chained up and whipped…fucked…" He sucked in a slow breath. "You're a rough sonofabitch, shitkicker."

205

"Done runnin' away?" Bart's drawl was quiet and honest. "It seems t' me that that's what you've been doin', stealin' cars an' gettin' locked up an' runnin' away."

"I guess so."

They lay still for several minutes. Bart's cock was still firm but no longer throbbing-hard in Tony's ass.

"Durn it!" he grumbled at last. "I'll never go all th' way soft—not as long as my pecker's makin' itself at home in your tail." He pulled up again, withdrawing his ram slowly from the warm clenching nest. "We can wash up down at th' creek. I like scrubbin' there better'n in th' house shower."

"Okay."

They got to their feet, and Bart seized the length of chain hung about the youth's neck, leading him from the barn.

The sun was setting, and Tony followed Bart across the clearing and into a stand of trees, head down.

He watched his cock flop between his thighs, wisps of straw come-stuck to the head and shaft, and he remembered the virile, demanding penetration of his asshole and the fury-pleasure of his climax.

Tony let his gaze move to the man leading him, the wide shoulders and long, tapering back, the slim hips, the easy rise and fall of the muscular butt, and he remembered the brutality of the flogging, the gentle stroking of the fingers as they examined every part of his stripped nakedness, the honest, shitkicker drawl, the unexpected willingness with which he'd let the sonofabitch lay him out on the mound of hay and screw his "fine little tail."

When they came to the bank of a fast-moving creek, Bart placed Tony at the edge of the water. Then he went to a wooden crate at the edge of the bushes, came back with a bar of soap, grinned at Tony...and shoved him face-forward into the pool.

Tony hit the water with a belly-spanking splash, went beneath the surface, held his breath in the darkness and fought with his manacled hands to right himself. Finally he got his feet planted on the rocky bottom and popped up, sucking for air.

"Goddamn! It's cold, Bart!"

"I reckon so, lad." Bart stood a few feet away, drenched, casually lathering his brawny torso and genitals, grinning. "When I was a young'un back home, my pappy used t' toss me int' th' creek every day till I got used t' it. He said it'd make a man outta me." Drizzling with soap foam, he came up to the shivering youth. "If Rusty don't come t' take you back t' th' camp, I reckon you'll get used t' it, too. In th' meantime, I'd best wash you proper-like."

He brought the soap up to Tony's chest and rubbed it slowly over the strong flesh-arcs, then downward.

Without question, he washed Tony's cock and balls, the runaway from the Sheriff's camp's most personal parts.

And Tony reached out to move the lather over Bart's hairy chest...into his armpits...down his muscular sides...into his exposed crotch...matching his movements...grasping his loose-hanging testicles....

Their eyes met, and Bart's gaze was steady and unafraid.

"Shitkicker," Tony muttered, releasing the man's sensitive nuts and turning away. "Wash my goddamn back. I can't reach it with these fucking handcuffs on."

Grinning, Bart finished scrubbing himself and the husky youth. Then they splashed in the chill water, rinsing themselves.

When Tony stumbled up onto the bank of the stream, Bart was already drying himself with a coarse towel.

"I've only got one towel," the man drawled. "I wasn't expectin' company."

"I don't mind using yours."

"I'll do it for you." He stepped forward and began

rubbing the damp cloth over the youth's muscular physique. "You was thinkin' about bustin' my rocks when you had ahold of them, right?"

"Maybe." Tony sucked in an audible breath. "You knew I wouldn't, didn't you?"

"Yup." He moved behind Tony and dried his welt-streaked back and ass. "Like I said before, you're learnin'." Finished, he tossed the towel over one shoulder and started toward the trees. "Come along, lad."

"Yes, sir."

Without thought, Tony had called the brawny man "sir," and as he followed, he realized Bart hadn't bothered to lead him by the chain around his neck this time.

They walked into the clearing in front of the house, and Bart spotted headlights approaching on the road.

"You'd best get inside, Tony. See if you can light th' fire in th' fireplace."

The youth went into the house, and Bart started to wrap his towel about his hips, then tossed it aside as he recognized the car coming into the clearing.

The sedan braked to a stop, its lights held on Bart's gleaming nakedness for a long moment before going dark, and a burly redhead in a khaki uniform swung from it.

"Goddamn, Bart!" he chuckled, sauntering forward.

"What're you doing standing around in your birthday suit?"

"Waitin' for you t' show up, Rusty."

"Goddamn!" the grinning sheriff repeated. and he reached out to grasp Bart's prick without hesitation. "Horny, pal?"

"I reckon I'm always horny," he acknowledged in an amused drawl. "Now, if you was t' drop your pants an'—"

"I haven't got time," he interrupted, tugging the thick flesh column gently. "I'm looking for another runaway from the camp."

"A fine-lookin' lad named Tony?"

"Yeah. You caught him, huh?" Rusty pulled back, chuckling. "That's why you're stripped bareass!"

"He's inside." Bart turned toward the house. "See for yourself."

They went through the front door and saw a small fire flickering in the fireplace. Tony sat on the floor in front of it, head down, staring at the flames, his whip-marked back exposed. The shifting light gleamed on the chain around his neck and the handcuffs on his wrists.

"Hey, Tony!" Rusty snickered. "You don't look so good, punk."

"That goddamn shitkicker worked me over," the youth growled. "He chained me up like this...used a whip on me...fucked me in the ass...." He wet his lips, still glowering. "Going to arrest him, Sheriff?"

"Jesus!" Rusty gasped in mock horror. "He worked you over? Screwed your skinny butt?" He laughed. "Man, just wait until I get you back to camp and tell your cock-hot pals that their hero's been whipped and fucked! They'll be all over you, twenty-four hours a day!"

Tony swallowed hard and shivered.

"I've been thinkin' about that," Bart said quietly. "Rusty, if you was t' forget about findin' Tony here, he could stay on an' help me out with th' work that's got t' be done." He reached down to stroke his hardening genitals. "Also, he can take care of my other needs."

"What if he tries to run away again? What if he doesn't do what you tell him to?"

"I reckon I'd have t' take him out in th' barn an' whomp on him some more. He knows that."

"I don't know about letting this punk loose," the sheriff muttered. "You really want to be responsible for him and his behavior? You really want him to stay?"

"Yup." There, Bart'd said it, straight-out and honest. "Yup, I wish that lad t' stay."

"Damn it, pal, if you're going to tell him what to do, and whip him if he doesn't do it...that's like having him as your slave! And slavery is illegal!"

"Lordy! I ain't about t' break th' law, no matter what!" He thought for a moment, then grinned at Rusty. "Would it still be slavery if Tony was t' agree?"

"Damned if I know."

"Then I'd best ask him." Bart moved over to Tony, patting him on the head. "Want t' stay, lad?"

"I sure as hell don't want to go back to the camp!" the youth muttered. "I—I don't mind staying here, shit-kicker."

"I guess that makes it legal," Rusty said with a shrug and turned toward the door. "I'd better get back to work."

"Stay on, if you wish," Bart offered. "Tony ain't shy about—"

"Maybe one night next week."

Bart watched the sheriff leave, then waited until the car motor sounded outside, growled and disappeared into the distance.

The fire crackled in the fireplace, and Tony hunched forward, staring at it.

"Bart? Did you mean what you said about wanting me to stay here?"

"Yup. I ain't much good at lyin'."

"And—what you and the sheriff said about me being your slave?"

"Yup." He bent down and unhooked the chain from Tony's neck. "I reckon you don't need t' wear this no more."

"Yes...sir."

"Put up your hands, lad."

Tony offered his manacled wrists, and Bart unfastened the handcuffs and tossed them aside.

"Bastard!" Tony muttered. "Belting me around...whipping me...fucking me...and wanting me to stick around!"

Tony raised his head slowly, gazing at the naked man's powerful legs, then his hair-filled groin and loose-flopping genitals. Suddenly he rocked forward and wrapped his arms about Bart's slim hips, pressing his face into the masculine crotch.

His lips found the bulging testicles, and he nuzzled them...licked them...sucked them gently...and then the potent, swelling cock.

He let the massive flesh column stiffen in his mouth, and he forced himself down on the thick shaft...all the way to the pubic hair at the base...

All the way!

"Lordy!" Bart gripped the back of Tony's head and

held him tight in place for a moment, then pulled back, cock-hard and grinning down at the youth sheepishly. "Durn it, havin' you gulp down on my pecker like that, it's got me mighty fired up again. Only—well, I reckon we'd best talk straight-out t' each other before our balls do our thinkin' instead of our brains!" He shoved Tony down on the floor and stepped away. "Also, I reckon both of us could use a cigarette."

Tony watched the shitkicker get a pair of cigarettes, light them, then settle beside him and stick one of them between his lips. He inhaled the smoke, held it in his lungs, then let it spew out.

"I'll have to get used to being your slave, shitkicker."

"An' I'll have t' get used t' havin' you call me 'shitkicker'." He dragged on his cigarette and let his free hand move to the naked youth lying back next to him. "T'morrow I'll show you what chores have t' be done around here."

"Okay." Tony spread his legs as Bart's fingers roamed toward his crotch. "Ever had a slave before?"

"Nope. Never wanted one."

"How come you wanted me?"

"Durned if I know." He toyed with Tony's genitals lazily, without hesitation. "Could be we need each other, lad."

They finished their cigarettes and flicked them into the glowing fire, and then Tony chuckled softly.

"Damn you, Bart! You're giving me a hard-on!"

"You're givin' it t' yourself," Bart drawled, turning on his side toward the youth. "I'm just helpin' it along."

He watched the youth's cock expand and rise full-hard, and he gave Tony one of those shitkicker-pleased grins.

Then he hunched down and took the bulging head into his mouth...licking...sucking...letting the powerful flesh column slide all the way into his throat.

"Shitkicker!" Tony gasped, shivering at the sensations churning inside him. "Goddamn—"

"Lordy!" Bart grumbled, pulling up. "You surely do have a mouthful of pecker on you!"

"Christ!" He lay back, gulping for air, and then he spoke softly, confused. "How come you did that? How come you went down on my dick?"

"'Cause I wanted t'." He lay back beside Tony again. "If you're my slave, I reckon I can make use of any part of you I wish t'. An' that includes your mighty fine dick!"

"Yeah?" He tried to sound like the tough punk in the Sheriff's camp. "You're a cocksucker, huh?"

"Sometimes," Bart admitted easily. "'Tain't often I've found one I've wished t' suck."

"How about taking it up the ass? Man, I bet you'd dig getting fucked right about now!"

"Nope," he replied honestly. "I've tried bein' rode, but it ain't my style." He grinned at the firelight flickering on the ceiling. "On th' other hand, I do believe Rusty'd be mighty pleased if you was t' mount him."

"The Sheriff?"

"Yup. He surely does enjoy bein' mounted, an' I do believe you could please him real fine." He chuckled happily. "Lordy, that'll be somethin' truly special, you takin' care of Rusty's needs while I'm pluggin' int' your little butt!"

"Awww—" Tony rolled over and clamped himself to Bart. "You bastard! You cocksucker! You sonofabitch!" He clung to the drawling stud and let go with his thoughts. "I wish to hell I'd run into you a long time ago…before I fouled up and got sent to the Sheriff's camp…before—"

"Don't try t' be friendly," Bart warned gruffly, denying his tone by embracing the youth, hard-on to hard-on. "You're stuck with bein' my slave, remember?"

"Yes, sir."

"An' I'm goin' t' whomp your ass if you don't act proper."

"Yes, sir!"

"An' do worse'n I've already done t' you."

"Yes, sir!"

"Durn it, lad!" Bart wanted to sound as tough as he thought Tony wanted...and he knew durned well he'd only be foolin' himself. "Like I said...lordy...you said you'd be my slave...an' we both agreed...an'—well, I reckon we're stuck with each other, lad."

"Yeahhh!...shitkicker!"

DEADHEADING

Dan pulled into the diesel stop to fuel up, stretch his legs, and take a leak

A tall, lean blond came from the station and took over filling the rig's tanks, and Dan swaggered trucker-style to the latrine to empty his.

Dan pissed long and hard in the small, urine-stinking latrine, and it'd felt damn good, letting his long, thick cock hang out and let go.

Dan was hung...and good-looking...and well-built... and he knew it!

Also, he was horny as hell!

The long hours alone pushing the rig always made his nuts work harder than ever, and he'd hoped to find a cocksucker waiting in the fuel-stop can...or maybe the blond would come in and take him off....

The guy didn't come in, so Dan finished taking his leak, washed up, and went back out into the evening gloom, still buttoning his Levi's.

Jimmy—Dan'd checked the name tag on the youth's shirt—Jimmy was standing beside the rig, grinning at the trucker.

"All set, chum?" Dan asked, buddy-like.

"You bet." The youth pushed the straight straw-colored hair out of his eyes, boyishly eager. "Where're you rolling, mister?"

"I'm deadheading to the city." He inhaled deeply, and his partially unbuttoned shirt spread from the broad hairy curves of his golden-tanned chest. "I don't have to be there until tomorrow night, so it's an easy run."

"You're lucky." Jimmy's gaze was fixed on the man's clearly outlined physique. "Going up to the city, I mean."

"Yeah, I guess so." Dan glanced about the station and the tree-studded hills beyond, giving the kid another chance to size him up. "Not much doing out here, huh?"

"Yeah, but I usually go into town for a beer after work. It's only a couple of miles."

"Shit, you're old enough to buy beer?"

"Sure. I'm eighteen. Almost nineteen!"

"Maybe I'll lay over overnight." Ignoring Jimmy, Dan rubbed one hand over his crotch, and he knew damn well the trucker-hungry teenager would get the message. "Any action in town?"

"Well—" He watched Dan's strong fingers dig into the coarse cloth, and he wet his youthful pink lips. "It—it depends...you know...on what you're looking for."

"Any port in a storm, that's what I always say," Dan chuckled, sure of himself. "Know what I mean, Jimmy?"

"I think so."

"How about having a beer with me right now? You've got a pretty good port right here."

"I—I guess so—but customers come in—I've gotta keep the place open—" The teenager shied away, but there was no doubt that he'd understood what Dan'd suggested. "When the boss comes by to close up for the night, he'll can me if—"

He fell silent, and Dan was sure the kid wanted to suck cock...maybe get fucked...take care of a horny trucker....

"Sure, pal." Dan dug out his wallet and handed a credit card to the youth. "Charge the refill...and I'll buy you a beer when you get to town tonight."

"You bet!"

Jimmy hustled toward the station office, and Dan smiled at the sharp rise and fall of the youth's trim ass beneath his overalls.

"Yeah," the trucker whispered to himself. "He knows the score! And if he doesn't, he's ready to learn."

He stared up at the darkening sky for a moment, and when he looked back at the brightly lit office, Jimmy was hunched forward over the telephone. The kid wasn't wearing a shirt under his overalls...bronzed, sturdy shoulders...maturing body...probably naked all the way down underneath—

Hell, Dan didn't care what the goddamn stud looked like, just as long as he sucked...or spread his buns!

And if he didn't—no sweat. Dan'd always been able to find something when he was horny...male or female... yeah, he didn't care how he got his rocks off...funny, he'd been doing it more and more with guys lately....

"Dan?" The kid'd come up behind him, grinning and

offering the credit card. "I got your name off the card. Mind signing?"

"Yeah…sure." They stood close, and as Dan scribbled his signature, he could inhale the sweat scent of the youth's body. "I'll see you in town…later…for that beer I owe you, huh?"

"Sure!" Jimmy pulled back, tauntingly sure of himself. "I'll check around until I find you, right?"

"Right!"

Dan swung back up into the cab of his rig. He checked, flicked, hammered the motor to life, set running lights and headlights, pulled out and rolled back onto the highway…and he knew damn well he'd lay over in the town ahead that night!

He mussed his curly sun-streaked hair and tugged a cigarette from his shirt pocket, lighting it without taking his eyes from the roadway ahead.

Dan was in his mid-twenties and had handsome features and a strong, well-muscled physique. He was proud of his body and kept in good shape…and he kept his prick in shape, too!

He filled his lungs with smoke and relaxed back against the worn leather seat, then dropped one hand from the steering wheel to finger his metal-buttoned fly.

"Maybe I ought to line up a cunt tonight," he mused aloud, then shrugged. "Hell, Jimmy's asshole'll be tighter than any cunt!"

He grinned, remembering the last bushy-tailed stud he'd had. Yeah, all Dan had done was strip and lie back on the bed, and that stud'd been all over him, worshiping his body with his fingers, then his lips. Man, the guy had given him one hell of an all-over tongue job, and finally he'd sucked cock like it was going out of style.

That was the kind of action Dan liked, just lying there and getting his rocks off.

Only the kid hadn't been satisfied with just drinking a churning load of come—shit, no! He'd worked Dan up again and greased his massive dick, and then he'd climbed up and sat on that goddamn iron. Jesus, that's been the greatest, watching his meat disappear up into the young stud's little butt, seeing him strain to take it all the way down, feeling the slippery muscle ring engulf his ram!

The youth had squirmed and bounced and twisted just about every direction there is, and finally Dan'd thrown him over on all fours and screwed him trucker-style until he creamed for all he was worth.

Afterward, the punk had wanted to trade places. Dan had told him to go to hell.

Dan didn't mind getting a blowjob or fucking a cock-sucker in the ass, but he wasn't about to do any of that queer crap.

Shit, no!

He finished his cigarette, and the rig rolled forward with an even hum, well below the speed limit.

The headlights picked up the city-limits sign, and he snickered.

"Another hick town! They always stick the city limits out in the middle of nowhere so they'll seem important."

The landscape was still trees and rolling hills in the fading twilight.

Suddenly headlights flashed in the rearview mirrors, pulling closer fast, then hanging on Dan's tail.

"Smokey Bear," he growled, and he checked his speed automatically—no sweat—then focused on the mirror again. "No, they're locals."

He was sure he was clean, and then the red light went on.

"Shit!"

He flipped the blinkers to show he was pulling over and braked gently, bringing the truck to a stop on the lip of the deserted highway.

With a sigh, he opened the cab door and swung out,

hopping from the high running board to the ground.

A uniformed officer was striding toward him.

"What's the trouble, pal?"

"May I see your license, sir?" the cop asked with formal politeness.

"Sure." Dan dug out his wallet and offered it. "But I don't know—"

"Thank you," he interrupted and took the wallet, opened it, checked the license and papers, then stuffed it in his shirt pocket. "I'm afraid I'll have to ask you to come with me, Dan."

Dan looked at the man—plain-looking stud, khaki uniform tailored to a good build, pistol holster clipped to wide leather belt, bulging crotch, gleaming boots—

"Look—sir—"

"I'm impounding your rig, Dan, so it'll be brought into town and kept in security," the officer acknowledged as if reading Dan's thoughts, then nodded to the prowl car parked behind the truck. "Now, if you'll get in the backseat and—"

"What the hell've I done?" Dan exploded.

"You know." His hand moved to his sheathed pistol, but his voice remained quiet and controlled. "Into the vehicle, please."

Dan saw the man's hand on the butt of the pistol, and he sure as hell didn't want to get his head blown off!

He walked to the black-and-white and got into the backseat.

The door locks snapped shut, and he was trapped.

There was another man in the front seat, on the copilot's side, and he sat motionless until his fellow officer had gotten behind the steering wheel.

"Back to the station, Ted." He fumbled the radio microphone in one hand. "Mitch's admitted he did the mutilation murders."

"Find the bodies this time, Mr. Wilson?"

"We'll go looking for the pieces tomorrow, in daylight. In the meantime, we've got Mitch locked up." Without turning, he spoke to the trucker in the back seat. "I'm Wilson, Chief of Police. We're taking you in."

"What for?" Dan asked, trying to sound pissed off.

"You know."

The officer called Ted started the car, and Dan studied the two men, puzzled.

It didn't make sense, getting hauled in by the fuzz and not having the goddamnedest idea why!

He rode in silence, and suddenly they were on the main street of the drab town…old-fashioned streetlights…

dark storefronts...a couple of bars...the police station.

"Inside," Wilson ordered, releasing the locks on the rear doors.

Dan got out, and for an instant he wanted to bolt and run. Then he saw the two men, hands on holstered pistols.

He followed Ted into the old stone building and down a short corridor to a well-lit office. For the first time, he could see his captors clearly.

Ted was about Dan's height and age, trim features, wide shoulders, tapering physique like a swimmer.

Wilson was older, black hair spike-cut, rugged looks, barrel-chested, burly...an ex-football player or wrestler... the chief of police.

"Want to confess, Dan?" Wilson asked quietly.

"To what?" Dan grasped at a straw. "How do you know my name, Wilson?"

"Shit," Ted muttered, pulling Dan's wallet from his shirt pocket, and he handed it to Wilson. "Here're his papers, Chief."

"Thanks." Wilson ignored the wallet, his dark eyes nailed on Dan. "I know plenty about you without checking your papers. That's why I'm the chief of this police force."

"Crap!" Dan exploded, and he was sure the cops had nothing on him...yeah, it was all some kind of frame-up! "I know my rights! You've got to tell me the charges and let me make a phone call and—"

"Fuck your rights!"

Ted's fist came out of nowhere and smashed into Dan's midsection.

The trucker doubled forward, stunned and hurting, and another blow straightened him.

He sucked for air, and he fought to control his temper.

Yeah, he had to keep cool until he figured out what the fuck was going on!

Another man came into the room, bare-chested, short and swarthy, built like a goddamn tank! "Telephone, Mr. Wilson."

"Thanks, Carl." The chief started toward the door. "Search him."

"Yes, sir." Carl waited until Wilson left, then viewed Dan and tossed Ted a grin. "Good-looking sonofabitch, huh?"

"No lie." Ted chuckled. "Wilson's going to have a ball with this one."

"We all will, if I know Wilson." He returned to Dan. "Strip, chum."

Dan felt a prickling tension grip him as he began to undress. Hell, he'd stripped in front of plenty of guys before—no sweat!—but there was something about what Ted had said: "Wilson's going to have a ball with this one."

A glaze of nervous sweat broke out on his tanned skin as he peeled off his clothes. His strong shoulders blended into the wide, solid curves of his chest, sparse peach fuzz spread between dark nipples, stomach was flat and hard. His tan dissolved into creamy paleness low on his hips, and his heavy genitals dangled loosely between his muscled thighs.

No matter what, Dan's prick always hung thick and long over his bulging nuts.

The two cops looked him over, and he felt naked as hell and defenseless as they took his clothing and inspected it, every pocket and seam.

Wilson returned. He looked at Dan, starting at his feet and working upward…pausing longer than necessary at the trucker's crotch.…

Dan wondered…maybe the rugged-looking police chief dug cocks…sucking…getting fucked.…

"Put the cuffs on him," Wilson ordered.

"Yeah!"

Ted and Carl moved in on Dan, seizing his arms and

wrenching them behind him, then handcuffing his wrists.

For some goddamned reason, Dan didn't fight them off.

"That was Jimmy on the phone," Wilson said, viewing his prisoner without emotion. "He's in line for a reward. He gave us the lead on where to pick you up."

Dan remembered the lean teenager at the fuel stop… wearing overalls…exchanging stares…horny kid, horny trucker…taking Dan's credit card and making a telephone call from the office—

"So what?" Dan asked warily. "I made a stop and bullshitted with him a little. That's all."

"Put the make on him?"

"Hell, no!"

"You should have," Wilson said calmly. "Jimmy would turn on to getting a cock like yours in his mouth or up his ass."

"Jesus!" He couldn't believe what the police chief had suggested so coolly…or maybe Wilson was trying to trap him. "Shit, I don't—"

"He goes both ways," Wilson interrupted casually. "If you want to go down on him or get screwed, Jimmy'll—"

"Fuck off!" Dan barked. "I've never—"

He didn't know who hit him first, but then all three men had closed in and were pummeling him.

Fists pounded his midsection, open palms slapped at him, fingers clawed and gouged at the most sensitive parts of his body.

One of the sonofabitches clipped him in the balls, and another tried to finger his asshole.

Christ, it was some kind of nightmare!

"Ready to confess, Dan?"

"Huh?" Dan had heard Wilson's voice, but it took him a moment to realize the torment had stopped. Then he focused and saw the three men—Ted and Carl...the police officers...and the burly, rugged-looking chief. "What am I supposed to confess to, dammit?"

"You know." Wilson's voice was still quiet and sure, and he nodded to his officers. "Lock him up."

Ted and Carl took Dan by his handcuffed arms and led him out of the brightly lit office...down a shadowed corridor...an open door to a small room with barred windows—

"Sorry, Dan," Ted said. "We've only got one cell in this goddamn jail."

They shoved him forward, and he stumbled and fell on the concrete...facedown...his nose was bleeding... his wrists were handcuffed behind him....

His eyes grew accustomed to the dimness, and he saw two men seated on the lower of two bunks hung against the far wall. One was short and dark, stripped to a pair of white Jockey shorts which emphasized his lean, wiry physique. The other man was younger—twenty or twenty-one—short-clipped blond hair, wide farmboy face, bare-chested, powerful muscles outlined beneath sun-bronzed skin.

"He's a fine-looking guy, Mitch," the blond observed, smiling at Dan. "But he's bleeding."

"I believe you're right, Bull." Mitch slid from the bunk and knelt beside Dan. "I'd better make sure he isn't badly hurt."

He gripped Dan's nose, squeezing hard. A spurt of blood splashed onto his fingers.

"Christ!" Dan hissed in pain. "That hurts, you bastard!"

"It isn't broken." He got to his feet and wiped his fingers on the pouch of his shorts, obviously pleased at the crimson stains soaking into the cloth. "I'm something of an expert when it comes to knowing which parts of a man's body are torn or ripped or broken." He turned to Bull. "Remember what I told you?"

"Sure...I think so." Bull hustled forward, gripped Dan's shoulders and flipped him easily onto his back.

"We start out checking his zones and stuff, right?"

"Right." Mitch stood over Dan, smiling down at him. "It looks like we have an excellent specimen for you to work on, Bull."

Dan stared up at the two figures looming over him in the semidarkness, and he frowned, confused. "Hey, what goes with you guys?"

"I've been trying to teach Bull about the more sophisticated forms of sex," Mitch answered proudly. "He's a little slow when it comes to thinking, and up until now he's been satisfied with just sticking his cock into any willing receptacle. What a waste!"

"Huh?" Dan felt a stab of fear in his guts...Mitch sounded weird—crazy! Mitch...back in the police car when Dan'd first been picked up, Wilson had said something to Ted about a mutilation murderer...Mitch! *Stay cool!* "Sure, Mitch," he agreed, struggling to sit up. "What say you guys help me up and—"

"Stay where you are!" He placed one foot against Dan's chest and rammed him down again. "Gag him, Bull!"

Dan felt real panic. For an instant, he wanted to scream for help... Mitch was insane!...no, Wilson knew about Mitch.... Wilson had put him in this cell with the madman and the simple blond....

Then Bull was hunched over him, forcing a foul-tasting cloth into his mouth.

Jesus, now what?

"Nobody'll hear him if he yells," Bull said cheerfully as he viewed the trucker's exposed nakedness. "He sure is a big guy. Big all over, huh?"

"Ideal!" Mitch whispered, crouching opposite the husky blond, his flashing eyes fixed on Dan. "He deserves the ultimate experience! The total blending of pain and ecstasy!"

"Like you told me about?"

"Exactly!" He placed one hand on Dan's chest, smoothed the soft hairs to the heaving curves, then gripped one taut nipple and twisted brutally. "The ultimate experience!" he repeated, watching the man writhe helplessly. "He's at the peak of his masculinity, the best of all times for what we're going to do, Bull!" He shifted to the other nipple and dug his fingernails into it, smiling at Dan's stifled cries. "See how well he reacts?"

"Yeah," Bull answered, unsure. "I guess so."

Dan tried to bellow into the gag in his mouth, tried to tell the blond farmboy to help him, to—

Mitch's fingers crawled downward...clawed at the coarse hair thicketing his groin...his thick, limp cock!

"The root of his manhood!" the man declared, twisting

Dan's prick gleefully. "He's hung almost as beautifully as you are, Bull! Think of the pleasure his dick has given him! Think of the pleasure your dick has given you!"

"Sure!"

Dan knew Bull didn't understand that Mitch was crazy…a mutilation murderer!…getting his kicks from cutting guys up…clenching his victim's cock.…

"Get the knife, Bull."

"Okay, Mitch."

Dan thrashed in terror, and Mitch twisted over to straddle his chest and pin him down.

"This will be your ultimate moment, Dan! I've taught Bull!" His eyes glowed with excitement. "First, your testicles! Then your penis! Then—" The blood-stained crotch of his shorts bulged, his cock stiffening. "Start the work, Bull!"

Dan stared up at the aroused man holding him down —the wiry physique, the insane look, the hard-on outlined inside the crumpled shorts—and then he felt Bull's fingers grip his nuts and pressure them painfully. He wanted to howl, but his voice was gagged and grated in his throat.

"He's got awful big balls," the blond murmured, behind Mitch. "It seems too bad to take them off."

"Pain and ecstasy!" Mitch gloated, bending forward over Dan. "The last one—he wasn't gagged, so I could hear him scream and beg…I did it all myself…he had an orgasm when I began cutting, a final, magnificent orgasm!"

Dan quivered with terror, but he couldn't take his eyes off the excited man.

"I enjoy watching the expression on my victim's face when the cutting begins. At first, it's very slow and doesn't hurt much. Then comes the real pain. I hope you don't pass out before we're done. I lose interest when my victim isn't awake." He ran his fingertips over Dan's sweat-streaked face, smiling. "All right, Bull, begin!"

Metallic coldness pressed against Dan's genitals… dull…not sharp or stabbing.…

With a strength born of fear, Dan arched his body upward, unseating the man riding him. His knees rammed into Bull's chest, knocking him back.

He saw Wilson standing in the open doorway to the cell. How long had the sonofabitch been watching?

Mitch and Bull retreated to the bunk, and a dull-edged table knife fell to the floor.

Wilson entered, pulled the gag from Dan's mouth, and hauled him to his feet.

"C'mon, Dan."

Dan followed the man, and his recent terror gave way to a strange numbness.

"Your chum Mitch is crazy, Wilson."

"Maybe. He's got this fantasy about cutting up guys."

"And Bull?"

"He's a good kid but—well, he isn't quite right when it comes to thinking. He's a boy in a man's body."

"He was going to cut my nuts off!"

"I doubt it," Wilson said unconcernedly. "Mitch told him about the mutilation murder, and Bull probably thought it was a game."

Dan followed the police chief back into the office where he'd first been stripped and punched around. Suddenly he was sure what Wilson was after.

"That murder—want me to confess to doing it?"

"Ever hack a stud to death, Dan?"

"Hell, no!"

"Then why confess to something you didn't do?" Wilson nodded to the straight-backed wooden chair set in the center of the room. "Sit down and I'll get you cleaned up."

His hands still locked behind him, Dan sat on the chair, and he watched Wilson walk to a washbasin in the corner of the room and begin to wet a towel.

For the first time, he realized the man had stripped off his shirt.

Wilson's torso and arms were etched with thick muscles. His thick chest was covered with swirling black hair. His pants hung low on his hips, no sign of shorts showing...and Dan wondered what Wilson had hidden inside his trousers...the size of his cock...soft or hard...the shape and taste—no, not the taste!

Wilson came back with the dripping towel and wiped Dan's blood- and sweat-glazed face.

"Thanks," Dan muttered, confused. "What do you want, Wilson?"

"The truth, so I can believe your confession when you make it." He stepped back, thoughtful. "Ever suck cock, Dan?"

"No," he lied automatically.

"Ever been fucked in the ass?"

"Shit, no!" He saw Wilson was staring at his heavy, exposed genitals, and he had a sudden feeling about the burly man...no one else was with them...maybe— He slouched back and spread his legs wider. "What say we work something out? Just you and me. I mean, if you want to play with my meat—"

Wilson snapped the towel, stinging Dan's lower

belly—almost his prick and nuts!—and the trucker doubled forward, more surprised than hurt.

"I can play with any part of you I want," the chief said quietly, pointedly. "You're here to confess, remember?"

Dan stayed slumped forward, trying to figure this nightmare out.

Dan didn't know how much later Ted and Carl returned.

"Jimmy's coming in, Mr. Wilson."

"Better chain Dan up."

"Yes, sir!"

They hoisted Dan to his feet and unlocked the handcuffs holding his hands behind him. For a moment, he was free, but before he could react, they'd replaced the cuffs with heavy metal bracelets...chains from his wrists to his ankles...about his waist and neck...he could move, but he couldn't escape.

They shoved him back against the wall, and he stood there, naked and chained and confused.

What next?

Jimmy, the punk from the fuel stop, came in, tanned and growing up and wearing those overalls. He grinned at Dan, then at Wilson.

"I told you Dan was what you're looking for, Chief.

Right?" Without waiting for an answer, the youth hustled up in front of Dan and began to rub his bared chest sensually. "Yeah, he sure is!"

Dan couldn't believe it—the cops standing around watching...the punk kid feeling him up...fingers crawling downward to his crotch...gripping his dick...all of them watching....

Jimmy stroked the man's prick with one hand and massaged his balls with the other, and in spite of his effort to control it, Dan felt his iron stretch and begin to stiffen.

Ted came up behind the youth and unfastened his overalls, letting them fall to his ankles. Then he pressed against Jimmy's back, crotch-to-ass.

Dan stared at the naked youth pumping his now-rigid iron—the slick, maturing chest plates, the hard little nipples, the still-boyish torso, the taut prick springing from the nest of soft pubic hair, marble-smooth and arrow-headed.

"How about it, pal?" Ted murmured, wrapping both arms about Jimmy from behind. "When you're finished playing with Dan's meat, I'm hot to drill mine into your tail."

"I'm finished!" Jimmy laughed, releasing Dan's massive

rod. "I just wanted to see what this trucker looked like hard." He kicked off his overalls and strode toward a side door from the office. "Let's go, Ted!"

Dan watched Ted follow Jimmy from the room. Suddenly the craziness of everything that had happened hit him.

He was chained up in the police station, naked and punched around—almost castrated, dammit!—and one of the cops was taking the punk who'd started it all into the other room to fuck him!

And Wilson, the burly chief of police, didn't seem to give a damn!

And neither did Carl, the other cop.

The two men stood talking casually, and Dan's aroused prick quivered as he heard the excited gasps and groans from beyond the open door.

Yeah, Jimmy was getting his butt plugged!

In spite of all that had happened to him, Dan was still trucker-horny...even more horny than usual, maybe.

Wilson sauntered across the office and closed the door, unperturbed.

The minutes ticked by. Finally Ted returned. His athletic torso was sweat-washed, and he was still fastening his trousers, grinning.

"That goddamn Jimmy's going to wear me out!"

"That'll be the day!" Wilson snickered, and he nodded toward Dan. "Take him outside and give him some exercise."

Ted and Carl hauled Dan through the doorway into a large, locker-lined room. Jimmy was showering lazily in an alcove, and several men were changing into khaki uniforms.

"One helluva lot of cops for a hick town," Dan muttered.

"Volunteers," Carl explained. "All of us're volunteers."

"Like you," Ted added, shoving Dan through a side door into a floodlit courtyard. "Get out there and run!"

And the nightmare began again.

They forced him to run the circuit of the yard, chained and naked... Ted running with him and slapping him along for the first round...then Carl...then another cop...and another....

The metal chains hung heavier on Dan step by step, and he stumbled and fell.

They beat him with straps...and he got up and ran...

chained...

stumbling again...

being beaten back to his feet...

243

running…

falling, exhausted…

being dragged up again…

weights hooked onto his balls…

running…

being whipped…

clamps on his nipples…

muscles aching with strain…

They let him rest, then began again.

Dan's brain felt numb and clouded, and he had no idea of how long the torment continued…maybe hours… maybe days. It didn't matter.

They dragged him back to Wilson's office and let him slump onto the wooden chair, a naked, beaten hunk of male flesh.

"Wake up, Dan." An open palm slapped across his face, and he looked up, focusing on Wilson's strong, almost-smiling features and burly physique. "When was the first time you sucked cock?"

"Years ago…Joey…" Dan's words came without effort to lie, and he remembered horsing around with his best buddy…jerking each other off…trading blowjobs… sharing the same sleeping bag on weekend camping trips, both of them naked and horny. Experimenting, that's all."

He recalled the other guys, the studs he'd messed with...gone down on...swallowed their come willingly... and the one who'd kicked him in the balls afterward and called him "queer."

"Queer!"

"Your pal, was he the first one to fuck you?"

"No, that was later. This stud...I was broke and needed the dough." Dan remembered going to the man's apartment, lying naked on the huge bed, feeling the stroking fingers on his back and ass, hearing the coaxing words and the offer of money. "I needed the dough." The first pain-shock of penetration...the male iron sliding deeper and deeper...the pulsing thrusts from the man hunched over him...the pain and the ecstasy...Dan's come spewing into the mattress beneath him before the man's load spewed into his guts. "I only went back 'cause I was broke. The other times, it was only because I needed the bread."

"Sure, Dan," Wilson agreed quietly, gently. "You went back to get fucked only because you needed the money, not because you wanted it." He shrugged. "Ready to confess?"

"To what?"

"To whatever I decide." Without waiting for an answer, he nodded to the others. "Tie him down."

The men pulled Dan up and forced him across the room, pressing him facedown on the chief's desk. His ankles were shackled to the legs on one side, his arms stretched, his wrists bound to the legs on the opposite side, his back and ass exposed.

Then nightmare began again.

He was bound and helpless, and Wilson was peeling his thick leather belt from his pants and moving to his right side. Ted and Carl followed suit, Ted taking a position on his left side, Carl disappearing behind him.

Wilson flexed his muscled arms, raised the belt, brought it crashing down. Dan writhed as the searing pain raked across his bare shoulders.

Ted hit him from the other side.

Carl laid a stroke on his taut buttocks.

It was all crazy, being stopped by the cops and being charged with an unknown crime, being stripped and tossed in a cell with a madman and the village idiot who'd threatened to cut off his balls, being questioned and beaten, now being flogged…and craziest of all, his goddamn cock was bobbling full-hard between his spread legs!

The lashes struck again and again from all sides with agonizing slowness.

He saw the men watching, most stripped to the waist,

some naked and stroking their genitals openly, smiling at his torture.

The whips ate over him, and his sweating body was stuck to the desk beneath him.

Yeah, it was all a nightmare!

The numbness crept back into his brain, and he wondered if he was screaming…howling in pain… groaning…whimpering…still with a hard-on.

Slowly, drifting in the cloud-filled escape, he realized the beating had ended.

"Hey, Bull," Wilson's voice echoed in Dan's ears. "Want to fuck this trucker?"

"Sure, Mr. Wilson! He's a fine-looking guy!"

Dan worked his eyes open and focused on the open-faced blond…tanned and bare-chested…smiling…fingers reaching downward and popping open his trousers… stripping…no shorts…massive, thick-shafted cock already rising over large heavy testicles.…

"Better grease that ram," Wilson advised gently. "You've got a real big one, remember?"

"I remember, Mr. Wilson!" He moved out of Dan's vision, pumping his swelling iron. "Is it okay if I play with his nuts, Mr. Wilson? He's got awful good ones."

"Okay, pal," the chief of police replied, maybe understanding Bull…maybe understanding Dan. "Go ahead, anyway you want!"

Dan, the all-male trucker tied down across the desk in the hick-town police station, felt the dumb blond move in behind him…

grip his asscheeks and spread them…

push the wrenching big head of his cock against the tender opening, slick and lubricated…

pressure it inward—

"AGGGHHHH!"

Bull was fucking him!…like that guy'd done when he'd needed the dough…prick jamming up his butt… awww—

Dan felt the arms wrap about his hips…powerful cock easing deeper…fingers clutching his balls…pain… ecstasy…cock shooting come…long, ropy strings of sperm spurting from Dan's rigid cock as Bull plowed deeper.…

"Dan! The boy-man's voice whispered hoarsely in Dan's ear, the massive ram plunging into his asshole frantically. "Dan! Danny! Awwww-Dannnnyyyy!"

Numbed in agony and pleasure, Dan remembered how his buddy had called him "Danny"…and how they'd traded blowjobs…and other guys he'd gone down on…the one who'd called him "queer".…

He closed his eyes, floating in a warm, secret world.

He was vaguely aware of Bull's murmurs of satisfaction, the work-roughened hands stroking his welted shoulders and back, the massive ram easing free from his throbbing asshole.

Another man took Bull's place.

And another.

Dan lay still, chained in place, semiconscious. He didn't care how many of the goddamn cops screwed him.

When he drifted back to reality, he was in the locker room showers, cool water drenching him. His handcuffs and shackles were gone, and several policemen were washing up with him, naked and male and cock-swinging.

"Mr. Wilson likes us guys to be clean and neat," Bull said, handing him a bar of soap. "Better scrub up, Danny."

Dan watched the burly young blond step back and lather his muscled physique and heavy, relaxed genitals. He matched Bull's movements, wanting to be clean and neat for Mr. Wilson.

He washed and rinsed, washed and rinsed again.

Bull smiled his approval and gave him a towel, and they both dried off.

He followed the blond through the locker room. The other men grinned at him.

He wondered if he was grinning back at them.

They went into Wilson's office, and the bare-chested chief viewed his nakedness for a moment.

"Ready to sign a confession, Dan?"

"Yes, sir."

Dan sat down in the chair by the desk, and a ball-point pen was shoved into his fingers. He stared down at the paper in front of him, and it was blank.

It didn't make any difference—Mr. Wilson would fill in any confession he wanted.

Dan wrote his name carefully, clearly. When he was done, he felt so goddamn free!

"Good enough," Wilson commented quietly. "You're going to be stuck here for a long, long time when the judge sees that confession, Dan."

"I—I know."

"Know what that means?"

"Yes, sir."

Dan raised his gaze slightly and watched Wilson unfasten his pants and let them drop. The man wore no shorts, and his full, mature genitals spilled out.

Wilson's hand cupped the back of Dan's head and drew him closer, and he let his face press into the chief's crotch.

Dan inhaled the scent of the masculine organs...

licked the hair-spiked sac holding the slippery testicles…
sucked them…shifted to the now-rigid cock… took it into
his mouth—and throat…all the way!

He gulped and swallowed…and Wilson mussed his
hair and pulled back.

Dan's prick stood up steel-hard. Wilson loomed over
him, brawny and virile, his cock glistening with Dan's
spit…and smiling…understanding.…

"C'mon." Bull tapped Dan on the shoulder from
behind. "If I know Mr. Wilson, he wants you to stay
with us guys, and I'm the only one who hasn't got a
full-time roommate. C'mon."

"Okay, Bull."

Dan knew the happy-faced blond was right, and he got
to his feet and followed him from the chief's office…
down the corridor…into a sparsely furnished bedroom.

"Lie down on the bunk, Danny. I've got some stuff
Mr. Wilson gave me. I'll spread it on your back, and
you'll heal up real fast."

"Thanks, pal."

Dan sprawled on his belly on the bed, and after a
moment, he felt Bull crouch beside him. A stinging lotion
spattered over his whip-raw back and ass, and then the
blond's paws were rubbing it in, gentle and soothing.

"I'm glad you're going to stay here, Danny," Bull said with simple honesty. "Some of the guys, they haven't wanted to do what Mr. Wilson says, but when he says—he's the chief."

"Yeah…I know."

"I'm glad. You're a fine-looking guy, Danny, and if it wasn't for Mr. Wilson, I wouldn't've been able to play with your balls and—"

"You and Mitch were going to cut off my balls!"

"That was Mitch's idea," Bill explained easily. "He said it was a game, pretending to do that." He drew back, and when he spoke again, his voice was troubled. "I liked playing with your nuts, Danny, and I liked fucking you. But Mr. Wilson says I don't think too good, not like the other guys."

"No sweat," Dan murmured, and he twisted over on his back and grinned up at the simple blond. "Are you in love with Wilson, Bull?"

"Sure. Aren't you?" He reached for a pair of cigarettes on the bedside table, lit them, and passed one to Dan. "Know what else I liked? I liked seeing you get hard when you were sucking Mr. Wilson."

"I haven't gone down on a guy…in a long time.…"

"Why not?"

"Dumb, I guess."

"Oh." He stretched out on his side next to Dan and put one hand on the man's solid chest. "I got into trouble with the law. That's why Mr. Wilson brought me here."

"What did you do?"

"I don't remember." He smiled, watching his fingers roam over Dan's naked torso. "Mr. Wilson's made me shape up. He'll do the same for you, Danny."

"He already has." He finished his cigarette and doused it. "Nobody's called me Danny since my buddy. I sucked him off—and some of the other guys—until one of them called me queer."

"That's what all of us call each other," Bull said cheerfully, and he put out his cigarette. "Sometimes we all get together in the locker room and call each other all sorts of names like that, and we all mess around and enjoy ourselves."

"That's that's what I've always wanted to do," Dan confessed, easing over to lie naked and aroused against the muscular blond. "Understand?"

"No."

"You're lucky!"

Dan envied the simple-talking young man who had no doubts or hang-ups when it came to male sex.

He slid downward and ran his lips over Bull's broad chest, and he remembered the countless times he'd wanted to let go with one of the horny studs at a truck stop. Instead, he'd always settled for a blowjob or for fucking ass.

Yeah, up until now, he'd always been the rough-and-tough trucker, screwing cunt and getting his rocks off with rest-stop fairies.

He nuzzled and licked lower over Bull's powerful physique. The younger man's cock swelled and hardened beneath him.

He worshiped the blond's maleness with his lips and tongue and fingers.

He inhaled the scent of his offered crotch...lapped his bulging testicles...sucked down on his massive, inflamed cock...wanted his come!

"Danny," Bull whispered, reaching down to grip Dan's shoulders, "I think Jimmy did the right thing, calling Mr. Wilson and telling him you needed to come here."

Dan remembered the straw-haired youth at the fuel stop, taunting him with his slender body, showing up later at the police station to get fucked while the other cops worked Dan over...and he knew he'd stay here, fucking Jimmy and getting fucked, sucking cock and getting sucked...

shacking up with Bull...
and Wilson!
and all the others!

THE HARDER HE FALLS

Road camp's no picnic, but it's a hell of a lot better than the county jail. I ought to know 'cause I've spent time in both.

The work's plenty hard at this camp, and if you screw up, you get your lumps. On the other hand, the chow's good, and each guy has his own room in the dorm. No shit! A while back, the county tore down the old barracks and built these jazzy new dorms with a private room for every one of us.

I bet the county never thought how convenient that'd be for a stud who wants to get a little action after lights-out!

Hell, the first night I was here, a real neat little guy sneaked into my room to give me an all-out blowjob. Christ, I was pissed off when that sonofabitch got paroled!

The guys here—well, there're like the guys at any of these goddamn camps. Good, bad, indifferent—know what I mean?

And then there's Chad.

I guess every "detention unit" has a Chad, a tough-as-nails bastard who calls the shots and keeps the rest of the guys in line.

Anyway, as soon as I landed here, I started hearing about how Chad ran the inside show, how he'd kicked the shit out of one fuckup and whipped another—all that crap—and I figured that sooner or later we'd have it out. You see, I don't make waves, but I don't kiss anybody's ass, either.

Know what I mean?

Well, one night, I went down the hall to take a

shower. The minute I walked into the latrine, I knew I was going to have it out with Chad.

Like I told you, we've all got private rooms in the dorm, but there's only one latrine and showers at the end of the hall. Usually there're guys shitting-shower-ing-and-shaving, but this night I'm telling you about, the place was deserted. That's what made me know I was going to tangle with Chad.

So I went ahead and started to shower, and I wasn't sur- prised when he marched in to scrub up, just him and me.

Look, I'd better tell you about Chad. He isn't one of these dumb slobs you see on television shows about jails and all. He's about my height and age, light-haired and pretty good looking, and he's got one of those weight-lifter builds that make most guys blink. Yeah, he's got big shoulders and arms and a real solid chest, and when he drops his pants—well, if his body doesn't make you blink, his dick sure will!

Me, I'm dark and kind of hairy and rugged enough to get by in a brawl, and I've never been shy about showing my meat. Soft, my cock's about average, I guess, but that goddamn Chad!

Okay, on the night I was telling you about, I was

showering, and Chad came in and started the spray across from mine, and I figured he was going to give me the rough-and-tough act. I was ready to fight it out with him, but he acted like I wasn't there, wetting down and starting to lather himself.

He had his back to me, and I eyeballed him like it was going out of style. He had a light golden tan, and every time he moved, his muscles would bulge and shift, sexy as hell. His body tapered from those big shoulders to his slim waist, and his little ass was smooth and pale and just right for fucking!

Christ, I dig a bubble-butt like Chad's, especially if it's locked up to my hard-on, and right away, I could feel my pecker twitch and stretch a little.

Then he turned around, and we both stood there, sizing each other up. Blond peach fuzz glistened across his broad chest, and his dark nipples stood up at each side, large and peaked. He had one of those washboard stomachs you always hear about, and his cock—

Shit, that sonofabitch was hung spelled with a capital H! No lie, it looked about as long and thick as the average hard-on, only it was soft and flopping down over egg-sized balls.

I figured Chad's dick must stand up like a goddamn

telephone pole when it got hard, and maybe that was why the others at the camp snapped-shit for him.

"Horny?" he growled, staring at my prick.

"I'm always horny."

"Want t' play with my meat?"

"I'd rather play with your little tail," I said, standing up to him. "That's the part of you that turns me on."

I guess nobody'd ever talked to him that way 'cause he blinked with surprise. Then he glared like he was ready to kill me.

"You're a cocky bastard," he said. "Maybe I ought t'—"

"I've been around." I got ready to fight it out with him then and there. "I don't suck up to anybody, chum."

Man, that sounded tough as nails, but it wasn't exactly true. I've been around, that's for sure, but I've also sucked…the right guy at the right time…know what I mean?

Anyway, Chad just went on glaring for a minute. Then he stepped back under his shower, rinsing off and flipping that goddamn big dick at me.

I was set to take him on, in case he tried to catch me off guard, but he just finished showering and went out into the latrine to dry off.

I still wasn't sure if Chad didn't have a trick up his

sleeve, so I took my time soaping and washing down and all. I mean, I was remembering that time in county jail when I thought nobody'd touch me, and I'd ended up fighting my way out of a rape…know what I mean?

Well, I was ready for anything when I went to dry off, but Chad just stood there watching and playing with his big dick and balls.

"Goin' t' th' movie in th' rec hall?" he asked all of a sudden.

"No." I had a feeling he was backing down, so I pushed him a little more. "I'm going to hit the sack and jerk off while I think about screwing your butt."

"Shit!" Chad blinked again and glared again. Then he gave me a weak grin, flipping his meat at me. "Want t' take turns? Want t' try sittin' on this, buddy?"

"I don't go that route," I said, tough-like. That was another lie, but he seemed to buy it. "When I fuck, I do the fucking."

"I've heard that crap before," he sneered, and headed for the door. "Have a good time pumpin' your rod.

And he just walked out.

Jesus, I couldn't be sure if Chad was going to round up his gang and come back to work me over, or if he figured I wasn't going to give in to him like the other guys had.

Or—maybe—he—

Look, something else happened that night, but I didn't connect it to Chad until later. I was in my room after lights-out, naked and horny, when one of the guys came in. Nothing said, he was all over me, licking and sucking and checking out everything I've got, front and rear, and I remember thinking that he was measuring me with his lips and tongue. Finally, he half-jerked and half-sucked me off. Afterward, I didn't think much about it.

Lots of studs've had a little trouble sucking me all the way down when I get full-hard.

Anyway, I got my rocks off, and the next day Chad showed up in the showers when the rest of us were washing off from sweating on the road crew, and he flicked that big prick of his around, saying nothing and showing off.

That's the way it went for a couple of days, and then there was this time when Chad caught up with me as we headed back from a work detail.

"Headed for th' showers, buddy?" He clapped me on the shoulder.

Chad had been doing that lately, clapping me on the shoulder and calling me buddy…and showing off his dick in the showers.

"Yeah," I said, "I need to wash up."

"Get your gear and meet me up at the old shower house, buddy."

The old shower house was the concrete-block building that had been left behind when the county built the new dorms. Back then, the guys at the road camp had to go down there when they wanted to piss or wash up or anything else...out in the boondocks from the new dorms...know what I mean?

Okay, so I got my gear and hiked up to the old showers. I realized it was far enough from the main camp so nobody would wander in or hear any noise.

The place was just one big room, a trough urinal and toilets and wash basins and plank benches along the walls, and at the far end, a row of showerheads showed where the guys'd cleaned up in front of all the other studs. The air was warm and musty smelling, and I couldn't help thinking about the horny bastards who must've messed around there and gotten their rocks off. Shit, I was plenty horny myself!

Then I spotted Chad. He was slouched back on one of the benches, naked, a cigarette dangling from between his thin lips. If I wasn't already turned on, seeing that sexy, big-pricked bastard sure would've done it!

But I wasn't about to let him know it.

"Cigarette, buddy?" he offered, looking at me real steady.

"I've got my own," I said, pulling a weed from my shirt pocket and lighting it.

I knew he wasn't trying to be friendly. Yeah, he was still trying to prove he was king-of-the-hill.

I started to strip down, staring at him just as hard as he was staring at me.

"I keep this shower room for myself," he growled, letting me know it was a big deal that he'd said I could come up there. "Durin' th' summer, like now, th' water tank on th' roof heats up enough so it's warm enough for showerin'."

"Yeah?" I peeled off my pants, playing it cool. "What do you do during the winter?"

"Bring th' fuckups here." He got to his feet and flexed his muscles and scratched his balls, showing off. "One of th' punks gets out of line, I bring him here, warm his tail, then cool him with an ice shower." He checked my crotch with his eyes and then headed for the showers. "Goin' t' be around next winter, pal?"

"Maybe." I knew damn well what he was hinting at, that he'd bring me up here for an ass-whipping and a cold shower—if I gave in to him—and I decided I'd better call his bluff again. "I'm going to stick around long enough to fuck that neat little butt of yours—that's for sure!"

I figured that would piss Chad off enough to fight it out with me, if that was what he'd planned on doing, but he just went ahead and flipped on one of the taps and started washing up.

So I did the same…but I sure didn't drop my guard.

No shit, I still couldn't figure the sonofabitch out! Maybe he was going to—

"We've got company." Chad nodded toward the doorway. "You know Windy?"

"Yeah." I glanced at the lean young stud coming into the room. "How's it going, Windy?"

"Okay."

"Strip down an' hit th' showers," Chad ordered, rough and tough.

Shit, I wasn't worried about having Windy jump me or anything like that. He had short brown hair and plain features with big blue-gray eyes, and he just wasn't the kind of guy who'd give anybody trouble.

Windy undressed, obeying Chad. He had a swimmer's build with wide, muscular shoulders and a long, trim physique, and his chest was tanned and smooth as glass. Yeah, he had a slick-muscled body, like a teenager, and his dick matched the rest of him, long and thin-shafted and kind of like mine.

Okay, so we sort of checked each other out with our eyes, and then he took one of the showers down away from Chad and me.

I went on washing up, waiting for whatever was going to happen next.

"Windy fucked up t'day," Chad said at last, stepping out to dry himself. "Didn't you, punk?"

"I—I was just horsing around with the guys."

"You know what fuckups get from me." He went over to his piled-up clothes, naked and cock-swinging, and he pulled the leather belt from his pants. "Assume th' position."

Windy swallowed fast, then moved out from under the shower, turned and bent forward, bracing himself against the wall on his outstretched arms. He was dripping wet, and the cheeks of his untanned ass were tight and glistening in the shadowed light.

Like I told you, I turn on to a stud with a neat-looking butt, which is exactly what Windy had, but I knew damn well Chad had brought him there for another reason.

Cool-like, Chad doubled his belt in his hand, stepped

up behind Windy and swatted his tail, laying the leather on him with a lot of noise. Windy winced, and a little pinkness showed up on his buns.

Chad belted Windy a couple of more times, and I knew he was putting on this show for my benefit. Hell, he was barely warming Windy's ass, in spite of all the noise.

Anyway, I wasn't surprised when Chad quit and turned to me.

"Ever discipline a fuckup, buddy?"

"Like I told you, I've been around." I knew he was challenging me again, and I took my time, strip-drying myself with my hands and meeting him eyeball-to-eyeball. "When I take care of a punk, he doesn't fuck up a second time."

"Yeah?" Chad sneered, slapping the belt against his palm. "Put up or shut up!"

Crap! Maybe he didn't believe it, but I'd made my share of studs crawl—and I sure as hell hadn't done it with a few love taps like Chad had given Windy!

So I went over and took his belt out of his hands, saying nothing, and I gripped the buckle end, letting it swing free. Then I got into position behind Windy.

Damn it, his little tail made a neat target!

"Grit your teeth, pal." I tapped him lightly with the whip.

He tensed, and I aimed and swung plenty hard.

Yeah, I don't play around when I go to work on a stud!

Windy gasped with pain, and a wide red welt cut into his creamy buns, turning a dark crimson.

I gave it time to sink in, and then I whomped him again.

And a third time.

"Enough!" Windy spluttered. "I've learned my lesson!"

"One more," I growled. I always give a guy one more stroke than he thinks he can take, and I really laid that last one on Windy. "Okay, chum, on your knees."

Windy went down slowly, and I moved around in front of him, showing him my stiffening dick. Yeah, I was plenty turned on, and then—well, he just rocked forward and started licking and sucking real hungry-like.

I mean, I'd just whipped his ass red hot, and there he was, gulping on me as if it was the best duty he'd ever had!

Look, I told you that I'm hung about average soft, but when I throw a hard-on—shit, it's longer and thicker than most, that's for sure. Believe me, I'm not bragging 'cause there've been times when I wanted to make the scene with a stud, only he'd chickened out when he's found out how big my prick gets.

Anyway, there I was with Windy sucking me up full-hard and taking every inch of my meat balls-deep. Suddenly he pulled partway back and looked up at me with those big blue-gray eyes. It was like—well, it was like he wasn't doing it 'cause I'd whipped him or anything like that...know what I mean?

Yeah, I was ready to go all the way with Windy. And then I spotted Chad. He was standing there, naked and muscled, just staring at Windy and me. And there was his cock, stiff as hell and begging for action.

Remember how Chad's hung big as a horse when he was flipping his meat around soft? Well, it turned out that he had the kind of cock that doesn't get much bigger when it gets hard. Shit, if it swelled up as much as mine does, it'd reach his ankles!

But the thing that got me was the look in Chad's eyes. Christ, the sonofabitch was plain begging to be in Windy's place!

Okay, I was hot to go for broke with Windy, but I knew this was the time to settle things between Chad and me.

So I shoved Windy off my rod. He sank back on his

heels, showing me that his prick was just as hard as mine. It was tall and thin-shafted with one helluva solid head, and I sure didn't want to do what I knew I had to.

"Fuckup!" I barked. "Get your butt out of here before I make hamburger out of it!"

Windy didn't say a word. He just got up, grabbed his clothes and hustled out of the latrine.

Hell, I knew I hadn't fooled him...know what I mean?

Anyway, then it was just Chad and me again, both of us squared off against each other and cock-hard, only I was still holding his belt and he was head-down and waiting.

Yeah, I was sure of what he wanted!

"Stick your hands out," I ordered. "It's your turn, punk!"

Chad offered his hands, and I used his belt to tie them together securely. He kept his head down, but I was sure he was watching as I got my own belt from my trousers. It was wider and heavier than his, and I saw his hefty cock quiver with excitement.

Yeah, he knew what was coming, and he wanted it!

"Against the wall, peckerhead!" I wrapped the buckle in my hand as he turned and pressed against the side of the shower, and there was that big back and tight little ass just waiting to be stroked. "You saw how I laid it on Windy. Well, you're going to get one hell of lot more than that!"

Christ, I was hot to make him crawl!

I took my time, lining up the first shot, tensing my muscles, then laying the lash across his shoulders full force.

Chad jerked back, and a wide dark welt rose on his tanned, muscled skin.

"Yes, sir!" he whispered. "I understand!"

Man, he knew he was in for a real flogging, and that's just what I gave him!

I wasn't kidding when I'd told him I'd been around, and I'd had plenty of experience in whipping a stud down to size...but Chad was one in a million! He wasn't going to give up easy, and we both knew it!

So I laid my belt on him...slow...giving him time to hurt...crisscrossing his back down to his ass...then across his thighs...and then—yeah, that fuckable tail!

Chad took everything I gave him...sure, he moaned and swore and tried to fight back...but after I'd burned his butt a few times, he let me know who was boss.

"Sir! Anything you say, sir!"

I knew he'd had enough, but I blistered his ass with that one extra stroke I always give a guy.

He went down on his hands and knees, and I gave him a minute to catch his breath. Then I moved around in front of him, showing him my hard-on.

"Suck, shitface!"

Chad obeyed slowly, bending forward, licking the head of my cock, then taking it into his mouth.

I wanted the rough-and-tough sonofabitch to remember that he'd given in to me, and I grabbed the back of his head and jammed him down on my rod. Like I told you, I throw a big hard-on, and he choked and gagged and might've thrown up if I hadn't let him go.

You know, it's odd about that. I wasn't really pissed off at Chad, but I wanted to make him crawl like a slave or something. On the other hand, I hadn't felt that way when I'd whipped Windy and fed him my dick. Odd, huh?

Anyway, I let Chad go, and he gulped for air.

"I'm sorry, sir," he mumbled, hunched over in front of me. "You're awful big. I know I should've sucked you off...anything you say, sir...."

"I don't give a damn," I said, turned on like crazy. "I'd rather have your ass, cocksucker." I moved around behind him. "Assume the position!"

Yeah, that's what Chad had ordered Windy to do before swatting the young stud's butt, and Chad rocked forward, sticking his heat-streaked tail up toward me.

He was asking to get fucked, and that's just what I was cock-hot to do to him! Only I wasn't going to do it easy and gentle—hell, no!

I got down behind him and spit on my fingers, and I added that to Chad's spit on my dick. Then I gripped his hot little buns, and there was his puckered asshole blinking up at me.

Shit, I plowed my meat into him, slow and steady and all the way until Chad had every inch.

Know what? That stud whimpered and groaned and cussed like crazy, but he took my dick all the way!

Christ, that turned out to be one of the fucks a guy never forgets—know what I mean?

Once Chad got used to having my rod up his butt, he started jumping back on it every time I humped forward. We cut loose like a couple of goddamn madmen. No lie, the rougher I plowed him, the more he wanted.

Man, I stiff-rammed him until my balls ached from slapping forward against his...I shifted to slow-fucking, pulling all the way back and sliding in again. I cork-screwed, twisting my meat in his guts... I held still, cooling a little to make it last...I laid him out and did push-ups into his squishy ass...yeah, and I raked my fingernails over the welts I'd raised on his shoulders and back...and he crawled!

"Yes, sir!" he whispered. "Anything you say, sir!"

"Damn right!" I wrapped my arms around Chad and jerked him back to sit upright on my iron. "Punk!"

"Yeah...anything...sir!"

He squirmed all the way down on my meat, and—Jesus, what a sensation! Like I told you, he had one hell of a build, and all I could feel was those bulging muscles quivering and shifting under his slick, sweat-streaked skin. I rubbed my palms over his solid chest and found his large, sharp-tipped nipples. I pinched and twisted them between my fingers, feeling him tense with pain.

"You like that?" I asked, twisting harder. "You like getting worked over, cocksucker?"

"I—I understand," he whimpered, his head back on my shoulder. "I– I deserve it, sir!"

"I'm going to rip you wide open!" I ran my hands down over his rugged torso and into his crotch. "I'm going to bust your nuts, peckerhead!"

"Yes, sir!"

I grabbed his super-hard cock in one hand and his tightened balls in the other, and when I clamped down—Christ, he shot his load like it was the end of the world!

No shit, Chad howled and creamed, and it would've been kind of funny except that—well, his asshole snapped down around my ram, tight as hell...man!

"Yeah!

Awww, I couldn't hold back anymore, and I let go, blasting my come into him...getting my rocks off... making him take it in the ass...

horny, belt-whipped show-off!

big-cocked stud!

slave!

Damn it, I shot off!

Well, when I came down—you know how it is after dropping a load—well, I came down and still wanted Chad to crawl!...you know... So I pulled my dick out of his ass and stood up and stepped around in front of him. He didn't say or do a thing while I untied his hands. Then I took a leak on him.

Shit, that was plenty wild, watching that hunky stud stay on his knees, naked and whipped, with my piss spraying all over him.

Know what he did when I was finished? He whispered, "Thank you, sir." That's what he did!

I'd taught him who was boss—that's for sure!

He didn't move while I cleaned up and got dressed. But just before I left, I saw he'd thrown another goddamn hard-on.

Well, I was in my room that night with the lights out, bareass and ready for bed, when there was a knock on the door.

It was Windy, bright-eyed and bushy-tailed and stripped to his shorts.

"Chad told me to come down here," he said, closing the door behind him. "Hell, I would've come down anyway."

"Yeah!" Christ, just being alone with the rangy stud was getting me turned on! "How's your butt?"

"A little sore." Giving me that real great smile of his, he dropped his shorts. "You're a lot rougher than Chad."

"You deserved it." Seeing him standing there naked in the darkness was making me horny as hell! "That's what you get for fucking up."

"I didn't really fuck up. I figured Chad wanted an excuse to check out how far you'd go."

"Maybe." I wanted Windy so goddamn badly, I was shaking. "Want me to get my belt?"

"No, thanks." He stepped up in front of me, our rigid pricks meeting. "I guess the rough stuff turns some guys on, but I don't need it." He eased forward until we were barely touching all the way down. "Okay?"

"You bet!"

We pressed together and held each other real tight for a while, and we sure fit great…you know…cocks and balls and bodies and…

Hell, Chad'll never understand how guys like Windy and me turn on to each other without one being "forced" to do what he wants to do with the other.

Know what I mean?

Anyway, Windy and I slid down and stretched out on the floor, and we spent a lot of time kind of exploring each other…"body-matching," that's what he calls it…

Hell, I don't have to tell you what it's like, taking your time and stroking a stud all over with your fingers and lips and tongue while he does the same to you.

Maybe it'll sound funny to you, but it was different from everything I'd done with any stud before. Sure, I'd fucked and gotten sucked—yeah, and sucked and been fucked once in a while—but with Windy, it was—

Well, he sure wasn't as good-looking as Chad, and he sure wasn't as muscular…but we fit so goddamn good!

So we body-matched and played with each other, we joked and talked, we shared a cigarette and compared hard-ons...and we sucked each other off...sixty-nined... he's got a real throat-choker, but it was damn special, taking him off and drinking his come and having him drink mine...falling asleep together...waking up and fucking...everything!

No matter what, Windy and I weren't about to quit after that first night!

Okay, I didn't pay much attention to Chad after that, and he seemed to steer clear of me. I did notice that he kept his shirt on when us guys were on work details, but I don't think anyone else paid any attention. Also, he didn't shower with the rest of us and show off that big dick of his, and I figured he was washing up alone in the old latrine so no one'd see the marks I'd left on his back and ass.

Then, about a week later, I was stretched out on my sack after lights out, having a cigarette and waiting for Windy to show up, and Chad came sneaking in. He wasn't wearing anything except a towel around his middle, and all those muscles rippled and humped as he came over and knelt down beside my bed.

"What do you want?" I growled, turning on to the way he was acting like a slave.

"Lemme talk to you."

"What about?"

"I'm goin' t' discipline a fuckup t'morrow." Chad kept his head down, but I knew he was eyeballing me hard. As far as I was concerned, that was another turn on. "Want t' help out?"

"Hell, no." I dragged on my cigarette, playing the rough-and-tough act he wanted and showing him that I was throwing a rod. "You can mess around with those punks all you want. I'm waiting to work you over again, punk."

"Yeah!" he whispered, and he put one hand on my chest, smoothing the dark hairs lightly. "Sir—"

"Next time, I'm going to take you out in the boon-docks…tie you down…use my belt on you, all over… clamp up your balls…fuck your goddamn ass…teach you to—"

"Yes, sir!" He dropped forward and ran his lips over my chest. "I understand."

Man, I sure dug making the roughest stud in the camp crawl! I lay back and finished my cigarette while he licked my chest hair and nipples. And then I reached out and jerked off the towel he was wearing. His prick stood out as stiff as mine, and I snapped the head and felt him wince at the pain.

"How come you haven't been showing off your dick in the showers, Chad?"

"I—I didn't want th' other guys t' see th' marks...you know." He gulped for breath. "Do—Do any of them know about—about what happened between you an' me?"

"Maybe." I gripped his slippery testicles, and he winced again as I let them squirt between my fingers. "Windy may've figured it out. He and I've been shacking up. He's a helluva lot better at sucking cock than you are." I pushed his head downward toward my crotch. "Get down there and put your goddamn mouth to work, peckerhead."

"Yes, sir!"

Shit, Chad acted like he couldn't wait! He swung onto the bed and knelt between my legs. A moment later, he was licking my prick, sucking my nuts—yeah, he even raised me up and stuck his face in my ass, kissing and tonguing for all he was worth!

And that was when Windy came in, stripped to his shorts, and—

Well, Chad didn't know we had company. For a moment, Windy just stared at me and the rugged stud rimming me. Then I guess he figured it out, and he gave me one of those great grins...and peeled off his shorts.

Damn it, Windy's dick was full-hard, and just seeing him naked and sexed-up got me balls-hot…know what I mean?

So he moved around to the end of the bed, wet his iron with spit, and rammed it into Chad's ass.

Yeah, Windy just plain rammed into Chad, nuts-deep, and Chad jerked up, gasping.

"No! Please! You're wreckin' me!"

"Crap!" Windy growled. "Get back down on my buddy's dick!"

"Y—Yes…sir…!"

Chad went down on my rod like it was a lollipop, and Windy and I traded grins.

Christ, Windy was the most special stud I'd ever traded come with, and both of us knew it!

"Hey, buddy?" he asked, looking me straight in the eye and almost laughing. "Is Chad as good a cocksucker as I am?"

"Hell, no!" I said. "Is his ass as good as mine?"

"Hell, no!!"

"Maybe we ought to train him, Windy. Maybe we ought to take him out to the old shower room and whip his butt and work him over and—"

"Yeahhhh!"

Man, Windy and I didn't have to say anything more.

He fucked, and I got sucked…sharing Chad…and a couple of days later, we took Chad out in the boondocks and gave him what he wanted.

Yeah, Chad ended up being slave to two of us… Windy and me.

BY THE BALLS

Whit and I hit it off right from the first, and that may sound odd because we're both topmen, know what I mean?

I met Whit at a leather bar up in the city one night, both of us wearing jackets and Levi's, and I didn't waste time because that's the way I operate.

"I'm Vic," I told him. "I dig the way you look and the bulge in your crotch. I figure you've got big balls, and I'll work on them, all the way."

"I'm Whit," he answered, no bullshit. "I dig the way you look and the hump of your ass. I figure you've got a hot little hole, and I'll plug it, all the way."

"No way, Whit."

"No way, Vic."

So we had a couple of beers, each one of us knowing we'd never hit the sack together. Yeah, we were both tops, but we found out we could be good buddies.

It turned out that Whit lived fairly close to me, and like me, he'd set up a workroom at his place. Pretty soon we were working together on guys who were into bondage and discipline, and Whit was damn good, believe me. He really turned on to butt-play, you know, warming a stud's buns with a whip, spreading his asshole with a dildo or plug or even a fist, then fucking hell out of it.

Hell, I dig plowing a slave's tail and getting my rocks off that way, but I guess I'm "balls-oriented"—that's what Whit calls it. Even in my jerk-off days, the best sessions were when I was pumping a hot cock with one hand and holding a pair of nuts in the other. Yeah, there's something super-personal about having your balls—

Anyway, Whit and I decided to take our vacations

from work at the same time, only we didn't really plan on what we'd do or where we'd go.

Hey, wait a minute, I'd better tell you about this crazy idea we joked about. All the guys we'd worked on were willing, so one of us came up with "What if we kidnap a stud who isn't willing?" Sure, it was just a joke, but we laughed about it a lot.

Well, on the first night of our vacation, Whit and I had a few drinks at my place and then hopped into my car and headed up the freeway to the city, hot to see what we could line up at one of the leather bars. Okay, so we were both a little high and horny as shit.

I took the usual off-ramp. We were cruising down the street when we both spotted this hitchhiker. He had wavy black hair, good-looking, eighteen or nineteen, white shirt, wash pants—

"Kidnap!" Whit said, reading my mind. "Let's grab that stud!"

I hung a right at the next corner, and as we circled back, we put together the plan. Whit climbed into the backseat and dug out the kit of equipment I always carried. He passed me a pair of handcuffs which I hid between my legs. Then he hunkered down out of sight, and I eased the car on around the block.

Luck! The guy was still standing under the street-light and waving his thumb, so I braked to a stop and reached over to open the door.

"Hop in, man." Jesus, this stud was even more of a hunk than I'd seen at first glance! "Where're you headed?"

"Uptown. There's a new flick showing at the—"

That's all he had time to say. I'd pulled forward into the shadows, and Whit popped up, locking a choke hold on the kid's neck. He jerked his hands up to break away, and that's when I brought out the handcuffs and snapped them on his wrists. Seconds later, Whit jammed a gag in his mouth and clamped my favorite blindfold over his eyes, and I roared the car back to the freeway.

Hey, I'd better tell you about blindfolds, especially the one I like best. A lot of guys panic the first time— they can't see what's happening—but after a while, they kinda like the darkness where they can cream off. This blinder Whit snapped on the stud is easy to take off, but only if you know where the locks and clamps are. Yeah, even without the handcuffs, our unwilling slave couldn't get out of his gag and blindfold!

"Play it cool, chum," Whit told him, rubbing his shoulders and also holding him in place. "We're going to show you a lot better time than any goddamn movie."

The kid just sat there like he was too stunned to move, and he made some whimpering sounds into his gag like he was scared shitless. Me, I kept thinking what I'd say if I screwed up driving and got hauled over by the highway patrol!

Anyway, we reached Whit's place without trouble, and we took the guy into the workroom by the back way, just the way we'd done with all those other hot-to-prove-something slaves.

We put him in place and traded the handcuffs on his wrists for the bindings attached to the chains hanging from the pulleys overhead, and we strung him up neat as hell. He tugged and tested a little, and then I went ahead with the usual act. You see, I like to start out by giving a slave a new name, make him forget who he really is; know what I mean?

"Hey, Whit?" I asked, sly-like. "What'll we name this stud?"

"How about calling him Rocky?" Whit answered, moving behind the kid.

"Why Rocky?"

"Rocky was my first asshole buddy." He rubbed his hands over the kid's back and down to his ass. "He gave me my first blowjob. And he spread his butt for my dick, later on."

"Okay," I agreed, "We'll call this one Rocky." I pawed the stud's chest, working up a hard-on. "Ever had a blowjob, Rocky?" He shook his head. "Ever suck cock?" He shook his head again, more violently. "Fuck? Get fucked?" He thrashed, finally getting the picture, and I started to unbutton his shirt. "Whit, I think we've got ourselves a virgin!"

"No lie!"

I finished opening Rocky's shirt, and Whit ripped it off. Man, we'd kidnapped a real hunk!

Rocky's solid shoulders humped into thick-muscled arms, and his wide armpits were filled with glossy black silk. His chest was full-broad and covered with a light growth of hair, and his nipples were broad and flat-tipped. His chunky frame narrowed slightly to the low-slung pants on his hips, and I sure wondered what he had hidden inside his fly.

I ran my palms over Rocky's stocky physique and played with his tits, and he broke out with a nervous sweat. Whit was examining his backside at the same time, and Rocky was beginning to realize his helplessness. Yeah, we could do anything we wanted with him.

At last, I unfastened Rocky's belt and opened his trousers, and when I pushed them down on his legs, his Jockey shorts showed against his creamy flesh, the pouch well filled in spite of his obvious fear. Damn right, I groped him, and he howled into his gag, then groaned as if accepting the inevitable.

Slowly, deliberately, I lowered his shorts. His swimming trunks were outlined against his golden tan, and a trickle of dark hair ran downward from his navel to merge with the spread of crisp hair at his groin. His cock flopped thick and heavy over his tight-sacked balls, and he damn near jumped out of his skin when I started feeling him up, especially his testicles. Christ, he had a fine pair!

"Rocky's hung damn good," I told Whit casually. "But we'll have to stretch his nuts so they'll hang low like yours and mine."

"Wait till you check his little tail. Maybe we'll stretch it prick-wide."

Like I told you, Whit's ass-oriented.

Well, we finished stripping Rocky, spread his legs and locked his ankles to the floor hooks. Then Whit and I took a break to have a drink in the living room and figure out just how to handle Rocky. Let's face it—we'd never kidnapped a goddamn virgin before!

"Think we can break Rocky, Whit?"

"We sure as hell can try." He began pecking open his shirt. "That'd be wild, huh? Training an innocent hunk like him. Awww, yeah!"

"We can turn him loose in a day or two. He won't be innocent by then, believe me." I started to undress. "I wonder if he'll suck my dick."

"I bet he'll bite it off!"

We made vague plans while we got out of our clothes, and both of us were sporting hard-ons when we peeled off our pants. Whit's got one of those wiry builds, almost thin, with sinewy muscles, but he's plenty strong. Also, he's loaded with body hair, a lot more than I have. On the other hand, his pecker's slim and sleek, arrow-tipped, not as long and fat as mine. Yeah, I remembered a dumb slave who said Whit wasn't hung worth shit until Whit hot-rammed his butt.

It isn't what you've got, it's how you use it. Right?

Another thing. A lot of times, Whit and I had worked on a stud wearing Levi's or a jockstrap, but this time we both stripped all the way. Hell, we both wanted Rocky to find out what serving a bareass man is like.

When we went back to the workroom, I checked out Rocky's backside while Whit played on his front. Damn it, the young stud had great back muscles, and Whit hadn't been kidding about Rocky's trim little tail. Man, that tight ass was baby-smooth and just begging to get fucked!

"I'm Vic," I told him, shoving my iron between his spread legs to rub noses with Whit's rod. "And this is my buddy Whit." I reached around Rocky to grab Whit and lock him up against the kid. "We're your masters, and we're going to teach you how to be the best goddamn slave in the whole world!"

Rocky tore at his chains and screamed into his gag. I bet he'd never heard of masters and slaves before, much less found himself trapped between two naked, horny studs!

After that, Whit and I took our time playing with every part of Rocky's chunky body, showing him we could do anything we wanted with him.

We introduced him to lightweight tit clamps and a narrow ball-stretcher. Nothing really rough. Not yet.

I teased his cock until he couldn't keep it from stiffening, and he ended up with one hell of a full, solid hard-on. Man, what a beauty!

"I'm going to bring you off," I told him, dropping down on my knees in front of him. "From now on, even your come belongs to your masters!"

Look, a lot of topmen won't go down on a slave, but I figure that making a guy cream his load is one way of showing my control over him.

I licked the blazing crown of Rocky's prick and had it collar-deep in my mouth before he seemed to realize what I was doing. I don't know why, but some guys get real upset when another man sucks his dick, and Rocky was one of those guys. He did everything he could to get away, which wasn't much. That's when Whit started whipping his ass with a belt—light at first, then harder and harder.

It's important that a slave learns pleasure and pain, and that's what we began teaching Rocky. I gulped on his meat while Whit warmed his butt, and when he started to pop, I grabbed his taut-sacked nuts and squeezed.

No shit—Rocky gushed like he hadn't unloaded in weeks, and afterward he went limp, worn out. Whit let him catch his breath, and then we went ahead with his training. Yeah, he'd gotten his rocks off, and now it was our turn.

We moved a waist-high table in front of Rocky, and before he figured out what was happening, we'd lowered him and stretched him out facedown, clamping his wrists to the table legs on the far side. His butt-cheeks glowed blood-hot from the belting Whit'd given him, right in position to get fucked.

Sure, I wanted to bust Rocky's cherry, but I decided it'd be easier for him if Whit went first. Like I told you, Whit's got a spikelike dick while mine's kind of big, especially for a goddamn virgin.

Anyway, I moved around in front of Rocky and shoved my crotch into his face while Whit took time out to grease up. I would've peeled off Rocky's gag and jammed my iron down his throat, but I remembered what Whit had said about getting it bitten off.

"Take a deep breath," I ordered. "Get used to the smell of your master, Rocky!"

He fought, but he had to breathe.

Damn right, he learned what a man's cock and balls smell like!

I held him there, and Whit moved in behind him, cock slicked and ready to screw. He spread Rocky's buns and finger-lubed his asshole, and I don't think Rocky knew what was coming up until he felt Whit's arrow-tipped prod poking into him.

Aww, yeah, Rocky howled into his gag, his nose in my crotch, Whit's spike slipping into his virgin tail!

"Open up!" Whit growled. "You're going to be one well-fucked slave when we turn you loose!"

Christ, what a turn-on! I could feel Rocky's gagged

moans against my genitals while I watched Whit screw him wide open. Whit may not have the biggest dick in the world, but he sure knows how to use it!

By the time Whit finally creamed, my pecker was dripping hot, so I greased up and took his place behind Rocky. I thought maybe Rocky had passed out because he'd gone real limp. But when I pressed my cock against his asshole, he tensed and groaned, maybe knowing he was going to get plowed even wider and deeper than before.

I plugged into Rocky real slow, mostly because I didn't want to shoot off in a hurry, and when I had my ram all the way into his tail, I gave him time to adjust to it. It was a damn tight fit, but suddenly, his asshole was pulsing and almost milking my iron.

Okay, so I fucked him for all I was worth. Long-dicking from tip to base, short chops, corkscrewing, you name it and I did it. Yeahhh!

All of a sudden, Rocky jerked his head up and howled into his gag, and I knew he was creaming again. Lots of studs pop from getting rear-ended.

After that, I jammed my hands under him and clamped against his sweaty back, and I pumped off one hell of a load—the best ever!

Maybe it sounds odd, but right then and there, I felt

that special oneness that a master shares with a slave, know what I mean?

On the other hand, Rocky wasn't the typical willing slave I was used to working on.

Later on, Whit and I hauled Rocky into the bathroom and gave him a shower while we cleaned up. Still chained, blindfolded, and gagged, he couldn't stop us from doing anything we wanted with him.

Of course, we had to take off the gag when we fed him and gave him something to drink. Right away, he started begging.

"Let me go, you guys," he mumbled. "I won't tell anyone what you've done. Honest!"

"Shit!" Whit snickered while I stuffed some food into Rocky's mouth with my fingers. "Don't you want to brag to your buddies about how you got kidnapped and fucked? Yeah, I bet they'd really dig knowing how you've served your masters!"

From then on, Rocky didn't do much begging.

We tied him down for the night, and Whit and I hit the sack for some sleep. When we woke up, we went back to work on our stud.

figure the best way to train a slave is to keep him off guard, never knowing what time it is, how long he's been with me, making him understand he's totally dependent on me for everything from food and drink to sex and discipline, even taking a shit. So that's how we treated Rocky.

Sometimes we went real easy on him, just playing around and keeping his prick up, and other times, we strung him up and went heavy. Yeah, he never knew what to expect.

Whit and I kept saying we'd turn Rocky loose "tomorrow," but we didn't. Hell, taking him to his limits was a real challenge.

We used tighter clamps on his nipples, keeping them supersensitive.

We fucked him whenever we felt like it, and we taught him about buttplugs and dildos.

We took turns whipping his back and ass in long, slow sessions.

We sucked and jerked his prick until it was damn near raw.

We switched to a gag with a cock-shaped insert to train him in doing some sucking of his own.

Sometimes, when we showered him, we pissed on him.

Remember what I said about liking to work on a stud's balls? Man, I stretched and weighted Rocky's nuts, making them hang lower than ever before.

Okay, so it was Whit's idea that we should shave Rocky. Maybe that's because Whit's so goddamn hairy. It seems as if a lot of guys think body fuzz shows manhood or something like that. Anyway, we had Rocky strapped down on his back, spread-eagled, and Whit scraped him razor-clean from neck to belly button. Christ, that made his muscles and tits stand out better than ever! Then I took over, shaving his ballsac and the line leading back to his asshole, and—yeah, legs-up, I screwed him face-to-face.

Rocky stopped begging us to let him go. We'd held him prisoner for more than a week, and maybe he was beginning to understand his new role. But I still wasn't sure about sticking my prick in his mouth.

One day I took off to the supermarket. When I got back, there was a note from Whit that he'd left Rocky chained up while he ran some errands. I stripped and found Rocky hung up in the workroom. Christ, he looked sexy, naked and muscled and glowing with a light sweat!

I released him from the cuffs on his wrists and ankles, and he slumped down on his knees in front of me. Then I peeled off his gag and fed him a drink of water.

"Thank you, sir," he whispered, and that was the first time he'd called me "sir!" "Thank you, Vic."

"How'd you know I'm Vic?"

"I've learned the smell of my masters' bodies, yours and Whit's."

Goddamn, he'd learned more than that!

So I took a chance and jammed his face into my crotch. For a little while he just breathed slow and deep. Then I felt his lips tracing over my genitals. Hard-on time, believe me!

I let him take his time, kissing and nibbling and licking. Finally he took my cockhead into his mouth. No doubt about it—from the way he choked and gagged, it was his first try at sucking a piece of hot male meat!

Anyway, Rocky kept trying, and I'll be damned if he didn't end up getting my ram throat-deep. That's when I reached down and unfastened his blindfold. Yeah, I wanted him to see what he was doing and who he was doing it to.

Well, for a few seconds, he didn't do a fucking thing. Then he sank back on his heels, my dripping dick still halfway in his mouth. That's when he looked up at me, maybe really seeing me for the first time. There was a really strange glaze in his eyes, like nothing I'd ever seen before in the eyes of a slave.

That goddamn Rocky! He ran his hands over me all the way up to my chest. Then he wrapped his arms around my waist and began sucking for all he was worth. Shit, his enthusiasm made up for whatever he lacked in experience!

Anyway, I was just about to cream when Whit walked in. You should've seen the expression on his face! He popped open his Levi's and hauled out his rod, and as soon as Rocky had swallowed my load, he went to work on Whit's.

After that, Rocky did whatever we ordered obediently, but his eyes kept that dazed look. We took him to bed with us, sticking him in the middle, and I swear he spent most of the night checking us out with his fingers and lips and tongue, first one and then the other.

Okay, so Whit and I were running out of vacation time.

"What're we going to do with Rocky?" I asked Whit one night. "Want to keep him?"

"Not me. I'm not the one-slave kind."

Maybe we should take him back to where we found him and turn him loose," I suggested.

"Don't do that, sir," Rocky begged, head down, his hands clamped behind his back as if chained. "I'm a slave. I need a master. You've taught me that."

"Okay." Hell, I guess I'd hoped the hunky young stud would say something like that. "Put on your goddamn pants and I'll take you to my place for a while."

"Yes, sir!"

I drove him over to my house. It was kind of odd that he didn't seem interested in where he was. We'd kidnapped him up in the city, remember?

Once inside, I had him strip down and leave his clothes folded by the front door.

"That's so you'll know where to find them when I throw you out," I told him. "Or when you want to leave."

"I won't want to leave," he murmured, slavelike. "I'm glad you're my master, Vic."

"You may change your mind after I've worked you over a few times!"

I gave him a tour of the joint and listed him his orders, like keeping everything spotless, making morning coffee for me, building a proper drink before dinner, shit like that. His only reaction was when I showed him my work irons; the sonofabitch started to throw a hard-on when he checked the equipment!

When we finally hit the sack that night, Rocky was real quiet, maybe because it was just him and me now. Then he started running his fingers over me lightly.

"Sir?" he asked at last, stroking my testicles. "Are you going to keep on stretching my balls?"

"Maybe. Why?"

"I want mine to hang low like yours do." He took a deep breath. "My nuts belong to you, sir."

Christ, he'd learned how I feel about ball-play! Yeah, he worshiped mine while I squeezed the hell out of his, and we ended up climbing all over each other and sharing our first sixty-nine. Man!

The next morning, Rocky was already banging around in the kitchen, and I hauled into the can to take a leak and wash up. I'd just hit the shower when he hopped in with me. For the first time, his eyes were clear and bright.

"The coffee's brewing, sir," he announced proudly, and he grabbed the soap. "Let me scrub you down, sir."

Hell, we scrubbed each other, and when we were both dripping with soap foam, Rocky grabbed me, his solid hard-on matching mine. I wrapped my arms about him and pawed the slick cheeks of his ass, and he didn't resist when I slid my fingertips into the warm cleft between them.

"Rocky," I warned him, "I'm going to fuck you like never before."

"Yes, sir!"

"Just as soon as we've had a cup of the coffee you're making."

"Shit!" he groaned. "Do it now! Please, Vic!"

Okay, so we postponed coffee for a while.

Look, some masters object to having a slave call them anything but "sir" or "master." Me, I don't care what he calls me just as long as he obeys. And Rocky sure obeyed!

The first day I went back to work, I left Rocky with his chores to do and a heavyweight stretcher on his testicles. When I got home that night, his chores were done...and his balls were tender as hell...and his clothes were gone from where I'd told him to leave them inside the front door.

"I put them away, sir," he explained softly. "I'm not going anywhere."

"Bullshit! You disobeyed me, and you're going to the workroom!"

I gave him a heavy working over, and I'll be damned if he didn't have a hard-on going the whole time. Yeah, he'd learned the pleasure of pain!

Another night, Rocky noted that his chest hair was growing back.

"It itches," he grumbled.

"Scratch it."

"Want me to keep it shaved?"

"I don't care," I yawned. "Shaving your chest was Whit's idea."

So Rocky let his chest hair grow back, but he kept his balls shaved. After all, I was the one who'd shaved them the first time, so it was his way of showing me that I was his master. Know what I mean?

A few days later, I came back from work to find Rocky dressed in his wash pants and a shirt I'd bought him, and I knew right off the bat that he'd been out of the house for the first time. Yeah, up until then he hadn't known where he was, much less tried to find out.

"I went out today," he explained nervously. "I got a job. At a gas station in town."

"How come?" I tried to sound master-rough. "Without my permission?"

"I thought you might say no, Vic. You've been buying everything since I came here, and I thought it's about time I paid my own way."

Maybe I should've punished Rocky, but I felt kind of proud of him.

Man, I couldn't believe the uniform the gas station gave Rocky to wear. The white shirt was so thin that the glow of his tan showed through and it fit like wallpaper, outlining every bulge and dip of his chunky thick-muscled physique. Sexy as hell, believe me!

On the other hand, the pants were cut loose, but not loose enough to hide the fact that he wasn't wearing shorts underneath. Yeah, I'd peeled his Jockeys off him that first night, and he wasn't going to wear them again without my permission. Maybe that's what gave me the idea to send him off to work every day with this special prick-and-balls trainer hung in place, a heavy strap stretching his nuts low, other bands locking his dick downward against them.

"Damn it!" he muttered. "That'll give me a hard-on I won't get rid of all day."

"You've already got one going."

"What if the guys at the station notice?"

"Maybe they'll pay you overtime!"

That goddamn Rocky! He went to work strapped and stretched. That night, we hit the sack and laughed and got our rocks off.

Yeah, I was his master, but Rocky and I had come to that point when we shared special times by relaxing and enjoying each other.

By the way, Rocky handed over his check every

payday, and I doled out whatever amount of cash I felt like. I called it "walking-around money," and he never knew ahead of time how much I'd give him, maybe just enough for lunch, maybe a hell of a lot more. I'd stick the cash inside the straps on his prick and nuts that I made him wear to work, knowing he'd have to dig it out before he could even buy a Coke on his morning break. But right from the first, he always accounted for every cent he'd spent. That's the kind of slave he'd become.

Sometimes we'd get together with Whit, and Rocky served Whit automatically, maybe showing off what a good slave the two of us'd made him. Man, we had some wild sessions, Rocky sucking one of us while the other one fucked his hot little ass!

But I guess the best times were when it was just the two of us. Maybe it would be when I had him chained down in the workroom, maybe when we were in the sack. I'd run my hands over his black hair and his handsome face, his chunky physique, his unprotected genitals, and I'd remember the first night when Whit and I'd kidnapped him, young and virgin-innocent. Yeah, we'd learned a lot about each other since then.

"Vic?" he asked one night when we were feeling lazy, stroking each other in bed. "You've met Ben, right?"

"Sure." I pictured the burly, rough-and-rugged blond who worked at the gas station with Rocky. "What about him?"

"We were horsing around today, and I groped him." He fingered my testicles gently. "His balls hang low like yours do, but they're not as tough as mine."

"Yours were tender as hell when I first went to work on them." I held him down on his back, still fondling his shadowed nakedness. "Ben did some groping of his own?"

"Yeah. He found out I was wearing that stretcher."

"So?"

"He wanted to try it on, but I told him you'd hung it on my nuts, so I can't take it off without your permission... sir." Rocky stayed in place, letting me find his rigid hard-on and bulging testicles. "It's up to you, sir."

"I'll think about it." I kept on fondling his heated genitals. "How come you're so hot to mess with Ben's jewels?"

"He's a good buddy—that's all. Nothing like you and me." He half-turned toward me and ran his fingers over my chest, his expression thoughtful. "There's something damn personal about playing with a stud's rocks. I remember the first time you grabbed mine. Christ, I was scared shitless! But it got to be sort of special, whether you squeezed them or stretched them or just held them in your hand." He paused, then took a deep breath. "Vic, can I make love to your balls?"

Hell, neither one of us had ever used the word "love" before, and I didn't know what to expect.

Rocky crawled down over me and crouched between my spread legs, and he buried his face in my crotch just as he had the first time he sucked my cock. After a minute or so, he slipped one hand under my testicles and raised them to his lips—and that's when I found out what he'd meant about making love to my nuts.

That goddamn slave!

He went so fucking slow, kissing and nibbling and licking my hairy-sacked balls, it seemed like forever before he finally took them into his mouth, first one, then the other, then both at the same time.

I remembered the time when I'd been afraid to stick my dick in his mouth because he might've bitten it off, and there I was, letting him work on my precious jewels!

Damn personal and special, believe me!

Shit, my prick was dripping like a leaky faucet by the time Rocky climbed up on it. He kept on playing with my nuts while he gave my hard-on a long tongue-job, like he was examining it for the first time, and then he went down on me.

All the way down!

Throat-deep in one gulp!!

"Rocky!"

I clamped him between my legs and stroked his dark, wavy hair, and he began sucking slow and steady.

Man, that was one blowjob I'll never forget! No, Rocky made it more than just another blowjob. He switched from my dick to my nuts and back, over and over, and—okay, so I creamed my guts out!

"AGGGHHHHH! ROCKKKYYYY!"

He drank down my come, then lay still until my iron went soft in his mouth. Finally he eased off, resting the side of his face against my belly.

"Vic?" he murmured at last.

"Yeah?"

"I shot my load all over the goddamn bed."

"Change the sheets in the morning."

"Yes, sir." Rocky lay still for a short time. Then: "I love your balls, Vic." And he scrambled up to me, flashing a big smile. "The rest of you is okay, too."

"Wise ass!" I tried to sound like a master, laughing inside. "I ought to take you down to the workroom for another session!"

"Whatever you say…sir."

"Tomorrow, maybe," I threatened. "Right now, get to sleep!"

Rocky stayed right where he was until I thought he'd gone to sleep, and then he gripped my wrist and hauled my hand over to his come-sticky testicles.

"Master," he whispered, "I told you before...my nuts belong to you."

"Damn right!"

WELL-TRAINED

It was Saturday. Tim was washing and drying last night's dinner dishes, then stacking them carefully on the kitchen shelves.

Everything had to be in place before Hack came home, Tim knew that.

Stripped to loose gym shorts, Tim had short-clipped black hair and a chunky muscled physique with strands of dark silk wisping across his wide-arched chest, more man than youth from the neck down.

Finished with the dishes, Tim paused to gaze out the window over the sink. Hot summer sunlight blazed on the street outside, and he stroked his crotch unconsciously as he saw two figures jogging down the sidewalk toward the house.

Hack was in front, a dark-haired, swarthy man in his late twenties, a sweat-stained T-shirt clinging to his powerful shoulders and broad chest, narrow shorts hugging his massive thighs. Following him was his friend Sam, a lean, boy-faced redhead only a few years older than Tim, slim and athletic, dressed like Hack.

Tim watched the two men trot up the driveway and enter the house.

"Hey, kid!" Hack bellowed from the garage. "Bring us a couple of beers!"

Tim blinked as he heard the man call him "kid," and then he hurried to get two beer cans from the refrigerator and hustled down the short hallway.

Hack had converted the garage into a miniature gym, complete with weights and body-building equipment, an alcoved shower room at the far end, even the scent of sweat and disinfectant—the sweat Tim and Hack and the others dripped after working out, the disinfectant Tim used to swab down the area as one of his chores. The only unusual feature was the net of chains dangling from the rafters in the shadowed corner.

Sam and Hack were slouched back side by side on the plank bench along one wall, and Tim recognized Hack's narrowed gaze as he passed the beer cans.

"Thanks, Tim," Sam said with a friendly smile. He took a long swallow of beer. "That sure hits the spot."

"Finish your chores, kid?" Hack asked coldly.

"Sure." Tim understood the glint in the man's eyes, and he looked down at the floor, obedient. "Yes…sir."

"Work out?" He nodded toward the exercise equipment. "The full routine?"

"Yes, sir."

"Okay." Hack peeled off his shirt and wiped his solid hairy chest and broad armpits, then tossed it to Tim. "Give him your shirt, Sam. He'll have it washed and clean for the next time we go jogging."

"Right." Sam squirmed out of his shirt. The redhead's hard-plated chest was slick and dotted with freckles with small pink-tipped nipples at each side. He moistened his lips as he watched Tim take the clothing to a hamper on the other side of the room. "It's real crazy, the way he does whatever you say."

"I've trained him," Hack acknowledged openly. "He was

a real screwup when I took him in a couple of years ago. I whipped him into shape."

"Whip?" A nervous frown creased Sam's forehead. "You mean—?"

"Hell, that's the best way to get a punk squared away." He drank, then pointed to the chains hanging from the rafters. "The first night, I strung him up over there and laid my belt on him. He took his licks like a man, but after a few heavy sessions like that, he got the picture." He grinned at the head-down youth. "Right, kid?"

"Yes, sir," Tim muttered. "I thought you two might be related. The way he's built, I mean."

"Crap!" Hack snorted. "He wasn't built worth a damn before I went to work on him."

"Weight lifting?"

"More than that. Check his tits." He drank again, viewing Tim's wide, dark nipples. "I used clamps and weights on them until they grew. The same goes for his cock and balls."

"You're joking," Sam suggested warily.

"No way! By the time I'm finished, he'll have the biggest dick and toughest nuts in town." Hack smiled at Tim. "Drop your shorts and give me those rocks, kid."

"Yes, sir," Tim whispered and obeyed quickly.

The youth hunched over and stripped. When he straightened, a band of untanned flesh showed at his hips. Wisps of black silk trailed downward from his deep-cleft navel to the pubic thicket at his groin, and his long, thick prick curled heavily over his loose-sacked testicles. Without a word, he stepped in front of Hack, his arms at his sides, his genitals offered.

"Jesus!" Sam hissed as he watched the man grip the balls and squeeze brutally. "You're wrecking him!"

"He's learned to take it," Hack said casually, and he pressured until Tim tensed, his head thrown back, his hands knotted into fists. "Anybody who gives this stud a knee in the crotch is in for a big surprise. That's part of the training I've given him." He released the pain-wracked youth and shrugged. "Stick your nuts in Sam's hands, kid. Show him how tough you are."

Tim took a deep breath, then moved in front of the redhead. Sam hesitated, his gaze fixed on the youth's crotch. After a moment, he reached up to grasp Tim's dangling balls. He clenched his fingers slowly, and Tim stiffened again, jaws locked, fighting the pain.

"Goddamn!" Sam murmured, letting go. "Those are real rocks!"

"How about his dick?" Hack asked with obvious pride. "He wasn't hung worth shit until I broke him in on the diet."

"Yeah, he's got plenty of meat," Sam admitted, hushed. "Uhh, what kind of diet? I mean, a guy ends up with whatever size cock he gets, right?

"Bullshit!" Hack tossed down the last of his beer. "Come and sweat, that's what made his pecker grow. He didn't dig it at first, but he's learned how good it is for him." He stretched his legs and pawed his shorts, grinning at Tim. "I worked up a real good sweat, jogging this morning with Sam. Want it, kid?"

"Yes, sir!"

Sam stared in disbelief as Tim knelt before Hack and began licking the linings of his hairy thighs, then buried his face in the man's mounded crotch.

"Hungry?" Hack asked with amusement, and he unfastened his shorts, spreading the flaps to reveal his sweat-stained jockstrap. "Wash me clean. It'll make your cock grow, right?"

Whimpering with eagerness, Tim jerked the strap down and tongue-lapped the forest of damp pubic hair, the loosened testicles, the swelling prick.

"Christ!" Sam exclaimed. "You've sure trained him!"

He watched wide-eyed as Tim finally pulled back, exposing Hack's thick, inflamed ram.

Hack gave Tim the hint of a grin, then nodded to the redhead beside him. "Climb over there and get another meal from Sam."

Automatically, the youth crawled to Sam and gripped his shorts. Sam raised his hips, making it easier for Tim to strip him. His rod was already heated, a glistening column of slick ivory flesh jutting from a patch of auburn crotch hair. Tim began licking willingly.

"Take it easy on my nuts!" Sam hissed. "They're not rocks like yours, damn it!"

Hack watched with satisfaction, then kicked off his clothing and got to his feet. Burly and naked, he sauntered across the room, took a tube of lubricant from the shelf, and he greased his soaring iron thoroughly. Turning back, he saw the husky youth kneeling between Sam's spread legs, head bobbing, tight-curved ass offered, and he moved into position behind him.

"You're going to get two loads of come this time, kid," the man growled. "That ought to add at least an inch to your pecker." He pulled Tim's buns apart and centered his bulging cockhead against the puckered opening. "Yeahhh!"

Tim took Sam's tool throat-deep and held it as the powerful ram probed into his tail, and his harsh groan was muffled by Sam's raging prong.

"I don't believe it!" the redhead gasped. "He's sucking me off—and you're plowing that iron up his butt at the same time!"

"I *told* you I'd trained him!"

The two men used the youth aggressively, Hack pumping the solid length of his rigid meat into the clenching asshole while Sam thrust his rod around the suctioning mouth.

"Awwhh!" the redhead groaned at last. "I'm going to pop!"

An instant later, he tensed and threw his head back. Then a hoarse cry broke from his throat, part pleasure, part pain.

"Drink that come, kid!" Hack ordered, clamping himself against Tim's back and humping feverishly. "You're going to get my load, too—NOW!"

He howled in climax, and his thick-muscled body shook with the force of each blast.

Exhausted, none of them moved for several minutes. Then Hack unpasted himself from Tim and mussed his dark hair affectionately. Looking up, he saw Sam slouched back on the plank bench, eyes closed. He ran his palms upward over the trim torso and tweaked the small nipples, grinning as the man winced.

"C'mon, Sam," Hack said, pulling back and sliding his heavy, relaxed cock free from Tim's butt, then swinging to his feet. "Let's hit the shower."

"Yeah…good idea."

Tim stayed on his knees while Sam stood up and jerked his shrunken dick away from his mouth. He waited until he was sure both men were in the shower alcove. Then he sank back on his haunches and gazed down at his still-rigid ram.

He forced his hard-on to cool down, and then got to his feet and walked to the shower entrance. Hack and Sam were trading places under the single spray and soaping themselves. When Hack spotted the youth, he pointed to the corner of the stall.

"Over there," Hack ordered. "Drinking beer makes me need to take a leak, kid."

Tim obeyed, backing into the corner and hunkering down, head lowered. Hack stepped in front of him, tugged his prick and began to piss. The hot, acrid stream sluiced over the youth's muscled torso and made golden puddles in his crotch. He stayed motionless until it ended.

"Thank you, sir," he mumbled as Hack shifted away.

"Your turn," Hack said to Sam, unconcerned. "Give him another bath."

Sam took Hack's place, ready to give Tim a second drenching, and Hack smiled with satisfaction as he lathered up his hands. Then he moved in close behind Sam, cupped the firm asscheeks in his foam-covered palms, and slid his fingers into the sharp crevice between them. Gently, he explored the hair-spiked passage and massaged the crinkled opening. He felt the young man shiver at the sensation.

Sure of himself, Hack moved back beneath the shower spray, rinsed, then stepped from the stall to grab a towel and dry himself. Minutes later, Sam joined him.

Tim stayed on his knees, young and muscular and piss-stinking, waiting until he was sure the two men had left the room. Then he stood under the pelting shower, soaping and scrubbing from head to toe repeatedly. He cleaned himself automatically, remembering the first time Hack had taken a leak on him and trained him to wash up thoroughly afterward.

Finished, he took his time drying off, then went into the main part of the house. He found Hack settled naked in his armchair in the living room, working on a can of beer.

"Where's Sam?" Tim asked warily.

"He cut out." Hack nodded to the coffee table. "I popped you a beer, pal. I figured you'd need it."

"Thanks." Tim picked up the waiting can and swallowed deeply, then faced the burly man. "You're working on something with Sam, right?"

"What makes you think so?"

"You started calling me 'kid' when you came back from jogging with him. You haven't called me that since you—"

"Since I trained you," Hack acknowledged, completing the youth's thought, and he grinned, viewing Tim's matured physique and genitals. "You sure aren't a kid anymore."

"Shit!" He drank again, feeling warm and proud. But at the same time, he went on being troubled about what had happened. "So…what about Sam?"

"Right now," Hack answered quietly, "I'd say he's wondering what it'd be like to take some heavy training."

"His balls are real tender."

"So were yours when I started working on them. You popped his nuts when he creamed, right?"

"Yeah. And you finger-fucked him while he was pissing on me."

"I only played with his asshole, just to give him the idea." Hack paused to drink. "Think you could train Sam, pal?"

"Me?" Tim was surprised. "How come?"

"It's time you used your experience. Also, I figure your first fuck ought to be into a virgin butt."

"Hot damn!" Tim tossed down the last of his beer and gazed at the man impishly. "Hey, Hack, how about letting me practice on your hunky tail? I've always wanted to—"

"Cool it!" Hack ordered sharply. "You can do anything you want with Sam, but nothing changes between you and me. Get the picture?"

"That's more like it. I'm going to go right on kicking the shit out of you whenever I feel like it, and you're going to do what I say." As if to enforce what he'd just said, Hack raised one hand. "Give me your balls, pal."

Tim shuffled forward, presenting his dangling genitals obediently. Hack grasped them, fingering his large, heavy testicles and cock tauntingly.

"Hack," he murmured moments later, "I'm getting a hard-on."

"Didn't you unload when you were sucking Sam and taking my load up your ass?"

"No," the youth admitted. "I would have, if you'd grabbed my dick like you usually do when you fuck me."

"That's why I didn't," Hack snickered. "I wanted you horny as hell when Sam and I were done with you, pal!"

Hack hunched forward and took the swelling cockhead into his mouth, rolling it over his tongue sensually. When the shaft was rigid with sex heat, he slid to his knees and took it throat-deep, wrapping his arms about Tim's hips and urging him downward.

"Hack!" the youth groaned, gripping the man's powerful shoulders for support as he lowered himself to the floor and settled on his back. "Keep that up and I'll cream in seconds!"

"Bullshit!" Hack barked, releasing Tim's spit-wet ram and watching it slam back against his belly. "If you shoot before I tell you to, I'll give you a training session you'll never forget!"

"Sonofabitch!" he replied, trying to hold back a grin. "*You're* the one who got me so goddamn hot!"

"And I'm going to keep you that way until your nuts ache." He stretched on his side next to Tim and ran his fingers over the youth's muscular chest. "Remember the first time I went down on you, pal? I barely got started before you popped."

"Hell, that was my first blowjob. Also, I was a punk kid."

"That's why I took you out in the garage and whipped

325

you like never before. So you'd learn to do what I say." He drew a deep breath. "We've come a long way since then."

"Yeah, I guess so." Tim brought one hand up to brush Hack's lush chest hair, avoiding his gaze. "If you hadn't taken over, I'd probably *still* be a punk kid."

"Probably," Hack agreed, still admiring the husky youth. "You're getting to be one hell of a stud."

"I'm trying to catch up with you."

"Keep right on trying," the man chuckled, then reached down to grip Tim's turgid prick. "We'll do some more bodybuilding in the garage this afternoon."

"Okay." He sighed kiddingly as Hack twisted down face-to-crotch, offering his potent iron to the youth at the same time. "How come I do whatever you say, Hack?"

"'Cause I've trained you."

"Bullshit." Tim fingered the man's testicles gently. "You've worked me over, whippings and tit clamps and all. But more than that, you've built me up and made me into the kind of guy who turns on a stud like Sam." He took a fast breath. "And you taught me that a punk kid sometimes needs a fucking sonofabitch like you!"

"Pal!"

They locked together, licking and caressing and

sucking, and they never did get around to that after-noon session of body building.

Unless you consider the size each added to his dick from that diet of come and sweat "body building."

MASQUERADE BOOKS

MASQUERADE

CLAIRE THOMPSON
SARAH'S SURRENDER
$6.95/620-0
Lovely Sarah denies her true desires for many years, hoping to find happiness with the pallid men who court her. Unable to hide her true feelings anymore, Sarah explores the SM scene—and tastes fulfillment for the first time. Gradually, her desires lead her to Lawrence, a discriminating man whose course of erotic training bring Sarah to a fuller realization of her submissive nature—and a deeper love—than she had ever imagined possible....

S. CRABB
CHATS ON OLD PEWTER
$6.95/611-1
A compendium of tales dedicated to dominant women. From domineering check-out girls to merciless flirts on the prowl, these women know what men like—and are highly skilled at reducing men to putty in their hands.

PAT CALIFIA
SENSUOUS MAGIC
$7.95/610-3
"Sensuous Magic is clear, succinct and engaging.... Califia is the Dr. Ruth of the alternative sexuality set...."
—*Lambda Book Report*

Erotic pioneer Pat Califia provides this unpretentious peek behind the mask of dominant/submissive sexuality. With her trademark wit and insight, Califia demystifies "the scene" for the novice, explaining the terms and techniques behind many misunderstood sexual practices.

ANAÏS NIN AND FRIENDS
WHITE STAINS
$6.95/609-X
A lost classic of 1940s erotica returns! Written by Anaïs Nin, Virginia Admiral, Caresse Crosby, and others for a dollar per page, this breathtakingly sensual volume was printed privately and soon became an underground legend. After more than fifty years, this priceless collection of explicit but sophisticated musings is back in print.

DENISE HALL
JUDGMENT
$6.95/590-5
Judgment—a forbidding edifice where unfortunate young women find themselves degraded and abandoned to their cruel masters. Callie MacGuire descends into the depths of this prison, discovering a capacity for sensuality she never dreamed existed.

CLAIRE WILLOWS
PRESENTED IN LEATHER
$6.95/576-X
At the age of nineteen, Flora Price is whisked to the south of France, where she is imprisoned in Villa Close, an institution devoted to the ways of the lash—not to mention the paddle, the strap, the rod...

ALISON TYLER & DANTE DAVIDSON
BONDAGE ON A BUDGET
$6.95/570-0
Filled with delicious scenarios requiring no more than simple household items and a little imagination, this guide to DIY S&M will explode the myth that adventurous sex requires a dungeonful of expensive custom-made paraphernalia.

JEAN SADDLER
THE FASCINATING TYRANT
$6.95/569-7
A reprint of a classic tale from the 1930s. Jean Saddler's most famous novel, *The Fascinating Tyrant* is a riveting glimpse of sexual extravagance in which a young man discovers his penchant for flagellation and sadomasochism.

ROBERT SEWALL
THE DEVIL'S ADVOCATE
$6.95/553-0
Clara Reeves appeals to Conrad Garnett, a New York district attorney, for help in tracking down her missing sister, Rita. Clara soon finds herself being "persuaded" to accompany Conrad on his descent into a modern-day hell, where unspeakable pleasures await....

LUCY TAYLOR
UNNATURAL ACTS
$7.95/552-2
"A topnotch collection" —*Science Fiction Chronicle*

Unnatural Acts plunges deep into the dark side of the psyche and brings to life a disturbing vision of erotic horror. Unrelenting angels and hungry gods play with souls and bodies in Taylor's murky cosmos: where heaven and hell are merely differences of perspective.

J. A. GUERRA, ED.
COME QUICKLY:
For Couples on the Go
$6.50/461-5
The increasing pace of daily life is no reason to forgo a little carnal pleasure whenever the mood strikes. Here are over sixty of the hottest fantasies around—all designed especially for modern couples on a hectic schedule.

MASQUERADE BOOKS

OLIVIA M. RAVENSWORTH
DOMESTIC SERVICE
$6.95/615-4

Though married for twenty-five years, Alan and Janet still manage to find sensual excitement in each other's arms. Sexy magazines fan the flames of their desire—so much so that Janet yearns to bring her own most private fantasy to life. She persuades Alan to hire live-in domestic help—and their home soon becomes the neighborhood's most infamous household!

THE DESIRES OF REBECCA
$6.50/532-8

Rebecca follows her passions from the simple love of the girl next door to the lechery of London's most notorious brothel, hoping for the ultimate thrill. She casts her lot with a crew of sapphic buccaneers, each of whom is more than capable of matching Rebecca's lust.

THE MISTRESS OF CASTLE ROHMENSTADT
$5.95/372-4

Lovely Katherine inherits a secluded European castle from a mysterious relative. Upon arrival she discovers, much to her delight, that the castle is a haven of sexual perversion. Before long, Katherine is truly Mistress of the house!

GERALD GREY
LONDON GIRLS
$6.50/531-X

In 1875, Samuel Brown arrives in London, determined to take the glorious city by storm. Samuel quickly distinguishes himself as one of the city's most notorious rakehells. Young Mr. Brown knows well the many ways of making a lady weak at the knees—and uses them not only to his delight, but to his enormous profit!

ATAULLAH MARDAAN
KAMA HOURI/DEVA DASI
$7.95/512-3

"Mardaan excels in crowding her pages with the sights and smells of India, and her erotic descriptions are convincingly realistic."
—Michael Perkins,
The Secret Record: Modern Erotic Literature

Kama Houri details the life of a sheltered Western woman who finds herself living within the confines of a harem. *Deva Dasi* is a tale dedicated to the sacred women of India who devoted their lives to the fulfillment of the senses.

ERICA BRONTE
LUST, INC.
$6.50/467-4

Explore the extremes of passion that lurk beneath even the most businesslike exteriors. Join in the sexy escapades of a group of professionals whose idea of office decorum is like nothing you've ever encountered!

VISCOUNT LADYWOOD
GYNECOCRACY
$9.95/511-5

Julian is sent to a private school, and discovers that his program of study has been devised by stern Mademoiselle de Chambonnard. In no time, Julian is learning the many ways of pleasure and pain—under the firm hand of this beautifully demanding headmistress.

N. T. MORLEY
THE OFFICE
$6.95/616-2

Lovely Suzette interviews for a desirable new position on the staff of a bondage magazine. Once hired, she discovers that her new employer's interest in dominance and submission extends beyond the printed page. Before long, Suzette and her fellow staffers are putting in long hours—and benefitting from some very specialized on-the-job training!

THE CONTRACT
$6.95/575-1

Meet Carlton and Sarah, two true connoisseurs of discipline. Sarah is experiencing some difficulty in training her current submissive. Carlton proposes an unusual wager: if Carlton is unsuccessful in bringing Tina to a full appreciation of Sarah's domination, Carlton himself will become Sarah's devoted slave....

THE LIMOUSINE
$6.95/555-7

Brenda was enthralled with her roommate Kristi's illicit sex life: a never ending parade of men who satisfied Kristi's desire to be dominated. Brenda decides to embark on a trip into submission, beginning in the long, white limousine where Kristi first met the Master.

THE CASTLE
$6.95/530-1

Tess Roberts is held captive by a crew of disciplinarians intent on making all her dreams come true—even those she'd never admitted to herself. While anyone can arrange for a stay at the Castle, Tess proves herself one of the most gifted applicants yet....

MASQUERADE BOOKS

THE PARLOR
$6.50/496-8
The mysterious John and Sarah ask Kathryn to be their slave—an idea that turns her on so much that she can't refuse! Little by little, Kathryn not only learns to serve, but comes to know the inner secrets of her keepers.

VANESSA DURIÈS
THE TIES THAT BIND
$6.50/510-7
This best-selling account of real-life dominance and submission will keep you gasping with its vivid depictions of sensual abandon. At the hand of Masters Georges, Patrick, Pierre and others, this submissive seductress experiences pleasures she never knew existed....

M. S. VALENTINE
THE GOVERNESS
$6.95/562-X
Lovely Miss Hunnicut eagerly embarks upon a career as a governess, hoping to escape the memories of her broken engagement. Little does she know that Crawleigh Manor is far from the upstanding household it appears. Mr. Crawleigh, in particular, devotes himself to Miss Hunnicut's thorough defiling.

AMANDA WARE
BOUND TO THE PAST
$6.50/452-6
Doing research in an old Tudor mansion, Anne finds herself aroused by James, a descendant of the property's owners. Together they uncover the perverse desires of the mansion's long-dead master—desires that bind Anne inexorably to the past—not to mention the bedpost!

SACHI MIZUNO
SHINJUKU NIGHTS
$6.50/493-3
Using Tokyo's infamous red light district as his backdrop, Sachi Mizuno weaves an intricate web of sensual desire, wherein many characters are ensnared by the demands of their carnal natures.

PASSION IN TOKYO
$6.50/454-2
Tokyo—one of Asia's most historic and seductive cities. Come behind the closed doors of its citizens, and witness the many pleasures that await intrepid explorers. Men and women from every stratum of society free themselves of all inhibitions in this thrilling tour through the libidinous East.

MARTINE GLOWINSKI
POINT OF VIEW
$6.50/433-X
The story of one woman's extraordinary erotic awakening. With the assistance of her new, unexpectedly kinky lover, she discovers and explores her exhibitionist tendencies—until there is virtually nothing she won't do before the horny audiences her man arranges. Soon she is infamous for her unabashed sexual performances!

RICHARD McGOWAN
A HARLOT OF VENUS
$6.50/425-9
A highly fanciful, epic tale of lust on Mars! Cavortia—the most famous and sought-after courtesan in the cosmopolitan city of Venus—finds love and much more during her adventures with some cosmic characters. A sexy, sci-fi fairytale.

M. ORLANDO
THE SLEEPING PALACE
$6.95/582-4
Another thrilling volume of erotic reveries from the author of *The Architecture of Desire*. *Maison Bizarre* is the scene of unspeakable erotic cruelty; the *Lust Akademie* holds captive only the most luscious students of the sensual arts; *Baden-Eros* is the luxurious retreat of one's nastiest dreams.

CHET ROTHWELL
KISS ME, KATHERINE
$5.95/410-0
Beautiful Katherine can hardly believe her luck. Not only is she married to the charming Nelson, she's free to live out all her erotic fantasies with other men. Katherine's desires are more than any one man can handle—and plenty of men wait to fulfill her extraordinary needs!

MARCO VASSI
THE STONED APOCALYPSE
$5.95/401-1/Mass market
"Marco Vassi is our champion sexual energist."   —*VLS*

During his lifetime, Marco Vassi's reputation as a champion of sexual experimentation was worldwide. Funded by his groundbreaking erotic writing, *The Stoned Apocalypse* is Vassi's autobiography; chronicling a cross-country trip on America's erotic byways, it offers a rare an stimulating glimpse of a generation's sexual imagination.

MASQUERADE BOOKS

THE SALINE SOLUTION
$6.95/568-9/Mass market

"I've always read Marco's work with interest and I have the highest opinion not only of his talent but his intellectual boldness."
—Norman Mailer

During the Sexual Revolution, Vassi established himself as an explorer of an uncharted sexual landscape. Through this story of one couple's brief affair and the events that lead them to desperately reassess their lives, Vassi examines the dangers of intimacy in an age of extraordinary freedom.

ROBIN WILDE
TABITHA'S TEASE
$6.95/597-2

When poor Robin arrives at The Valentine Academy, he finds himself subject to the torturous teasing of Tabitha—the Academy's most notoriously domineering co-ed. Adding to Robin's delicious suffering is the fact that Tabitha is pledge-mistress of a secret sorority dedicated to enslaving young men. Robin finds himself the and wildly excited captive of Tabitha & Company's weird desires!

TABITHA'S TICKLE
$6.50/468-2

Tabitha's back! Once again, men fall under the spell of scrumptious co-eds and find themselves enslaved to demands and desires they never dreamed existed. Think it's a man's world? Guess again. With Tabitha around, no man gets what he wants until she's completely satisfied....

CHARLES G. WOOD
HELLFIRE
$5.95/358-9

A vicious murderer is running amok in New York's sexual underground—and Nick O'Shay, a virile detective with the NYPD, plunges deep into the case. He soon becomes embroiled in the Big Apples notorious nightworld of dungeons and sex clubs, hunting a madman seeking to purge America with fire and blood sacrifices.

CHARISSE VAN DER LYN
SEX ON THE NET
$5.95/399-6

Electrifying erotica from one of the Internet's hottest authors. Encounters of all kinds—straight, lesbian, dominant/submissive and all sorts of extreme passions—are explored in thrilling detail.

STANLEY CARTEN
NAUGHTY MESSAGE
$5.95/333-3

Wesley Arthur discovers a lascivious message on his answering machine. Aroused beyond his wildest dreams by the acts described, he becomes obsessed with tracking down the woman behind the seductive voice. His search takes him through strip clubs, sex parlors and no-tell motels—before finally leading him to his randy reward....

CAROLE REMY
FANTASY IMPROMPTU
$6.50/513-1

Kidnapped to a remote island retreat, Chantal finds herself catering to every sexual whim of the mysterious Bran. Bran is determined to bring Chantal to a full embracing of her sensual nature, even while revealing himself to be something far more than human....

BEAUTY OF THE BEAST
$5.95/332-5

A shocking tell-all, written from the point-of-view of a prize-winning reporter. All the licentious secrets of an uninhibited life are revealed.

ANONYMOUS
DANIELLE: DIARY OF A SLAVE GIRL
$6.95/591-3

At the age of 19, Danielle Appleton vanishes. The frantic efforts of her family notwithstanding, she is never seen by them again. After her disappearance, Danielle finds herself doomed to a life of sexual slavery, obliged to become the ultimate instrument of pleasure to the man—or men—who own her and dictate her every move and desire.

ROMANCE OF LUST
$9.95/604-9

"Truly remarkable...all the pleasure of fine historical fiction combined with the most intimate descriptions of explicit love-making."
—The Times

One of the most famous erotic novels of the century! First issued between 1873 and 1876, this titillating collaborative work of sexual awakening in Victorian England was repeatedly been banned for its "immorality"—and much sought after for its vivid portrayals of sodomy, sexual initiation, and flagellation. Romance of Lust not only offers the reader a linguistic tour de force, but also delivers a long look at the many possibilities of sexual love.

MASQUERADE BOOKS

SUBURBAN SOULS
$9.95/563-8

One of American erotica's first classics. Focusing on the May–December sexual relationship of nubile Lillian and the more experienced Jack, all three volumes of *Suburban Souls* now appear in one special edition—guaranteed to enrapture modern readers with its lurid detail.

THE MISFORTUNES OF COLETTE
$7.95/564-6

The tale of one woman's erotic suffering at the hands of the sadistic man and woman who take her in hand. Beautiful Colette is the victim of an obscene plot guaranteed to keep her in erotic servitude—first to her punishing guardian, then to the man who takes her as his wife. Passed from one lustful tormentor to another, Colette wonders whether she is destined to find her greatest pleasures in punishment!

LOVE'S ILLUSION
$6.95/549-2

Elizabeth Renard yearned for the body of rich and successful Dan Harrington. Then she discovered Harrington's secret weakness: a need to be humiliated and punished. She makes him her slave, and together they commence a thrilling journey into depravity that leaves nothing to the imagination!

NADIA
$5.95/267-1

Follow the delicious but neglected Nadia as she works to wring every drop of pleasure out of life—despite an unhappy marriage. With the help of some very eager men, Nadia soon experiences the erotic pleasures she had always dreamed of.... A classic title providing a peek into the sexual lives of another time and place.

TITIAN BERESFORD
CHIDEWELL HOUSE AND OTHER STORIES
$6.95/554-9

What keeps Cecil a virtual, if willing, prisoner of Chidewell House? One man has been sent to investigate the sexy situation—and reports back with tales of such depravity that no expense is spared in attempting Cecil's rescue. But what man would possibly desire release from the breathtakingly corrupt Elizabeth?

CINDERELLA
$6.50/500-X

Beresford triumphs again with this intoxicating tale, filled with castle dungeons and tightly corseted ladies-in-waiting, naughty viscounts and impossibly cruel masturbatrixes—nearly every conceivable method of erotic torture is explored and described in lush, vivid detail.

JUDITH BOSTON
$6.50/525-5

A bestselling chronicle of female domination. Edward would have been lucky to get the stodgy companion he thought his parents had hired for him. But an exquisite woman arrives at his door, and Edward finds—to his increasing delight—that his lewd behavior never goes unpunished by the unflinchingly severe Judith Boston! An underground classic—from the Victorian mold.

AKBAR DEL PIOMBO
THE FETISH CROWD
$6.95/556-5

An infamous trilogy presented in one volume guaranteed to appeal to the modern sophisticate. Separately, *Paula the Piquõse*, the infamous *Duke Cosimo*, and *The Double-Bellied Companion* are rightly considered individual masterpieces—together they make for an unforgettably lusty volume.

TINY ALICE
THE GEEK
$5.95/341-4

An offbeat classic of modern erotica, *The Geek* is told from the point of view of, well, a chicken who reports on the various perversities he witnesses as part of a traveling carnival. When a gang of renegade lesbians kidnaps Chicken and his geek, all hell breaks loose. A strange but highly arousing tale, filled with outrageous erotic oddities, that finally returns to print after years of infamy.

LYN DAVENPORT
THE GUARDIAN II
$6.50/505-0

The tale of submissive Felicia Brookes continues. No sooner has Felicia come to love Rodney than she discovers that she has been sold—and must now accustom herself to the guardianship of the debauched Duke of Smithton. Surely Rodney will rescue her from the domination of this depraved stranger. *Won't he?*

GWYNETH JAMES
DREAM CRUISE
$4.95/3045-8

Angelia has it all—exciting career and breathtaking beauty. But she longs to kick up her high heels and have some fun, so she takes an island vacation and vows to leave her inhibitions behind. From the moment her plane takes off, she finds herself in one steamy encounter after another—and wishes her horny holiday would never end!

MASQUERADE BOOKS

LIZBETH DUSSEAU

THE BEST OF LIZBETH DUSSEAU
$6.95/630-8

A special collection of this popular writer's best work. *Member of the Club, Spanish Holiday, Caroline's Contract* and *The Applicant* have made Lizbeth Dusseau a favorite with fans of contemporary erotica. This volume is full of heroines who are unafraid to put everything on the line in order to experience pleasure at the hands of a virile man...

MEMBER OF THE CLUB
$6.95/608-1

A restless woman yearns to realize her most secret, licentious desires. There is a club that exists for the fulfillment of such fantasies—a club devoted to the pleasures of the flesh, and the gratification of every hunger. When its members call she is compelled to answer—and serve each in an endless quest for satisfaction....

SPANISH HOLIDAY
$4.95/185-3

Lauren didn't mean to fall in love with the enigmatic Sam, but a once-in-a-lifetime European vacation gives her all the evidence she needs that this hot, insatiable man might be the one for her....Soon, both lovers are exploring the furthest reaches of their desires.

JOCELYN JOYCE

PRIVATE LIVES
$4.95/309-0

The dirty habits of the illustrious make for a sizzling tale of French erotic life. A widow has a craving for a young busboy; he's sleeping with a rich businessman's wife; her husband is minding his sex business elsewhere!

SABINE
$4.95/3046-6

There is no one who can refuse her once she casts her spell; no lover can do anything less than give up his whole life for her. Great men and empires fall at her feet; but she is haughty, distracted, impervious. It is the eve of WW II, and Sabine must find a new lover equal to her talents and her tastes.

SARA H. FRENCH

MASTER OF TIMBERLAND
$6.95/595-6

A tale of sexual slavery at the ultimate paradise resort—where sizzling submissives serve their masters without question. One of our bestselling titles, this trek to Timberland has ignited passions the world over.

MARY LOVE

ANGELA
$6.95/545-X

Angela's game is "look but don't touch," and she drives everyone mad with desire, dancing for their pleasure but never allowing a single caress. Soon her sensual spell is cast, and she's the only one who can break it!

MASTERING MARY SUE
$5.95/351-1

Mary Sue is a rich nymphomaniac whose husband is determined to declare her mentally incompetent and gain control of her fortune. He brings her to a castle where, to Mary Sue's delight, she is unleashed for a veritable sex-fest! No one could have predicted the depth of Mary Sue's hungers.

AMARANTHA KNIGHT

THE DARKER PASSIONS: FRANKENSTEIN
$6.95/617-0

The mistress of erotic horror sets her sights on Mary Shelley's darkest creation. What if you could create a living, breathing human? What shocking acts could it be taught to perform, to desire, to love? Find out what pleasures await those who play God in another breathtaking journey through the Darker Passions.

The Darker Passions: CARMILLA
$6.95/578-6

Captivated by the portrait of a beautiful woman, a young man finds himself becoming obsessed with her remarkable story. Little by little, he uncovers the many blasphemies and debaucheries with which the beauteous Laura filled her hours—even as an otherworldly presence began feasting upon her....

The Darker Passions: THE PICTURE OF DORIAN GRAY
$6.50/342-2

One woman finds her most secret desires laid bare by a portrait far more revealing than she could have imagined. Soon she benefits from a skillful masquerade, indulging her previously hidden and unusual whims.

The Darker Passions: DR. JEKYLL AND MR. HYDE
$4.95/227-2

It is a sexy story of incredible transformations. Explore the steamy possibilities of a tale where no one is quite who—or what—they seem. Victorian bedrooms explode with hidden demons!

MASQUERADE BOOKS

THE DARKER PASSIONS READER
$6.50/432-1

Here are the most eerily erotic passages from the acclaimed sexual reworkings of *Dracula*, *Frankenstein*, *Dr. Jekyll & Mr. Hyde* and *The Fall of the House of Usher*.

THE PAUL LITTLE LIBRARY
SLAVE ISLAND
$6.95/655-3

A tale of ultimate sexual license from this modern master. A leisure cruise is waylaid by Lord Henry Philbrock, a sadistic genius. The ship's passengers are kidnapped and spirited to his island prison, where the women are trained to accommodate the most bizarre sexual cravings of the rich and perverted.

DOUBLE NOVEL
$7.95/647-2

Two best-selling novels of illicit desire combined into one spell-binding volume! Paul Little's *The Metamorphosis of Lisette Joyaux* tells the story of an innocent young woman seduced by a group of beautiful and experienced lesbians. *The Story of Monique* explores an underground society's clandestine rituals and scandalous encounters.

TEARS OF THE INQUISITION
$6.95/612-X

"There was a tickling inside her as her nervous system reminded her she was ready for sex. But before her was...the Inquisitor!" Titillating accusations ring through the chambers of the Inquisitor as men and women confess their every desire....

CHINESE JUSTICE
$6.95/596-4

The notorious Paul Little indulges his penchant for discipline in these wild tales. *Chinese Justice* is already a classic—the story of the excruciating pleasures and delicious punishments inflicted on foreigners under the tyrannical leaders of the Boxer Rebellion.

FIT FOR A KING/BEGINNER'S LUST
$8.95/571-9/Trade paperback

Two complete novels. Voluptuous and exquisite, she is a woman *Fit for a King*—but could she withstand the fantastic force of his carnality? *Beginner's Lust* pays off handsomely for a novice in the many ways of sensuality.

SENTENCED TO SERVITUDE
$8.95/565-4/Trade paperback

A haughty young aristocrat learns what becomes of excessive pride when she is abducted and forced to submit to ordeals of sensual torment. Trained to accept her submissive state, the icy young woman soon melts under the heat of her owners, discovering a talent for love she never knew existed....

ROOMMATE'S SECRET
$8.95/557-3/Trade paperback

A woman is forced to make ends meet by the most ancient of methods. From the misery of early impoverishment to the delight of ill-gotten gains, Elda learns to rely on her considerable sensual talents.

TUTORED IN LUST
$6.95/547-6

This tale of the initiation and instruction of a carnal college co-ed and her fellow students unlocks the sex secrets of the classroom.

LOVE SLAVE/
PECULIAR PASSIONS OF MEG
$8.95/529-8/Trade paperback

What does it take to acquire a willing *Love Slave* of one's own? What are the appetites that lurk within *Meg*? The notoriously depraved Paul Little spares no lascivious detail in these two relentless tales!

CELESTE
$6.95/544-1

It's definitely all in the family for this female duo of sexual dynamics. While traveling through Europe, these two try everything and everyone on their horny holiday.

ALL THE WAY
$6.95/509-3

Two hot Little tales in one big volume! *Going All the Way* features an unhappy man who tries to purge himself of the memory of his lover with a series of quirky and uninhibited vixens. *Pushover* tells the story of a serial spanker and his celebrated exploits.

THE END OF INNOCENCE
$6.95/546-8

The early days of Women's Emancipation are the setting for this story of very independent ladies. These women were willing to go to any lengths to fight for their sexual freedom, and willing to endure any punishment in their desire for total liberation.

THE BEST OF PAUL LITTLE
$6.50/469-0

Known for his fantastic portrayals of punishment and pleasure, Little never fails to push readers over the edge of sensual excitement. His best scenes are here collected for the enjoyment of all erotic connoisseurs.

CAPTIVE MAIDENS
$5.95/440-2

The scandalously sexy story of three independent and beautiful young women who find themselves powerless against the debauched landowners of 1824 England. The unlucky lovelies find themselves banished to a sex colony, where they are subjected to unspeakable perversions.

MASQUERADE BOOKS

THE PRISONER
$5.95/330-9
Judge Black has built a secret room below a penitentiary, where he sentences his female prisoners to hours of exhibition while his friends watch. Judge Black's justice keeps his captives on the brink of utter pleasure!

DOUBLE NOVEL
$6.95/86-6
The Metamorphosis of Lisette Joyaux tells the story of a young woman initiated into an incredible world world of lesbian lusts. *The Story of Monique* reveals the twisted sexual rituals that beckon the willing Monique.

....

ALIZARIN LAKE
MISS HIGH HEELS
$6.95/632-4
Forced by his wicked sisters to dress and behave like a proper lady, Dennis Beryl finds he enjoys life as Denise much more! Petticoats and punishments make for one kinky romp!

CLARA
$6.95/548-4
The mysterious death of a beautiful woman leads her old boyfriend on a harrowing journey of discovery. His search uncovers an unimaginably sensuous woman embarked on a quest for deeper and more unusual sensations, each more shocking than the one before!

SEX ON DOCTOR'S ORDERS
$5.95/402-X
Naughty nurse Beth uses her considerable skills to further medical science by offering insatiable assistance in the gathering of specimens. Soon she's involved everyone in her horny work—and no one leaves without surrendering what Beth wants!

THE EROTIC ADVENTURES OF HARRY TEMPLE
$4.95/127-6
Harry Temple's memoirs chronicle his incredibly amorous adventures—from his initiation at the hands of insatiable sirens, through his stay at a house of hot repute, to his encounters with a chastity-belted nympho, and much more!

....

LUSCIDIA WALLACE
THE ICE MAIDEN
$6.95/613-8
Edward Canton has everything he wants in life, with one exception: Rebecca Esterbrook. He whisks her away to his remote island compound, where she learns to shed her inhibitions. Fully aroused for the first time in her life, she becomes a slave to desire!

....

JOHN NORMAN
HUNTERS OF GOR
$6.95/592-1
Tarl Cabot ventures into the wilderness of Gor, pitting his skill against brutal outlaws and sly warriors. His life on Gor been complicated by three beautiful, very different women: Talena, Tarl's one-time queen; Elizabeth, his fearless comrade; and Verna, chief of the feral panther women. In this installment of Norman's million-selling sci-fi phenomenon, the fates of these uncommon women are finally revealed....

CAPTIVE OF GOR
$6.95/581-6
On Earth, Elinor Brinton was accustomed to having it all—wealth, beauty, and a host of men wrapped around her little finger. But Elinor's spoiled existence is a thing of the past. She is now a pleasure slave of Gor—a world whose society insists on her subservience to any man who calls her his own. And despite her headstrong past, Elinor finds herself succumbing—with pleasure—to her powerful Master....

RAIDERS OF GOR
$6.95/558-1
Tarl Cabot descends into the depths of Port Kar—the most degenerate port city of the Counter-Earth. There Cabot learns the ways of Kar, whose residents are renowned for the grip in which they hold their voluptuous slaves....

ASSASSIN OF GOR
$6.95/538-7
The chronicles of Counter-Earth continue with this examination of Gorean society. Here is the caste system of Gor: from the Assassin Kuurus, on a mission of vengeance, to Pleasure Slaves, trained in the ways of personal ecstasy.

NOMADS OF GOR
$6.95/527-1
Cabot finds his way across Gor, pledged to serve the Priest-Kings. Unfortunately for Cabot, his mission leads him to the savage Wagon People—nomads who may very well kill before surrendering any secrets....

PRIEST-KINGS OF GOR
$6.95/488-7
Tarl Cabot searches for his lovely wife Talena. Does she live, or was she destroyed by the all-powerful Priest-Kings? Cabot is determined to find out—though no one who has approached the mountain stronghold of the Priest-Kings has ever returned alive....

RHINOCEROS

M. CHRISTIAN, ED.
EROS EX MACHINA
$7.95/593-X

As the millennium approaches, technology is not only an inevitable, but a deeply desirable addition to daily life. *Eros Ex Machina* explores the thrill and danger of machines—our literal and literary love of technology. Join over 25 of today's hottest writers as they explore erotic relationships with all kinds of gizmos, gadgets, and devices.

LEOPOLD VON SACHER-MASOCH
VENUS IN FURS
$7.95/589-1

The alliance of Severin and Wanda epitomizes Sacher-Masoch's obsession with a cruel goddess and the urges that drive the man held in her thrall. Exclusive to this edition are letters exchanged between Sacher-Masoch and Emilie Mataja—an aspiring writer he sought as the avatar of his desires.

JOHN NORMAN
IMAGINATIVE SEX
$7.95/561-1

The author of the Gor novels outlines his philosophy on relations between the sexes, and presents fifty-three scenarios designed to reintroduce fantasy to the bedroom.

KATHLEEN K.
SWEET TALKERS
$6.95/516-6

"If you enjoy eavesdropping on explicit conversations about sex... this book is for you."
— *Spectator*

A explicit look at the burgeoning phenomenon of phone sex. Kathleen K. ran a phone-sex company in the late 80s, and she opens up her diary for a peek at the life of a phone-sex operator. Transcripts of actual conversations are included.
Trade /$12.95/192-6

THOMAS S. ROCHE
NOIROTICA 2: Pulp Friction (Ed.)
$7.95/584-0

Another volume of criminally seductive stories set in the murky terrain of the erotic and noir genres. Thomas Roche has gathered the darkest jewels from today's edgiest writers to create this provocative collection. A must for all fans of contemporary erotica.

NOIROTICA: An Anthology of Erotic Crime Stories (Ed.)
$6.95/390-2

A collection of darkly sexy tales, taking place at the crossroads of the crime and erotic genres. Here are some of today's finest writers, all of whom explore the extraordinary and arousing terrain where desire runs irrevocably afoul of the law.

DARK MATTER
$6.95/484-4

"*Dark Matter* is sure to please gender outlaws, bodymod junkies, goth vampires, boys who wish they were dykes, and anybody who's not to sure where the fine line should be drawn between pleasure and pain. It's a handful."—Pat Califia

"Here is the erotica of the cumming millennium.... You will be deliciously disturbed, but never disappointed."
— Poppy Z. Brite

DAVID MELTZER
UNDER
$6.95/290-6

The story of a 21st century sex professional living at the bottom of the social heap. After surgeries designed to increase his physical allure, corrupt government forces drive the cyber-gigolo underground, where even more bizarre cultures await.... A thrilling, disturbing look at the future.

LAURA ANTONIOU, ED.
SOME WOMEN
$7.95/573-5
Introduction by Pat Califia

"Makes the reader think about the wide range of SM experiences, beyond the glamour of fiction and fantasy, or the clever-clever prose of the perverati." — *SKIN TWO*

Over forty essays written by women actively involved in consensual dominance and submission. Professional mistresses, lifestyle leatherdykes, whipmakers, titleholders—women from every conceivable walk of life lay bare their true feelings about issues as explosive as feminism, abuse, pleasure and public image. A bestselling title and valuable resource for anyone interested in sexuality.

NO OTHER TRIBUTE
$7.95/603-0

A volume sure to challenge Political Correctness. Tales of women kept in bondage to their lovers by their deepest passions. Love pushes these women beyond acceptable limits, rendering them helpless to deny anything to the men and women they adore.

MASQUERADE BOOKS

BY HER SUBDUED
$6.95/281-7
These tales all involve women in control—of their lives and their lovers. So much in control that they can remorselessly break rules to become powerful goddesses of those who sacrifice all to worship at their feet.

AMELIA G, ED.
BACKSTAGE PASSES:
Rock n' Roll Erotica from the Pages of *Blue Blood* Magazine
$6.95/438-0
Amelia G, editor of the goth-sex journal *Blue Blood*, has brought together some of today's most irreverent writers, each of whom has outdone themselves with an edgy, antic tale of modern lust.

ROMY ROSEN
SPUNK
$6.95/492-5
Casey, a lovely model poised upon the verge of super-celebrity, falls for an insatiable young rock singer—not suspecting that his sexual appetite has led him to experiment with a dangerous new aphrodisiac. Soon, Casey becomes addicted to the drug, and her craving plunges her into a strange underworld....

MOLLY WEATHERFIELD
CARRIE'S STORY
$6.95/485-2
"I was stunned by how well it was written and how intensely foreign I found its sexual world.... And, since this is a world I don't frequent... I thoroughly enjoyed the National Geo tour."
—*bOING bOING*

"Hilarious and harrowing... just when you think things can't get any wilder, they do." —*Black Sheets*

Weatherfield's bestselling examination of dominance and submission. "I had been Jonathan's slave for about a year when he told me he wanted to sell me at an auction...." A rare piece of erotica, both thoughtful and hot!

CYBERSEX CONSORTIUM
CYBERSEX: The Perv's Guide to Finding Sex on the Internet
$6.95/471-2
You've heard the objections: cyberspace is soaked with sex, mired in immorality. Okay—so where is it!? Tracking down the good stuff—the real good stuff—can waste an awful lot of expensive time, and frequently leave you high and dry. The Cybersex Consortium presents an easy-to-use guide for those intrepid adults who know what they want.

LAURA ANTONIOU
("Sara Adamson")
"Ms. Adamson creates a wonderfully diverse world of lesbian, gay, straight, bi and transgendered characters, all mixing delightfully in the melting pot of sadomasochism and planting the genre more firmly in the culture at large. I for one am cheering her on!" —Kate Bornstein

THE MARKETPLACE
$7.95/602-2
The first title in Antoniou's thrilling Marketplace Trilogy, following the lives and lusts of those who have been deemed worthy to participate in the ultimate BD/SM arena.

THE SLAVE
$7.95/601-4
The Slave covers the experience of one talented submissive who longs to join the ranks of those who have proven themselves worthy of entry into the Marketplace. But the price, while delicious, is staggeringly high....

THE TRAINER
$6.95/249-3
The Marketplace Trilogy concludes with the story of the trainers, and the desires and paths that led them to become the ultimate figures of authority.

THE CATALYST
$6.95/621-9
A kinky art movie inspires the audience members—het and queer—to try some SM play of their own. Different from a lot of SM smut in that it depicts actual consensual SM scenes between just plain folks rather than wild impossible fantasies, *The Catalyst* is both sweet-natured and nastily perverse. The "why don't we give this kinky stuff a try" tone is a true delight.
—*Blowfish*

After viewing an explicitly kinky film full of images of bondage and submission, several audience members find themselves deeply moved by the erotic suggestions they've seen on the screen. Bondage, discipline, and unimaginable sexual perversity are explored as long-denied urges explode with new intensity. The first of this author's best-selling BD/SM titles.

TAMMY JO ECKHART
AMAZONS: Erotic Explorations of Ancient Myths
$7.95/534-4
The Amazon—the fierce woman warrior—appears in the traditions of many cultures, but never before has the erotic potential of this archetype been explored with such energy and imagination. Powerful pleasures await anyone lucky enough to encounter Eckhart's legendary spitfires.

MASQUERADE BOOKS

PUNISHMENT FOR THE CRIME
$6.95/427-5
Stories that explore dominance and submission. From an encounter between two of society's most despised individuals, to the explorations of longtime friends, these tales take you where few others have ever dared....

GERI NETTICK
WITH BETH ELLIOT
MIRRORS: Portrait of a Lesbian Transsexual
$6.95/435-6
Born a male, Geri Nettick knew something just didn't fit. Even after coming to terms with her own gender dysphoria she still fought to be accepted by the lesbian feminist community to which she felt she belonged. A remarkable and inspiring true story of self-discover and acceptance.

TRISTAN TAORMINO & DAVID AARON CLARK, EDS.
RITUAL SEX
$6.95/391-0
The contributors to *Ritual Sex* know that body and soul share more common ground than society feels comfortable acknowledging. From memoirs of ecstatic revelation, to quests to reconcile sex and spirit, *Ritual Sex* provides an unprecedented look at private life.

AMARANTHA KNIGHT, ED.
DEMON SEX
$7.95/594-8
Examining the dark forces of humankind's oldest stories, the contributors to *Demon Sex* reveal the strange symbiosis of dread and desire. Stories include a streetwalker's deal with the devil; a visit with the stripper from Hell; the secrets behind an aging rocker's timeless appeal; and many more guaranteed to shatter preconceptions about modern lust.

SEDUCTIVE SPECTRES
$6.95/464-X
Tours through the erotic supernatural via the imaginations of today's best writers. Never have ghostly encounters been so alluring, thanks to otherworldly characters well-acquainted with the pleasures of the flesh.

SEX MACABRE
$6.95/392-9
Horror tales designed for dark and sexy nights—sure to make your skin crawl, and heart beat faster.

FLESH FANTASTIC
$6.95/352-X
Humans have long toyed with the idea of "playing God": creating life from nothingness, bringing life to the inanimate. Now Amarantha Knight collects stories exploring not only the act of Creation, but the lust that follows.

GARY BOWEN
DIARY OF A VAMPIRE
$6.95/331-7
"Gifted with a darkly sensual vision and a fresh voice, [Bowen] is a writer to watch out for."   —Cecilia Tan

Rafael, a red-blooded male with an insatiable hunger for the same, is the perfect antidote to the effete malcontents haunting bookstores today. The emergence of a bold and brilliant vision, rooted in past and present.

GRANT ANTREWS
LEGACIES
$7.95/605-7
Kathi Lawton discovers that she has inherited the troubling secret of her late mother's scandalous sexuality. In an effort to understand what motivated her mother's desires, Kathi embarks on an exploration of SM that leads her into the arms of Horace Moore, a mysterious man who seems to see into her very soul. As she begins falling for her new master, Kathi finds herself wondering just how far she'll go to prove her love.... Another moving exploration of adult love and desire from the author of *My Darling Dominatrix*.

SUBMISSIONS
$7.95/618-9
Antrews portrays the very special elements of the dominant/submissive relationship with restraint—this time with the story of a lonely man, a winning lottery ticket, and a demanding dominatrix. Suddenly finding himself a millionaire, Kevin Donovan thinks his worries are over—until his restless soul tires of the high life. He turns to the icy Maitresse Genevieve, hoping that her ministrations will guide him to some deeper peace....

ROGUES GALLERY
$6.95/522-0
A stirring evocation of dominant/submissive love. Two doctors meet and slowly fall in love. Once lovely Beth reveals her hidden, kinky desires to Jim, the two explore the forbidden acts that will come to define their distinctly exotic affair.

BUY ANY 4 BOOKS & CHOOSE 1 ADDITIONAL BOOK, OF EQUAL OR LESSER VALUE, AS YOUR FREE GIFT

MASQUERADE BOOKS

MY DARLING DOMINATRIX
$7.95/566-2
When a man and a woman fall in love, it's supposed to be simple, uncomplicated, easy—unless that woman happens to be a dominatrix. This highly praised and unpretentious love story captures the richness and depth of this very special kind of love without leering or smirking.

JEAN STINE
THRILL CITY
$6.95/411-9
Thrill City is the seat of the world's increasing depravity, and this classic novel transports you there with a vivid style you'd be hard pressed to ignore. No writer is better suited to describe the extremes of this modern Babylon.

JOHN WARREN
THE TORQUEMADA KILLER
$6.95/367-8
Detective Eva Hernandez gets her first "big case": a string of murders taking place within New York's SM community. Eva assembles the evidence, revealing a picture of a world misunderstood and under attack—and gradually comes to face her own hidden longings.
THE LOVING DOMINANT
$7.95/600-6
Everything you need to know about an infamous sexual variation, and an unspoken type of love. Warren, a scene veteran, guides readers through this rarely seen world, and offers clear-eyed advice guaranteed to enlighten any erotic explorer.

DAVID AARON CLARK
SISTER RADIANCE
$6.95/215-9
A meditation on love, sex, and death. The vicissitudes of lust and romance are examined against a backdrop of urban decay in this testament to the allure—and inevitability of the forbidden.
THE WET FOREVER
$6.95/117-9
The story of Janus and Madchen—a small-time hood and a beautiful sex worker on the run—examines themes of loyalty, sacrifice, redemption and obsession amidst Manhattan's sex parlors and underground S/M clubs.

MICHAEL PERKINS
EVIL COMPANIONS
$6.95/3067-9
Evil Companions has been hailed as "a frightening classic." A young couple explores the nether reaches of the erotic unconscious in a confrontation with the extremes of passion.

THE SECRET RECORD:
Modern Erotic Literature
$6.95/3039-3
Michael Perkins surveys the field with authority and unique insight. Updated and revised to include the latest trends, tastes, and developments in this misunderstood genre.
AN ANTHOLOGY OF CLASSIC ANONYMOUS EROTIC WRITING
$6.95/140-3
Michael Perkins has collected the best passages from the world's erotic writing. "Anonymous" is one of the most infamous bylines in publishing history—and these excerpts show why!

HELEN HENLEY
ENTER WITH TRUMPETS
$6.95/197-7
Helen Henley was told that women just don't write about sex. So Henley did it alone, flying in the face of "tradition" by writing this touching tale of arousal and devotion in one couple's kinky relationship.

ALICE JOANOU
THE BEST OF ALICE JOANOU
$7.95/623-5
"Joanou has created a series of sumptuous, brooding, dark visions of sexual obsession and is undoubtedly a name to look out for in the future."
—*Redeemer*

"Outstanding erotic fiction."
—*Susie Bright*

A major name in the renaissance of American erotica, Joanou is responsible for some of the decade's most unforgettable images. This volume includes excerpts from *Cannibal Flower*, *Tourniquet* and *Black Tongue*—the titles that announced her talent to the world.
BLACK TONGUE
$6.95/258-2
"Joanou has created a series of sumptuous, brooding, dark visions of sexual obsession, and is undoubtedly a name to look out for in the future."
—*Redeemer*

Exploring lust at its most florid and unsparing, *Black Tongue* is redolent of forbidden passions.

PHILIP JOSÉ FARMER
A FEAST UNKNOWN
$6.95/276-0
"Sprawling, brawling, shocking, suspenseful, hilarious..."
—*Theodore Sturgeon*
Lord Grandrith—armed with the belief that he is the son of Jack the Ripper—tells the story of his remarkable life. His story progresses to encompass the furthest extremes of human behavior.

MASQUERADE BOOKS

FLESH
$6.95/303-1
Stagg explored the galaxies for 800 years. Upon his return, the hero Stagg is made the centerpiece of an incredible public ritual—one that will take him to the heights of ecstasy, and drag him toward the depths of hell.

SAMUEL R. DELANY
THE MAD MAN
$8.99/408-9/Mass market
"Delany develops an insightful dichotomy between [his protagonist]'s two worlds: the one of cerebral philosophy and dry academia, the other of heedless, 'impersonal' obsessive sexual extremism. When these worlds finally collide...the novel achieves a surprisingly satisfying resolution...."
—*Publishers Weekly*

Graduate student John Marr researches the life of Timothy Hasler: a philosopher whose career was cut tragically short over a decade earlier. Marr begins to find himself increasingly drawn toward shocking sexual encounters with the homeless men, until it begins to seem that Hasler's death might hold some key to his own life as a gay man in the age of AIDS. Surely this legendary writer's most mind-blowing novel.

TUPPY OWENS
SENSATIONS
$6.95/3081-4
Tuppy Owens takes a rare peek behind the scenes of *Sensations*—the first big-budget sex flick. Originally commissioned to appear in book form after the release of the film in 1975, *Sensations* is finally available.

DANIEL VIAN
ILLUSIONS
$6.95/3074-1
Two tales of danger and desire in Berlin on the eve of WWII. From private homes to lurid cafés, passion is stark contrast to the brutal violence of the time, as desperate people explore their darkest sexual desires.
PERSUASIONS
$4.95/183-7
"The stockings are drawn tight by the suspender belt, tight enough to be stretched to the limit just above the middle part of her thighs, tight enough so that her calves glow through the sheer silk..." A double novel, including the classics *Adagio* and *Gabriela and the General*, this volume traces lust around the globe.

LIESEL KULIG
LOVE IN WARTIME
$6.95/3044-X
Madeleine knew that the handsome SS officer was dangerous, but she was just a cabaret singer in Nazi-occupied Paris, trying to survive in a perilous time. When Josef fell in love with her, he discovered that a beautiful woman can be as dangerous as any warrior.

SOPHIE GALLEYMORE BIRD
MANEATER
$6.95/103-9
Through a bizarre act of creation, a man attains the "perfect" lover—by all appearances a beautiful, sensuous woman, but in reality something far darker. Once brought to life she will accept no mate, seeking instead the prey that will sate her hunger.

BADBOY

DAVID MAY
MADRUGADA
$6.95/574-3
Set in San Francisco's gay leather community, *Madrugada* follows the lives of a group of friends—and their many acquaintances—as they tangle with the thorny issues of love and lust. Uncompromising, mysterious, and arousing, David May weaves a complex web of relationships in this unique story cycle.

PETER HEISTER
ISLANDS OF DESIRE
$6.95/480-1
Red-blooded lust on the wine-dark seas of classical Greece. Anacraeon yearns to leave his small, isolated island and find adventure in one of the overseas kingdoms. Accompanied by some randy friends, Anacraeon makes his dream come true—and discovers pleasures he never dreamed of!

KITTY TSUI WRITING AS "ERIC NORTON"
SPARKS FLY
$6.95/551-4
The highest highs—and most wretched depths—of life as Eric Norton, a beautiful wanton living San Francisco's high life. *Sparks Fly* traces Norton's rise, fall, and resurrection, vividly marking the way with the personal affairs that give life meaning.

MASQUERADE BOOKS

BARRY ALEXANDER
ALL THE RIGHT PLACES
$6.95/482-8
Stories filled with hot studs in lust and love. From modern masters and slaves to medieval royals and their subjects, Alexander explores the mating rituals men have engaged in for centuries—all in the name of desire...

MICHAEL FORD, ED.
BUTCHBOYS:
Stories For Men Who Need It Bad
$6.50/523-9
A big volume of tales dedicated to the rough-and-tumble type who can make a man weak at the knees. Some of today's best erotic writers explore the many possible variations on the age-old fantasy of the thoroughly dominating man.

WILLIAM J. MANN, ED.
GRAVE PASSIONS:
Gay Tales of the Supernatural
$6.50/405-4
A collection of the most chilling tales of passion currently being penned by today's most provocative gay writers. Unnatural transformations, otherworldly encounters, and deathless desires make for a collection sure to keep readers up late at night.

J. A. GUERRA, ED.
COME QUICKLY:
For Boys on the Go
$6.50/413-5
Here are over sixty of the hottest fantasies around—all designed to get you going in less time than it takes to dial 976. Julian. Anthony Guerra has put together this volume especially for you—a busy man on a modern schedule, who still appreciates a little old-fashioned action.

JOHN PRESTON
HUSTLING: A Gentleman's Guide to the Fine Art of Homosexual Prostitution
$6.50/517-4
"Fun and highly literary. What more could you expect form such an accomplished activist, author and editor?"—*Drummer*

John Preston solicited the advice and opinions of "working boys" from across the country in his effort to produce the ultimate guide to the hustler's world. *Hustling* covers every practical aspect of the business, from clientele and payment to "specialties," and drawbacks. A must for men on either side of the transaction. Trade $12.95/137-3

MR. BENSON
$4.95/3041-5
Jamie is an aimless young man lucky enough to encounter Mr. Benson. He is soon learns to accept this man as his master. Jamie's incredible adventures never fail to excite—especially when the going gets rough!

TALES FROM THE DARK LORD
$5.95/323-6
Twelve stunning works from the man *Lambda Book Report* called "the Dark Lord of gay erotica." The ritual of lust and surrender is explored in all its manifestations in this heart-stopping triumph of authority and vision.

TALES FROM THE DARK LORD II
$4.95/176-1

THE ARENA
$4.95/3083-0
Preston's take on the ultimate sex club–where men go to abolish all personal limits. Only the author of *Mr. Benson* could have imagined so perfect an institution for the satisfaction of male desire.

THE HEIR•THE KING
$4.95/3048-2
The Heir, written in the lyric voice of the ancient myths, tells the story of a world where slaves and masters create a new sexual society. *The King* tells the story of a soldier who discovers his monarch's most secret desires.

THE MISSION OF ALEX KANE
GOLDEN YEARS
$4.95/3069-5
When evil threatens the plans of a group of older gay men, Kane's got the muscle to take it head on. Along the way, he wins the support—and very specialized attentions—of a cowboy plucked right out of the Old West.

DEADLY LIES
$4.95/3076-8
Politics is a dirty business and the dirt becomes deadly when a smear campaign targets gay men. Who better to clean things up than Alex Kane!

STOLEN MOMENTS
$4.95/3098-9
Houston's evolving gay community is victimized by a malicious newspaper editor who is more than willing to boost circulation by printing homophobic slander. He never counted on Alex Kane, fearless defender of gay dreams and desires.

SECRET DANGER
$4.95/111-X
Alex Kane and the faithful Danny are called to a small European country, where a group of gay tourists is being held hostage by brutal terrorists.

MASQUERADE BOOKS

LETHAL SILENCE
$4.95/125-X
Chicago becomes the scene of the right-wing's most noxious plan—facilitated by unholy political alliances. Alex and Danny head to the Windy City to battle the mercenaries who would squash gay men underfoot.

MATT TOWNSEND
SOLIDLY BUILT
$6.50/416-X
The tale of the relationship between Jeff, a young photographer, and Mark, the butch electrician hired to wire Jeff's new home. For Jeff, it's love at first sight; Mark, however, has more than a few hang-ups.

JAY SHAFFER
ANIMAL HANDLERS
$4.95/264-7
In Shaffer's world, every man finally succumbs to the animal urges deep inside. And if there's any creature that promises a wild time, it's a beast who's been caged for far too long.

FULL SERVICE
$4.95/150-0
One of today's best chroniclers of masculine passion. No-nonsense guys bear down hard on each other as they work their way toward release in this finely detailed assortment of fantasies.

D. V. SADERO
IN THE ALLEY
$4.95/144-6
Hardworking men bring their special skills and impressive tools to the most satisfying job of all: capturing and breaking the male animal.

SCOTT O'HARA
DO-IT-YOURSELF PISTON POLISHING
$6.50/489-5
Longtime sex-pro Scott O'Hara draws upon his acute powers of seduction to lure you into a world of hard, horny men long overdue for a tune-up.

SUTTER POWELL
EXECUTIVE PRIVILEGES
$6.50/383-X
No matter how serious or sexy a predicament his characters find themselves in, Powell conveys the sheer exuberance of their encounters with a warm humor rarely seen in contemporary gay erotica.

GARY BOWEN
WESTERN TRAILS
$6.50/477-1
Some of gay literature's brightest stars tell the sexy truth about the many ways a rugged stud found to satisfy himself—and his buddy—in the Very Wild West.

MAN HUNGRY
$5.95/374-0
A riveting collection of stories from one of gay erotica's new stars. Dipping into a variety of genres, Bowen crafts tales of lust unlike anything being published today.

ROBERT BAHR
SEX SHOW
$4.95/225-6
Luscious dancing boys. Brazen, explicit acts. Take a seat, and get very comfortable, because the curtain's going up on a very special show no discriminating appetite can afford to miss.

KYLE STONE
THE HIDDEN SLAVE
$6.95/580-8
"This perceptive and finely-crafted work is a joy to discover. Kyle Stone's fiction belongs on the shelf of every serious fan of gay literature."
—Pat Califia

A young man searches for the perfect master. An electrifying tale of erotic discovery.

HOT BAUDS 2
$6.50/479-8
Stone conducted another heated search through the world's randiest gay bulletin boards, resulting in one of the most scalding follow-ups ever published.

HOT BAUDS
$5.95/285-X
Stone combed cyberspace for the hottest fantasies of the world's horniest hackers. Sexy, shameless, and eminently user-friendly.

FIRE & ICE
$5.95/297-3
A collection of stories from the author of the adventures of PB 500. Stone's characters always promise one thing: enough hot action to burn away your desire for anyone else....

FANTASY BOARD
$4.95/212-4
Explore the future—through the intertwined lives of a collection of randy computer hackers. On the Lambda Gate BBS, every horny male is in search of virtual satisfaction!

MASQUERADE BOOKS

THE CITADEL
$4.95/198-5
The sequel to *PB 500*. Micah faces new challenges after entering the Citadel. Only his master knows what awaits....

THE INITIATION OF PB 500
$4.95/141-1
He is a stranger on their planet, unschooled in their language, and ignorant of their customs. But Micah will soon be trained in every detail of erotic service. When his training is complete, he must prove himself worthy of the master who has chosen him....

RITUALS
$4.95/168-3
Via a computer bulletin board, a young man finds himself drawn into sexual rites that transform him into the willing slave of a mysterious stranger. His former life is thrown off, and he learns to live for his Master's touch....

JASON FURY
THE ROPE ABOVE, THE BED BELOW
$4.95/269-8
A vicious murderer is preying upon New York's go-go boys. In order to solve this mystery and save lives, each shady suspect must lay bare his soul—and more!

ERIC'S BODY
$4.95/151-9
Follow the irresistible Jason through sexual adventures unlike any you have ever read—touching on the raunchy, the romantic, and a number of highly sensitive areas in between....

1 900 745-HUNG

THE connection for hot handfuls of eager guys! No credit card needed—so call now for access to the hottest party line around. Spill it all to bad boys from across the country! (Must be over 18.) Pick one up now.... $3.98 per min.

LARS EIGHNER
WANK: THE TAPES
$6.95/588-3
Lars Eighner gets back to basics with this look at every guy's favorite pastime. Horny studs bare it all and work up a healthy sweat during these provocative discussions about masturbation.

WHISPERED IN THE DARK
$5.95/286-8
A volume demonstrating Eighner's unique combination of strengths: poetic descriptive power, an unfailing ear for dialogue, and a finely tuned feeling for the nuances of male passion. An extraordinary collection of this influential writer's work.

AMERICAN PRELUDE
$4.95/170-5
Eighner is one of gay erotica's true masters, producing wonderfully written tales of all-American lust, peopled with red-blooded, oversexed studs.

DAVID LAURENTS, ED.
SOUTHERN COMFORT
$6.50/466-6
Editor David Laurents now unleashes a collection of tales focusing on the American South—stories reflecting not only the Southern literary tradition, but the many sexy contributions the region has made to the iconography of the American Male.

WANDERLUST:
Homoerotic Tales of Travel
$5.95/395-3
A volume dedicated to the special pleasures of faraway places—and the horny men who lie in wait for intrepid tourists. Celebrate the freedom of the open road, and the allure of men who stray from the beaten path....

THE BADBOY BOOK
OF EROTIC POETRY
$5.95/382-1
Erotic poetry has long been the problem child of the literary world—highly creative and provocative, but somehow too frank to be "art." *The Badboy Book of Erotic Poetry* restores eros to its place of honor in gay writing.

AARON TRAVIS
BIG SHOTS
$5.95/448-8
Two fierce tales in one electrifying volume. In *Beirut*, Travis tells the story of ultimate military power and erotic subjugation; *Kip*, Travis' hypersexed and sinister take on *film noir*, appears in unexpurgated form for the first time.

EXPOSED
$4.95/126-8
Cops, college jocks, ancient Romans—even Sherlock Holmes and his loyal Watson—cruise these pages, fresh from the pen of one of our hottest authors.

IN THE BLOOD
$5.95/283-3
Early tales from this master of the genre. Includes "In the Blood"—a heart-pounding descent into sexual vampirism.

THE FLESH FABLES
$4.95/243-6
One of Travis' best collections. Includes "Blue Light," as well as other masterpieces that established him as one of gay erotica's master storytellers.

MASQUERADE BOOKS

BOB VICKERY

SKIN DEEP
$4.95/265-5

So many varied beauties no one will go away unsatisfied. No tantalizing morsel of manflesh is overlooked—or left unexplored!

JR

FRENCH QUARTER NIGHTS
$5.95/337-6

Sensual snapshots of the many places where men get down and dirty—from the steamy French Quarter to the steam room at the old Everard baths.

TOM BACCHUS

RAHM
$5.95/315-5

Tom Bacchus brings to life an extraordinary assortment of characters, from the Father of Us All to the cowpoke next door, the early gay literati to rude, queercore mosh rats.

BONE
$4.95/177-2

Queer musings from the pen of one of today's hottest young talents. Tom Bacchus maps out the tricking ground of a new generation.

KEY LINCOLN

SUBMISSION HOLDS
$4.95/266-3

From tough to tender, the men between these covers stop at nothing to get what they want. These sweat-soaked tales show just how bad boys can really get.

CALDWELL/EIGHNER

QSFX2
$5.95/278-7

Other-worldly yarns from two master story-tellers—Clay Caldwell and Lars Eighner. Both eroticists take a trip to the furthest reaches of the sexual imagination, sending back ten scalding sci-fi stories of male desire.

CLAY CALDWELL

SOME LIKE IT ROUGH
$6.95/544-1

A new collection of stories from a master of gay eroticism. Here are the best of Clay Caldwell's darkest tales—thrilling explorations of dominance and submission. Hot and heavy, Some Like It Rough is filled with enough virile masters and willing slaves to satisfy the the most demanding reader.

JOCK STUDS
$6.95/472-0

Scalding tales of pumped bodies and raging libidos. Swimmers, runners, football players—whatever your sport might be, there's a man here waiting to work up a little sweat, peel off his uniform, and claim his reward for a game well-played....

ASK OL' BUDDY
$5.95/346-5

Set in the underground SM world—where men initiate one another into the secrets of the rawest sexual realm of all. And when each stud's initiation is complete, he takes part in the training of another hungry soul....

STUD SHORTS
$5.95/320-1

"If anything, Caldwell's charm is more powerful, his nostalgia more poignant, the horniness he captures more sweetly, achingly acute than ever." —Aaron Travis

A new collection of this legend's latest sex-fiction. Caldwell tells all about cops, cadets, truckers, farmboys (and many more) in these dirty jewels.

TAILPIPE TRUCKER
$5.95/296-5

Trucker porn! Caldwell tells the truth about Trag and Curly—two men hot for the feeling of sweaty manflesh. Together, they pick up—and turn out—a couple of thrill-seeking punks.

SERVICE, STUD
$5.95/336-8

Another look at the gay future. The setting is the Los Angeles of a distant future. Here the all-male populace is divided between the served and the servants—guaranteeing erotic satisfaction of all involved.

QUEERS LIKE US
$4.95/262-0

For years the name Clay Caldwell has been synonymous with the hottest, most finely crafted gay tales available. Queers Like Us is one of his best: the story of a randy mailman's trek through a landscape of available studs.

ALL-STUD
$4.95/104-7

This classic, sex-soaked tale takes place under the watchful eye of Number Ten: an omniscient figure who has decreed unabashed promiscuity as the law of his all-male land. Love is outlawed—and two passionate men find themselves pitted against an oppressive system.

MASQUERADE BOOKS

CLAY CALDWELL & AARON TRAVIS
TAG TEAM STUDS
$6.50/465-8

Wrestling will never seem the same, once you've made your way through this assortment of sweaty studs. But you'd better be wary—should one catch you off guard, you might spend the night pinned to the mat....

LARRY TOWNSEND
LEATHER AD: M
$5.95/380-5

John's curious about what goes on between the leatherclad men he's fantasized about. He takes out a personal ad, and starts a journey of discovery that will leave no part of his life unchanged.

LEATHER AD: S
$5.95/407-0

The tale continues—this time told from a Top's perspective. A simple ad generates many responses, and one man puts these studs through their paces....

1 800 906-HUNK

Hardcore phone action for real men. A scorching assembly of studs is waiting for your call—and eager to give you the headtrip of your life! Totally live, guaranteed one-on-one action. (Must be over 18.) No credit card needed. $3.98 per minute.

BEWARE THE GOD WHO SMILES
$5.95/321-X

Two lusty young Americans are transported to ancient Egypt—where they are embroiled in warfare and taken as slaves by barbarians. The two finally discover that the key to escape lies within their own rampant libidos.

MIND MASTER
$4.95/209-4

Who better to explore the territory of erotic dominance than an author who helped define the genre—and knows that ultimate mastery always transcends the physical. One gifted man exploits his ability to control others.

THE LONG LEATHER CORD
$4.95/201-9

Chuck's stepfather never lacks money or male visitors with whom he enacts intense sexual rituals. As Chuck comes to terms with his own desires, he begins to unravel the mystery behind his stepfather's secret life.

THE SCORPIUS EQUATION
$4.95/119-5

The story of a man caught between the demands of two galactic empires. Our randy hero must match wits—and more—with the incredible forces that rule his world.

MAN SWORD
$4.95/188-8

The *trés gai* tale of France's King Henri III, who encounters enough sexual schemers and politicos to alter one's picture of history forever! Witness the unbridled licentiousness of one of Europe's most notorious courts.

THE FAUSTUS CONTRACT
$4.95/167-5

Another thrilling tale of leather lust. Two cocky young hustlers get more than they bargained for in this story of lust and its discontents.

CHAINS
$4.95/158-6

Picking up street punks has always been risky, but here it sets off a string of events that must be read to be believed. The legendary Townsend at his grittiest.

RUN, LITTLE LEATHER BOY
$4.95/143-8

The famous tale of sexual awakening. A chronic underachiever, Wayne seems to be going nowhere fast. While exploring the gay leather underground, he discovers a sense of fulfillment he had never known before.

RUN NO MORE
$4.95/152-7

The sequel to *Run, Little Leather Boy*. This volume follows the further adventures of Townsend's leatherclad narrator as he travels every sexual byway available to the S/M male.

THE SEXUAL ADVENTURES OF SHERLOCK HOLMES
$4.95/3097-0

A scandalously sexy take on the notorious sleuth. Via the diary of Holmes' horny sidekick Watson, experience Holmes' most challenging—and arousing–adventures! An underground classic

THE GAY ADVENTURES OF CAPTAIN GOOSE
$4.95/169-1

Jerome Gander is sentenced to serve aboard a ship manned by the most hardened criminals. In no time, Gander becomes one of the most notorious rakehells Olde England had ever seen. On land or sea, Gander hunts down the Empire's hottest studs.

DONALD VINING
CABIN FEVER AND OTHER STORIES
$5.95/338-4

"Demonstrates the wisdom experience combined with insight and optimism can create."
—*Bay Area Reporter*

Eighteen blistering stories in celebration of the most intimate of male bonding, reaffirming both love and lust in modern gay life.

MASQUERADE BOOKS

DEREK ADAMS

MILES DIAMOND AND THE CASE OF THE CRETAN APOLLO
$6.95/381-3
Hired to track a cheating lover, Miles finds himself involved in a highly unprofessional capacity! When the jealous Callahan threatens not only Diamond but his studly assistant, Miles counters with a little undercover work—involving as many horny informants as he can get his hands on!

THE MARK OF THE WOLF
$5.95/361-9
The past comes back to haunt one well-off stud, whose desires lead him into the arms of many men—and the midst of a mystery.

MY DOUBLE LIFE
$5.95/314-7
Every man leads a double life, dividing his hours between the mundanities of the day and the pursuits of the night. Derek Adams shines a little light on the wicked things men do when no one's looking.

HEAT WAVE
$4.95/159-4
Derek Adams sexy short stories are guaranteed to jump start any libido—and *Heatwave* contains his very best.

MILES DIAMOND AND THE DEMON OF DEATH
$4.95/251-5
Miles always find himself in the stickiest situations—with any stud he meets! This adventure promises another carnal carnival, as Diamond investigates a host of horny guys—each of whom hides a secret Miles is only too willing to expose!

THE ADVENTURES OF MILES DIAMOND
$4.95/118-7
The debut of this popular gay gumshoe. To Diamond's delight, "The Case of the Missing Twin" is packed with randy studs. Miles sets about uncovering all as he tracks down the delectable Daniel Travis.

KELVIN BELIELE

IF THE SHOE FITS
$4.95/223-X
An essential volume of tales exploring a world where randy boys can't help but do what comes naturally—as often as possible! Sweaty male bodies grapple in pleasure.

JAMES MEDLEY

THE REVOLUTIONARY & OTHER STORIES
$6.50/417-8
Billy, the son of the station chief of the American Embassy in Guatemala, is kidnapped and held for ransom. Billy gradually develops an unimaginably close relationship with Juan, the revolutionary assigned to guard him.

HUCK AND BILLY
$4.95/245-0
Young lust knows no bounds—and is often the hottest of one's life! Huck and Billy explore the desires that course through their bodies, determined to plumb the depths of passion. A thrilling look at desire between men.

FLEDERMAUS

FLEDERFICTION: STORIES OF MEN AND TORTURE
$5.95/355-4
Fifteen blistering paeans to men and their suffering. Unafraid of exploring the furthest reaches of pain and pleasure, Fledermaus unleashes his most thrilling tales in this volume.

VICTOR TERRY

MASTERS
$6.50/418-6
Terry's butchest tales. A powerhouse volume of boot-wearing, whip-wielding, bone-crunching bruisers who've got what it takes to make a grown man grovel.

SM/SD
$6.50/406-2
Set around a South Dakota town called Prairie, these tales offer evidence that the real rough stuff can still be found where men take what they want despite all rules.

WHiPs
$4.95/254-X
Cruising for a hot man? You'd better be, because these WHiPs—officers of the Wyoming Highway Patrol—are gonna pull you over for a little impromptu interrogation....

MAX EXANDER

DEEDS OF THE NIGHT: Tales of Eros and Passion
$5.95/348-1
MAXimum porn! Exander's a writer who's seen it all—and is more than happy to describe every inch of it in pulsating detail. A whirlwind tour of the hypermasculine libido.

BUY ANY 4 BOOKS & CHOOSE 1 ADDITIONAL BOOK, OF EQUAL OR LESSER VALUE, AS YOUR FREE GIFT

MASQUERADE BOOKS

LEATHERSEX
$4.95/210-8
Hard-hitting tales from merciless Max. This time he focuses on the leather clad lust that draws together only the most willing and talented of tops and bottoms—for an all-out orgy of limitless surrender and control....

MANSEX
$4.95/160-8
"Mark was the classic leatherman: a huge, dark stud in chaps, with a big black moustache, hairy chest and enormous muscles. Exactly the kind of men Todd liked—strong, hunky, masculine, ready to take control...."

TOM CAFFREY
TALES FROM THE MEN'S ROOM
$5.95/364-3
Male lust at its most elemental and arousing. The Men's Room is less a place than a state of mind—one that every man finds himself in, day after day....

HITTING HOME
$4.95/222-1
Titillating and compelling, the stories in *Hitting Home* make a strong case for there being only one thing on a man's mind. Hot studs via the imagination of this new talent.

"BIG" BILL JACKSON
EIGHTH WONDER
$4.95/200-0
"Big" Bill Jackson's always the randiest guy in town—no matter what town he's in. From the bright lights and back rooms of New York to the open fields and sweaty bods of a small Southern town, "Big" Bill always manages to cause a scene!

TORSTEN BARRING
CONFESSIONS OF A NAKED PIANO PLAYER
$6.95/626-X
Frederic Danton is a musical prodigy—and currently the highest paid and most sought-after concert pianist in the world. At the height of his fame, Frederic withdraws from the limelight, and many fear he will never return. And why would he? Frederic books passage on the *S. S. Yeoman*, bound for the isle of Corrigia—home of the most depraved gay sex resort known to man!

GUY TRAYNOR
$6.50/414-3
Some call Guy Traynor a theatrical genius; others say he was a madman. All anyone knows for certain is that his productions were the result of blood, sweat and outrageous erotic torture!

SHADOWMAN
$4.95/178-0
From spoiled aristocrats to randy youths sowing wild oats at the local picture show, Barring's imagination works overtime in these steamy vignettes of homolust.

PETER THORNWELL
$4.95/149-7
Follow the exploits of Peter Thornwell and his outrageously horny cohorts as he goes from misspent youth to scandalous stardom, all thanks to an insatiable libido and love for the lash. The first of Torsten Barring's popular SM novels.

THE SWITCH
$4.95/3061-X
Some of the most brutally thrilling erotica available today. Sometimes a man needs a good whipping, and *The Switch* certainly makes a case! Packed with hot studs and unrelenting passions, these stories established Barring as a writer to be watched.

BERT McKENZIE
FRINGE BENEFITS
$5.95/354-6
From the pen of a widely published short story writer comes a volume of highly immodest tales. Not afraid of getting down and dirty, McKenzie produces some of today's most visceral sextales.

CHRISTOPHER MORGAN
STEAM GAUGE
$6.50/473-9
This volume abounds in manly men doing what they do best—to, with, or for any hot stud who crosses their paths.

THE SPORTSMEN
$5.95/385-6
A collection of super-hot stories dedicated to the all-American athlete. These writers know just the type of guys that make up every red-blooded male's starting line-up....

MUSCLE BOUND
$4.95/3028-8
Tommy joins forces with sexy Will Rodriguez in a battle of wits and biceps at the hottest gym in town, where the weak are bound and crushed by iron-pumping gods.

SONNY FORD
REUNION IN FLORENCE
$4.95/3070-9
Follow Adrian and Tristan an a sexual odyssey that takes in all ports known to ancient man. From lustful Turks to insatiable Mamluks, these two spread pleasure throughout the classical world!

MASQUERADE BOOKS

ROGER HARMAN
FIRST PERSON
$4.95/179-9
Each story takes the form of a confessional—told by men who've got plenty to confess! From the "first time ever" to firsts of different kinds....

J. A. GUERRA, ED.
SLOW BURN
$4.95/3042-3
Torsos get lean and hard, pecs widen, and stomachs ripple in these sexy stories of the power and perils of physical perfection.

DAVE KINNICK
SORRY I ASKED
$4.95/3090-3
Unexpurgated interviews with gay porn's rank and file. Get personal with the men behind (and under) the "stars," and discover the hot truth about the porn business.

SEAN MARTIN
SCRAPBOOK
$4.95/224-8
From the creator of *Doc and Raider* comes this hot collection of life's horniest moments—all involving studs sure to set your pulse racing!

CARO SOLES & STAN TAL, EDS.
BIZARRE DREAMS
$4.95/187-X
An anthology of voices dedicated to exploring the dark side of human fantasy. Here are the most talented practitioners of "dark fantasy," the most forbidden sexual realm of all.

MICHAEL LOWENTHAL, ED.
THE BADBOY EROTIC LIBRARY
Volume 1
$4.95/190-X
Excerpts from *A Secret Life, Imre, Sins of the Cities of the Plain, Teleny* and others.
THE BADBOY EROTIC LIBRARY
Volume 2
$4.95/211-6
This time, selections are taken from *Mike and Me, Muscle Bound, Men at Work, Badboy Fantasies,* and *Slowburn.*

ERIC BOYD
MIKE AND ME
$5.95/419-4
Mike joined the gym squad to bulk up on muscle. Little did he know he'd be turning on every sexy muscle jock in Minnesota! Hard bodies collide in a series of horny workouts.

MIKE AND THE MARINES
$6.50/497-6
Mike takes on America's most elite corps of studs! Join in on the never-ending sexual escapades of this singularly lustful platoon!

ANONYMOUS
A SECRET LIFE
$4.95/3017-2
Meet Master Charles: eighteen and quite innocent, until his arrival at the Sir Percival's Academy, where the lessons are supplemented with a crash course in pure sexual heat!

SINS OF THE CITIES OF THE PLAIN
$5.95/322-8
Indulge yourself in the scorching memoirs of young man-about-town Jack Saul. Jack's sinful escapades grow wilder with every chapter!

IMRE
$4.95/3019-9
An extraordinary lost classic of gay desire and romance in a small European town on the eve of WWI. An early look at gay love and lust.

THE SCARLET PANSY
$4.95/189-6
Randall Etrange travels the world in search of true love. Along the way, his journey becomes a sexual odyssey of truly epic proportions.

HARD CANDY

ELISE D'HAENE
LICKING OUR WOUNDS
$7.95/605-7
"A fresh, engagingly sarcastic and determinedly bawdy voice. D'Haene is blessed with a savvy, iconoclastic view of the world that is mordant but never mean." —*Publisher's Weekly*

This acclaimed debut novel is the story of Maria, a young woman coming to terms with the complexities of life in the age of AIDS. Abandoned by her lover and faced with the deaths of her friends, Maria struggles along with the help of Peter, HIV-positive and deeply conflicted about the changes in his own life, and Christie, a lover who is full of her own ideas about truth and the meaning of life.

MASQUERADE BOOKS

CHEA VILLANUEVA
BULLETPROOF BUTCHES
$7.95/560-3

"...Gutsy, hungry, and outrageous, but with a tender core...
Villanueva is a writer to watch out for: she will teach us something."
—Joan Nestle

One of lesbian literature's most uncompromising voices. Never afraid to address the harsh realities of working-class lesbian life, Chea Villanueva charts territory frequently overlooked in the age of "lesbian chic."

KEVIN KILLIAN
ARCTIC SUMMER
$6.95/514-X

A critically acclaimed examination of the emptiness lying beneath the rich exterior of America in the 50s. With the story of Liam Reilly—a young gay man of considerable means and numerous secrets—Killian exposes the complexities and contradictions of the American Dream.

STAN LEVENTHAL
BARBIE IN BONDAGE
$6.95/415-1

Widely regarded as one of the most clear-eyed interpreters of big city gay male life, Leventhal here provides a series of explorations of love and desire between men.

**SKYDIVING ON
CHRISTOPHER STREET**
$6.95/287-6

"Positively addictive." —Dennis Cooper

Aside from a hateful job, a hateful apartment, a hateful world and an increasingly hateful lover, life seems, well, all right for the protagonist of Stan Leventhal's latest novel. An insightful tale of contemporary urban gay life.

MICHAEL ROWE
**WRITING BELOW THE BELT:
Conversations with Erotic Authors**
$7.95/540-9

"An in-depth and enlightening tour of society's love/hate relationship with sex, morality, and censorship."
—James White Review

Award-winning journalist Michael Rowe interviewed the best and brightest erotic writers and presents the collected wisdom in *Writing Below the Belt*. Includes interviews with such cult sensations as John Preston, Larry Townsend, Pat Califia, as well as new voices such as Will Leber, Michael Lowenthal and others. An illuminating look at some of today's most challenging writers.

PAUL T. ROGERS
SAUL'S BOOK
$7.95/462-3
Winner of the Editors' Book Award

"A first novel of considerable power... Speaks to us all."
—New York Times Book Review

The story of a Times Square hustler, Sinbad the Sailor, and Saul, a brilliant, self-destructive, dominating character who may be the only love Sinbad will ever know. A classic tale of desire, obsession and the wages of love.

PATRICK MOORE
IOWA
$6.95/423-2

"Full of terrific characters etched in acid-sharp prose, soaked through with just enough ambivalence to make it thoroughly romantic."
—Felice Picano

The tale of one gay man's journey into adulthood, and the roads that bring him home.

LARS EIGHNER
GAY COSMOS
$6.95/236-1

An analysis of gay culture. Praised by the press, *Gay Cosmos* is an important contribution to the area of Gay and Lesbian Studies.

WALTER R. HOLLAND
THE MARCH
$6.95/429-1

Beginning on a hot summer night in 1980, *The March* revolves around a circle of young gay men, and the many others their lives touch. Over time, each character changes in unexpected ways; lives and loves come together and fall apart, as society itself is horribly altered by the onslaught of AIDS.

BRAD GOOCH
THE GOLDEN AGE OF PROMISCUITY
$7.95/550-6

"The next best thing to taking a time-machine trip to grovel in the glorious '70s gutter."
—San Francisco Chronicle

"A solid, unblinking, unsentimental look at a vanished era. Gooch tells us everything we ever wanted to know about the dark and decadent gay subculture in Manhattan before AIDS altered the landscape."
—Kirkus Reviews

RED JORDAN AROBATEAU
DIRTY PICTURES
$5.95/345-7
Dirty Pictures is the story of a lonely butch tending bar—and the femme she finally calls her own.